Other Books by

The Broken World Series:
Broken World
Shattered World
Mad World
Lost World
New World
Forgotten World
Silent World
Broken Stories

The Twisted Series:
Twisted World
Twisted Mind
Twisted Memories
Twisted Fate

The Outliers Saga:
Outliers
Uprising

Zombie Apocalypse Love Story Novellas:
More than Survival
Fighting to Forget
Playing the Odds
Key to Survival
The Things We Cannot Change
Surviving the Storm

The Blood Will Dry

Collision

The College of Charleston Series:
The List
No Regrets
Moving On
Letting Go

When We Were Human

Alone: A Zombie Novel

The Moonchild Series:
Moonchild
Liberation

Anthologies:
Prep For Doom
Gone with the Dead

For my best friend, who is so different from me but has taught me so much about love, friendship, and acceptance.

UPRISING

Book Two in the OUTLIERS Saga

KATE L. MARY

Twisted Press

Published by Twisted Press, LLC, an independently owned company.

This book is a work of fiction. The names, characters, places, and incidents are fictitious or have been used fictitiously, and are not to be construed as real in any way. Any resemblance to person, living or dead, actual events, locales, or organizations is entirely coincidental.

Copyright © 2018 by Kate L. Mary
ISBN-13: 978-1986495516
ISBN-10: 1986495515
Cover Art by Kate L. Mary
Edited by Lori Whitwam

All rights reserved. This book or any portion thereof may not be reproduced or used in any manner without the express permission of the author, except for the use of brief quotations in a book review.

ONE

I STOOD AT THE EDGE OF THE VILLAGE, WATCHING the sun rise over the wilds while I waited for Mira. The chill in the air told me that winter was once again on its way, and I found myself thinking back to the year before. To the day of the first snowfall, which had also been the day I received my first punishment from Saffron in almost three years. I had not known it at the time, but that day had been the beginning of something new. It had started a chain of events that had changed me so thoroughly that I found the life I was now living completely unrecognizable at times. The person I had become was nothing like the old Indra. She had been timid and weak, scared to go out into the wilds even with her husband. Now, though, I had found strength buried deep inside me that I had never known I could possess. If I went back to the city now, if I once again put myself in a position where the Sovereign and Fortis had power over me, would it change me even more? Would it make me stronger, or more vulnerable? Did I really have the strength to make a difference in the lives of my people, or was I fooling myself?

Until last night when Mira came to me, delivering Saffron's request that I return to my job, I had never considered returning to the city. Not after everything they had stolen from me. Not after watching my husband lose his life on my last day there. But I could do so much more for my people inside those walls than out here in the wilds, and not going back would be an act of cowardice. It was what the old Indra would have done, and I was no longer that person.

While my mind was made up, thinking about that punishment, as well as all the other things that had transpired over the last year, I still found myself wondering *why* I would ever choose to head back into the city when I had barely escaped with my life the last time. The reasons to stay away numbered more than the stars in the sky—the threat of Lysander, the brutality of the guards, the cruelty of Saffron—but every time I thought about them, the reasons I had to return pushed at my doubts until they were carried away like the dust in the wind.

By the time Mira emerged from between the huts, her passage markings dark against her pale skin in the early morning light, my mind was made up. When she saw me waiting at the edge of the village, a smile spread across her face that illuminated her blue eyes. I was fairly certain it was the first genuine smile she had given me since Bodhi's death, and I added it to the list of things that had changed over the last year.

She stopped in front of me just as a breeze swept through the wilds, rustling her blond hair. "You are sure?"

"I am," I replied.

The words came out firm and confident, and they gave me strength. Strength I would need on the long walk ahead of us, as well as throughout the day. Just being in the city would challenge me emotionally, but being around Saffron and Lysander, the very people who were responsible for the death of my husband, would no doubt test me to my very limits of self-control.

Mira and I set off, and the cool morning air clung to us all the way through the wilds to the borderland. By the time the wastelands came into view, the sun was well over the horizon, and the warmth of its rays sucked every ounce of chill from the air.

I had not set eyes on the dry earth of the wastelands for more than six months, and it shocked me how blinding it seemed after emerging from the cover of the trees. My hand went to my eyes on its own, shading them from the rays, and I had the sudden recollection of doing this same thing four years ago on my very first trip to Sovereign City. Even though I had been well into my twenties back then, I had still been a child, naïve, my fears superficial compared to what they were now. I was better equipped to deal with the concerns that plagued my life now, but compared to the worries of that day, they were as massive as the Lygan Cliffs at my side.

Despite the long walk, when the wall came into view, looming in the distance and dwarfing even the cliffs, it seemed as if only minutes had passed. Then the tops of the houses that signified the Fortis village were visible as well, and the dread I had been trying to keep at bay balled into a rock and settled in the bottom of my stomach. Mira and I paused to stash our weapons like we usually did, neither of us saying a word, and I was grateful for the silence. I was focused on what I would need to do to get through the day, and Mira no doubt knew that.

Last time I left the city, the building that was to be quarters for the Outliers had been little more than a shell. Now, six months later, it was well underway. It towered over the homes in the village. Three stories high, it had a walkway on each level and rows of doors lined up one after the other. So many that I could not comprehend it, but the numbers were no doubt correct. It would be enough to hold every Outlier who worked in the city, and when that happened, we would be nothing but slaves for the Sovereign.

Thankfully, the progress seemed to be very slow.

"I thought it would be further along," I said as Mira and I started walking again.

"They do just enough work to please the Sovereign, but they are dragging it out," she replied. "As long as it is being built, they receive more from inside the city."

"Then let us hope it takes them years to finish."

My time away had not been long enough to wash the sights and smells of the Fortis village from my mind, but I still wrinkled my nose in disgust when we reached the outskirts. It was the stench of rotting food and too many people living together, as well as the stink of waste, from both animals and people. It was enough to make me second-guess my decision, even though I knew I had been right to return to the city. Still, no matter how vivid my memories of the brutality I had witnessed and been subjected to at the hands of the Fortis, it was not until this moment that I was able to once again fully appreciate just how repulsive these people were. They lived like animals, took little to no care with themselves or their homes, and their stench was as rotten as their souls.

Thankfully, as usual, the village was quiet in the dawn of a new morning, and we made it through without incident. Then the gate was in front of me, opening so Mira and I could pass through, and I suddenly found myself ready to cross the threshold into Sovereign City for the first time in six months. It took a great deal of effort to put one foot in front of the other, because all at once my legs felt as weighed down as my stomach. I managed it though, lifting one foot after the other until I was finally inside and the doors had shut behind me, and I knew there was no going back.

The city had not changed in all the months I had been away, and yet it had. Mira and I walked down the street, surrounded by the same world I had visited nearly every day for more than three years. On the surface, nothing had really changed, but everything about it looked different to me now. Or maybe it only felt different.

The streets were already busy despite the early hour. Outliers hurried to jobs or ran errands for the houses they worked in, while Fortis guards leaned against walls, watching with cool eyes. I spied the occasional Sovereign among the crowd, cloaked in the thick robes they wore, the hoods pulled up to protect them from the sun, electroprods in their hands.

At the first sight of them, my heart pounded faster and I found myself being transported back in time, back to the day I knelt in front of dozens of people, waiting for my husband's punishment. The memory of the crack of the whip against my back caused me to break out into a sweat, and a tremble moved through my body. I wanted to turn and run, to get away from this city and these people. To never return.

Then I saw an Outlier, a member of the Huni tribe, standing in front of two Fortis guards. Her shaved head was lowered, and surrounded by the massive forms of the men, she seemed impossibly small and helpless. Anger surged through me when one of the men took the basket from her hand and dumped it on the ground, spilling the contents on the street. The other man grabbed her arm, jerking her forward until his face was nearly pressed up against hers. His lips moved, and even though I could not make out his words, I knew the tone with which they would be flung at the poor girl. The hatred, the rage. Directed at her simply because she was an Outlier, and within these walls she had no rights. She was helpless.

But I was not. I had killed men just like the ones standing in front of her. Had raised my bow and released my arrow, and watched as they bled to death on the forest floor. Inside these walls I might not have had the power to put a stop to this, but that did not mean it would always be that way. This was why I had come back. To find a way to turn the tables on the Fortis. To find a way to free my people.

After that, I kept my head high as I walked, refusing to lower my eyes when I passed the Fortis guards, refusing to steer clear of the Sovereign the way I always had before.

They no longer scared me, because not only had I been through the worst they could do to me and survived, I also knew the scars they had left behind were just that. Scars. The marks on my back no longer hurt, the bruises had healed, and the cracks in my heart would heal over time as well. I would always miss Bodhi, but he was with me in spirit and that was something no one could take from me. Not even the Sovereign.

Mira and I arrived at the house to find my new uniform waiting in the mudroom. My friend was silent as I changed my clothes, the worry in her blue eyes feeling louder than a scream in the small space.

"I will be okay," I told her.

Mira's expression did not ease. "Saffron will want to see you."

"I know." I exhaled as I ran my hands down my uniform.

The stiff fabric of the dress against my skin brought a new rush of memories, and for a moment I had to close my eyes. Wearing this dress seemed to transfer me back to the person I used to be. It made me vulnerable. Weak, even.

It was only a dress, though. Nothing about it changed who I was now or erased the things I had done. I was strong, and I would not let Saffron break me.

"I will be okay," I murmured, almost to myself.

When I reopened my eyes, I felt stronger. More prepared to face the day.

"We should go in," Mira said, turning toward the door.

Even though we were silent when we stepped into the kitchen, most of the Outliers in the room turned, almost as if they had been waiting for my arrival. No one spoke, but the gazes of the other women followed my progress as I crossed the room, their eyes filled with pity. If only I could tell them how unnecessary it was. If only I could explain to them it was not me they should pity, but the Fortis.

I said nothing as I passed through the kitchen and out into the dining room, heading for Saffron's office. Months had passed since I had last seen the woman who wore my husband's blood on her hands, and I felt like a totally different person when I stepped into the room. The last time I was here, I had been beaten and bruised from Lysander's attack, and facing the death of my husband. I had felt on the verge of dying myself and had been very certain it would be at the hands of the Fortis. Now, though, I walked with confidence. The blood that ran through Saffron ran through my veins as well. I was Sovereign, I had been born inside these walls, but I was stronger than they were because I was an Outlier as well. I knew what it meant to suffer and struggle, and I had the strength to drag myself up off the ground even in the face of extreme despair. I had the power to be as strong as the woman who ran this house. Not cold and unemotional, but persuasive and determined. Someone who did what needed to be done no matter the cost.

Just as I had expected, Saffron was sitting behind her desk when I stepped into her office, waiting for me. Her eyes, which were the same steely gray as her hair, swept over me when I stopped in front of her, and her lips twitched as if she were working to hold in a smile. In front of her sat the electroprod, menacing even in its silence.

"I'm glad you decided to return," she said after only a beat of silence.

I lowered my head, but not nearly as low as it used to be. My eyes, however, were not focused on the wood floors gleaming beneath my feet, but instead on the woman in front of me. Her skin appeared twice as pale in the dim light of the room, and I was once again struck by how smooth it was despite having lived more than a half a century.

"Thank you for the opportunity." I intentionally left off the word *mistress*.

If Saffron noticed, she made no mention of it. Instead, she stood from her chair and crossed to the front of the desk, her eyes on me the whole time. I watched as she did it, my gaze focused and steady. Not once did it waiver from her face, and not once did I consider lowering it to the ground.

She frowned, pulling her waxy skin down as her eyes swept over me again. Saffron had put on weight over the last six months, although she was still nowhere near as plump as most of the Sovereign, and her face was rounder than it had been. It made her look more like her son, which should have scared me, but instead made my back stiffen even more as my determination to stand up to this woman grew in intensity. She and I were the same height, short by the standards of both the Fortis and the Outliers, but average among the Sovereign.

I had always been the shortest among my people, though, and it suddenly made sense why that was. Outliers tended to be tall and wiry, while the Sovereign were short and much rounder. Their thickness stemmed from their gluttonous lifestyles, but the height was something that had come about over centuries, perhaps due to the lack of variety in their bloodlines, and it explained why I was such a small person. Only last night, right after Mira had returned to the city and told me Saffron wanted me to return to my post, I discovered I had been born within these very walls. That I was Sovereign by birth but had been smuggled out of the city and raised as an Outlier.

Saffron stood in front of me, her emotionless eyes silently taking me in for another moment before saying, "Six months? That's how long it's been?" She paused so I could nod. "I thought you would need the time to not only recover, but to think about how you would proceed once you were back in my good graces. I take it you now understand that defiance of any kind will not be tolerated?"

"I now know that Outliers are expected to bend to the will of the Sovereign no matter what the circumstances are."

Saffron's left eyebrow lifted just a tad, and I could tell that she was trying to decide if my words meant I agreed with her, or if I was making a point.

After a moment she said, "Very well, then. You may return to your post."

I bowed my head slightly as I took a step back. "Thank you."

This time when I left *mistress* off, Saffron's eyes did narrow. She said nothing, but her gaze followed me as I turned away and dug into my back like the claws of a lygan. I kept my head high, though, and my spine straight as I left her office, and I had no intention of changing that, no matter what I faced today or any other day. From now on, I would be stronger than even the strongest of the Fortis guards.

Two

I HAD NOT THOUGHT OF ASA, THE FORTIS GUARD who had worked so hard to protect me in the past, once when considering whether to return to my job. Had not thought of him during my walk to the city, or when I passed through the gates and made my way to Saffron's house. The second I stepped out of the mistress's office, however, my mind wandered to him. Did he know I had returned? Would he care? How would I feel when I saw him again, knowing he had risked so much to get me home safely the last time we were together?

I barely remembered that day, or at least I barely remembered what had transpired after my husband was put to death and I was whipped to within an inch of my life. What I did know was that Asa had felt the pain of my punishment more than a person not connected with the events should have. We barely knew one another, yet he had put his safety on the line for me over and over again. He had even continued to help Mira after I was gone, and had often asked about me. Though I could not comprehend where this man's feelings for me came from, I was sure that not even all these months apart could have erased them.

After my punishment, Asa had met Mira and me with a horse and accompanied us through the borderland, even staying at my side for hours once he had gotten me home safely, waiting to make sure I was okay. Even now, my heart was raw from Bodhi's loss, and a part of me doubted there would ever be room in it for love again, but I could not deny that Asa held a part of it now. He had watched over me the best he could, and he had kept Mira safe since then. I owed him a lot, which made no sense. He was a Fortis, and I was an Outlier. Our people did not mix. Except we had, and we had formed a bond some people might even call friendship.

I was in the kitchen when Asa saw me for the first time. He stepped into the room with a few other guards, and froze. His bronzed skin was darker than I remembered, which I attributed more to the heat from the summer's sun than to my own memory. His black hair was as short as ever, cut close to the scalp so he almost appeared bald, and the strong facial features I remembered so well were softened by the expression in his brown eyes. They seemed to grab me from all the way across the room, holding me prisoner.

The emotion in his eyes told me that until this moment, he had been completely unaware of my return. The feeling in them was as intense as ever, as sharp and penetrating as the last time I saw him and it made the hair on my scalp prickle. It stripped me and left me naked and exposed.

It only took a second for him to start walking again, but he seemed unable to wipe the emotion from his expression. It remained as if carved on his face while he got his plate, while he ate at the table with the other Fortis guards—his eyes on me most of the time—and was still there after he had finished his lunch and brought his plate to me to wash.

When Asa stopped in front of me, the heat from his body wrapped around me, and as always, I found myself nearly overwhelmed by his size. The Fortis in general were large, but Asa seemed to tower over even the tallest of his people. The top of my head barely reached his shoulders, and I had to look up to meet his gaze. Again, his eyes were on me, dark and swimming with feeling, causing a flush to move up my cheeks.

Asa held his plate out, and when I took it, our fingers brushed. His skin was dark compared to mine, brown where mine was pale even after months of hunting in the forest. The warmth of his skin brought back the memory of my hand in his on my last day here, of the calluses that decorated his palms, and how comforting his touch had been when everything else in my life had seemed so hopeless.

We were unable to talk in the kitchen, surrounded by other guards and housemaids, and when he left with nothing more than a nod, it felt as if I had lost something important yet again. We would have time, I told myself. Later, I would find him and thank him for helping me, for helping Mira after I left. For being something I never knew could exist—a Fortis man who saw me not as a worthless Outlier, but as a human being.

After lunch ended and the kitchen had been cleaned up, I headed out in search of him, knowing he would not be hard to find. He would be waiting for me; I was sure of it. Like me, Asa would have things he wanted to say.

As usual, he did not disappoint, and when I stepped into the hall that led to the servants' bathroom, he was already there, already waiting, and the emotion in his brown eyes wrapped me in comfort.

Asa took a step toward me but kept his distance. "You came back."

"I did."

His gaze moved over me, and I knew without him having to say anything that he was remembering how I had looked the last time he saw me. How broken and bruised I had been. How he had been certain I was on the brink of death.

"I am better," I assured him.

Asa nodded, and I smiled, remembering his silence and how it used to unnerve me. It no longer did. Now it was as familiar and comfortable as his brown eyes on me.

"You have new markings," he said after a moment.

Asa reached out like he was going to touch my face, but I pulled away before his fingers could find their mark. The thought of his touch sent conflicting emotions swirling through me. It was wrong because of who we both were and because my husband had only been gone six months, but it also warmed me, remembering how gentle Asa had been with me before, and knowing it would be the same now.

"They are passage markings. The ones on my cheeks are for the people I have lost." My hand went to my face on its own, my fingers tracing the raised area. The marks for the birth parents I had never known, for my father, and the new ones. The ones that represented Bodhi. "For my husband."

Asa's gaze moved to the floor the way it usually did when I mentioned Bodhi. "I'm sorry about him."

I believed him.

I knew Asa loved me, but I also believed he felt genuinely bad that I had lost the man I loved, and it made him even more endearing to me. Made me understand that he had the potential to take up even more of my heart than he already did, and that scared me. Scared me because it made no sense, a Fortis and an Outlier, and because I was not yet ready to think about anyone else being in my life the way Bodhi had. The wounds were healing, but it was going to take time. A long time.

I stepped back, putting more space between us, and Asa lifted his head.

"What is it?" he asked.

"I wanted to thank you for taking me back to my village, and for being so worried. My mother told me that you waited for hours. I am sorry I did not wake before you left. I would have liked to have been able to thank you."

"There's nothing to thank. If I had been here, it never would've happened."

"No." My hand jerked when I almost reached out to touch him, and instead I curled my fingers into a fist. "You cannot think that, Asa. What happened was not your fault. You tried."

"I didn't try hard enough."

Suddenly, a memory came back to me. That day he had not shown up for work, which was what opened the door for Lysander's attack. The next day, after Bodhi was in custody, Asa had been there to comfort me, but like me, he had been covered in bruises. As if he had been in a fight. How could I have forgotten that?

"What happened to you?" I asked. "When you came back to work, you were hurt."

"Thorin." Asa's brown eyes clouded over at the mention of the Fortis man who had tormented me the day I dragged Ronan through his village. "He and his friends have seen me escort you from the city. They don't like it. Fortis aren't supposed to help Outliers. We're enemies. He attacked me that morning before I went in to work, something he'd done before, but this time he brought friends. I fought back, but not hard enough. I woke in our healer's house after hours of being unconscious. I was too hurt to go to work." Asa shook his head, and his gaze moved to the floor like he could not bring himself to look at me. "I should've gone anyway. I should've crawled through the city to get to you."

His words touched me more than anything he had ever said or done, but I could not help feeling bad that he carried so much guilt over what had happened. It was unfair. Asa was not responsible for me, and it was not his fault we lived in a world where so much evil existed.

Hesitantly, I took a step closer to him. "Asa. Look at me."

He lifted his head, and when his brown eyes met mine, the intensity of his feelings nearly took my breath away.

I swallowed and whispered, "Stop blaming yourself. Please. I cannot be responsible for anyone else's pain. I have enough of my own."

His gaze held mine for a beat longer, and when he finally looked away, it seemed as if it was a very difficult thing for him to do. Like he was afraid that if he looked away, I would once again disappear.

"I'll be waiting for you in the mudroom as usual," he said, his brown eyes still focused on the floor.

I paused for a moment, studying him. Remembering how much he had scared me at first. How cold he had seemed. Now, looking him over, I saw something very different. He was Fortis, but he was not hard and angry like the rest of his people. Asa had a vulnerability to him, and a softness in his eyes that made his size less overpowering—and almost desirable.

The thought took me by surprise, but I could not deny the truth in it. I found Asa attractive. He was the opposite of Bodhi in every way, dark and silent while my husband had been blond and open, but they shared one very important trait. Kindness. Asa was kind, and that was what made him stand out among his people. He cared about other human beings, even a lowly Outlier like me.

I looked away from the man in front of me, from his strong jaw and dark skin and wide shoulders that suddenly interested me more than ever before, and whispered, "Thank you."

Asa's head bobbed once, and then he turned away. I did not move, watching him until he disappeared through the door at the end of the hall, the entire time thinking about what this man was to me. And what he could be.

I thought about Asa the rest of the day as I worked, about his feelings for me, about what it had led him to do—betray his people. It still seemed impossible, thinking about a Fortis helping an Outlier, but it was true. It defied all logic, but it was impossible to deny.

Even more troubling were the feelings swirling through me. I could not put names to them, or perhaps I simply did not want to, but they had the potential to grow into something big with time. I was unsure if I wanted that, or if it would be a betrayal to my dead husband when it did happen. In fact, there was very little about Asa that I was sure of.

I WAS ON MY HANDS AND KNEES SCRUBBING THE floor when footsteps entered the dining room behind me, and I looked up just as a group of Fortis guards stepped in. There were four of them, three men and the lone woman who worked in Saffron's house, and Greer was among the men.

He had been there that day, had tried to force Mira and me to strip. Had he not stopped us, had we been allowed to leave the house without interference, perhaps Lysander would not have gotten what he wanted. Instead, Greer had cornered us, and then Saffron's son had come in, demanding we allow him to search us. The sneer on his face as he looked Mira over had left little doubt what was about to happen, and in an instant my mind was made up. I had been at Lysander's mercy before, but Mira had not, and even if it meant putting myself in danger, I would not allow Lysander to have his way with her.

At the sight of Greer, the memories came back in a rush, falling on me in a flood of emotions that nearly knocked me to the ground. If he saw me right now, the Fortis guard would not hesitate to torment me, and I wanted to slink back into the shadows of the room, wanted to avoid his notice for one more day. Before I had a chance, though, one of the men said something that caught my attention, and I found myself frozen in place, on my hands and knees, the rag in my hand forgotten as I listened to his words.

"Thane's been missing for three days," the man said. "Since the hunting party."

"Something isn't right." The woman shook her head, and the twisted knots she tried to pass off as hair brushed her shoulders.

They were talking about *me*.

"It's a predator," Greer growled.

"What else can it be?" another man said as the group moved across the room, heading for the door that led into the kitchen.

Greer let out a deep laugh that echoed through the room. "Nothing. Nothing else could take out a Fortis. It's probably a pack of cats. We're not hunting them enough, and the population's gotten too big again."

"We should send a big group out to hunt the bastards down before they kill more of our people," the woman said.

"It might be a good idea."

They went by without looking down, too caught up in their conversation to notice me, which I was more than thankful for. A beat later, they had moved out of the room, and I was able to let out the breath I had been holding.

Over fifty Fortis hunters had died by my hands since Bodhi's death. I had started going into the forest out of desperation, hoping to take my mind off my pain while at the same time providing meat for my family. Not once had I considered killing Fortis hunters until the moment I released that first arrow. When I did, when I saw the man fall, it had awoken something in me. It had given me strength even though I had always been told I was weak. I was nothing. A Winta woman. An Outlier. Useless. But that day, I learned the truth about myself.

I was strong.

Of course, I had known the deaths would not go unnoticed forever, but to hear the very men and women I was hunting talk about it still made my heart beat faster. But it was a good thing, too. It told me what they were thinking, and what they were going to do about the missing men and women. Sooner or later they were going to send a large party into the wilds to hunt, but it would not be *me* they were hunting. No, I was something they would never consider. They were Fortis and much too strong to be killed by anything other than a wild creature. Especially not an Outlier.

They were fools, but at that moment, I was thankful for it.

Three

RETURNING TO WORK HELPED MY FAMILY, BUT IT did not stop me from hunting in the evenings. Not only did my mother and sister need the meat, but with Bodhi gone, my people were struggling, and I felt compelled to do something about it. My husband had been the best hunter in the village, and the game he used to provide was missed.

There was more to it, though. Now that I was back in Saffron's house, I found I longed for the peacefulness the forest provided, not to mention how close it made me feel to Bodhi. He had been the first one to take me into the forest, back when we were just children, and then after we were married. He had shown me how to hunt. Shown me how strong I could be. Going into the forest kept his memory alive. It made me feel closer to him.

I also could not bring myself to stop hunting the Fortis. Not even after overhearing the conversation in Saffron's house. If anything, returning to the city made the need in me grow. I was able to see their abuse firsthand. I witnessed Outliers being stripped and taken advantage of on their way out of the city, heard the insults thrown at us as we made our way through the Fortis village. Every instance made me itch for a weapon so I could take the men and women down the way I did in the forest, but not only was I empty-handed, in the city I was outnumbered, and it made me feel useless.

Not in the wilds. Out there I knew where to go and what to do to take the Fortis by surprise. Out there I could show anyone I came across exactly how strong I was.

Returning to work meant my time in the forest was cut short, though, and I no longer had the luxury of spending hours searching for hunting parties. Not if I wanted to bring game in as well. Still, if I happened upon a small group while I was in the woods, I killed them without hesitation. Not only did they deserve to die for what they had done to my people for centuries, but I also needed their game. I usually only had a couple hours of good daylight left by the time I returned from the city, and winter was on its way. When it came, things would be even more difficult. Tracking an animal in the snow was easier, assuming one could be found, but many of the forest creatures slept during winter. Depending on the few short hours of sunlight I had at the end of each day meant I would come home with almost nothing, but the Fortis hunting parties I came upon in the wilds had usually been out for hours, and it was not uncommon to find their horses overflowing with game.

Just like the horses of the men in front of me right now.

The first one, a man with long gray hair and tan skin that reminded me of an animal's hide, had four rodents and a string with at least a dozen rawlins dangling from it, their red feathers brilliant against the horse's dark coat. The second man had just as many of the birds hanging from his own horse, as well as a rat big enough to feed two families.

Killing these men could result in the Fortis sending a search party out, but it was a risk I needed to take. More than a week had passed since I had stumbled upon a hunting party, and a month since I had returned to Saffron's house. I knew from the gossip I overheard on a daily basis that the Fortis hunters had been out searching for whatever creature they thought was killing their people. They had found nothing, of course, but as the deaths became less and less frequent, they had begun to suspect they had at least succeeded in scaring the animal off. They had no way of knowing the drop in Fortis deaths was because I had returned to my job in Sovereign City. No one did.

I was hidden by a group of bushes when I released my arrow, but it found my target without issue. The man with the rat let out a grunt when the point sank into his neck, and the thump of his body hitting the forest floor seemed to echo through the air.

Before his friend had even hit the ground, the second man was on alert. He jumped from his horse, pulling his sword out at the same time, and looked around as if trying to figure out where the arrow had come from. The way his upper lip curled reminded me of the looks Greer shot me, and I had no qualms about notching a second arrow. Only, the man was moving too much for me to get a good shot off, and the horse was stomping around at his side, refusing to stay still and succeeding in blocking his master from view.

I shifted my position in hopes of getting a better angle, but between the horse and the bushes in front of me, it was impossible. If I wanted to take this man out—and I *did*—I was going to have to make myself known.

I got to my feet, my back straight and my arrow ready.

The man spotted me and let out an animalistic growl that made the hair on my arms stand up. "What do you think you're doing, *Outlier*?"

His mocking tone made it impossible to keep my mouth shut, and I called out, "The same thing I have been doing for months."

He blinked, confused by my words, but only a moment later understanding flashed in his gray eyes. He took at step toward me, his knuckles tightening on the hilt of his sword. "You? You're the one who's been taking our hunters out?" The man looked me over before shaking his head. "I don't believe it. You're too puny. Too pathetic."

"Ask your friend," I said, nodding to the dead man at his back.

The Fortis man glanced down, and the second his eyes were no longer focused on me, I released my arrow. It hit him in the heart, and he had just enough time to look up before he dropped to the ground beside his friend. The expression of shock was frozen on his face as he left this world.

My process of unloading the horses had not changed over the months, but my habit of taking one or two items from the dead men had. Stripping them clean would draw suspicion, but it hurt no one to take a sword on occasion or something else that might be useful down the road. Over the months, I had managed to gather an impressive cache of weapons, all of which were currently stored in my cave. What I was saving them for, I did not yet know; I just knew that I was going to need them at some point.

I was in the middle of ridding the dead men of their weapons when the beat of hooves broke through the silence. My bow was lying on the ground at my side, and I reached for it, but before I could wrap my fingers around it, the horse and its rider had already broken through the trees in font of me. The man pulled on the horse's reins when he saw me, and the animal let out a snort.

"What's this?" the Fortis man bellowed as he looked around, his gaze going from me to the dead men.

He let out a roar and kicked his heels against the horse's flanks, and then he was charging me. There was no time to grab an arrow, let alone notch one, and since I already had a knife in my hand, I did the only thing I could think to do. I jumped to my feet and charged the man.

When he was close enough, I jumped. My free hand grabbed hold of his shirt while I slashed the knife at him with my other. The blade made contact with his arm as his body toppled toward me, slipping from the horse and falling, taking me down with him. He landed on top of me, and the weight of his body on my chest forced all the air from my lungs, but he was injured, too. He was bleeding all over me and groaning instead of trying to get back to his feet.

I gasped, desperately trying to fill my lungs while kicking my legs, trying to get the man off me. He grunted and moved enough that I was able to free my hands, giving me the chance to swing my knife at him again. I got him in the side this time, but giving up was not in his nature. His hands found my neck, and he started to squeeze.

Panic surged through me, taking over my thoughts and instincts, and for an instant I could do nothing but struggle for air and try to get his hands from my neck. When I reached up and tried to claw at his fingers, hoping to free myself from his grasp, it hit me that I still had the knife. That was when instinct kicked in.

I brought the knife down, and when the blade sank into his back, he let out a scream. Still, he did not release me. So I did it again, and then again, driving the blade into his back over and over until his grip finally loosened enough to allow me to breathe. When it did, I filled my lungs, gasping for air greedily before stabbing the man on top of me one final time.

He stopped moving, but he was still alive. I could feel the sporadic rise and fall of his chest against mine. The man was still on top of me; weighing me down until I thought I would suffocate. Putting all my strength into it, I shoved him, and he rolled off, flopping onto his back at my side. His eyes were wide and glassy, but he was staring at me, and somewhere behind the fear and pain swimming in his eyes, there was a look of shock that matched the one the other Fortis hunters had given me.

It was impossible to say how many times I had stabbed him, a dozen at least, and I was too shaken by what had happened to move right away. This man was more than twice my size, and I should not have been able to take him out, and yet I had. It had been close, and I very well could have died, but I had won. The thought had me frozen in a combination of awe and terror.

I was still lying on my back when a fourth horse broke through the trees and skittered to a stop right in front of me. Finally, my senses returned and I rolled to my side. I pushed myself up, but I was still on my knees in the clearing when my gaze landed on the newcomer. The sight of him made me freeze yet again. I was unarmed, vulnerable, and covered in the blood of the Fortis men I had just killed, but I could do nothing but stare.

"Asa." His name was all I could get out, and even that was little more than a gasp of surprise.

He said nothing, and he stared down at me without moving for so long that I started to wonder if he recognized me. His gaze went to the three men I had killed before once again looking me over, and then he was sliding off his horse and hurrying to my side.

"Indra, where are you hurt?"

"I am fine." The words came out hoarse, though, and I had to clear my throat. "I am okay, Asa."

He seemed to not believe me. He touched first my arms and then my face, and then he repeated the process, desperate to find the source of the blood. It was the worry swimming in his brown eyes that made me realize what the situation looked like to him. He thought these men had attacked me. That I had defended myself. He thought I was the victim.

He could not have been more wrong.

"Stop." I pushed his hands away and got to my feet.

"What did they do to you?" he asked, looking up at me from his position on the ground.

"Nothing. I killed them."

Asa blinked, and the questions in his eyes told me that he still did not understand.

"I have been killing them for months. Your hunting parties." I waved to my bow, sitting on the ground at his side. "I hide in the trees and shoot them, then steal their game. Your people think a wild animal is responsible, but I am."

Understanding dawned on his face, but I could not read him well enough to know what he was thinking, if he was angry or appalled, or if he thought I was brave.

"You did this?" he said after a moment. "You're the one responsible for the missing and dead Fortis hunters?"

I lifted my head and squared my shoulders. "I am."

Asa said nothing, and for a moment we stood in silence, staring at one another. His expression made it seem as if he was seeing me for the first time, but I still could not figure out what he was thinking.

He opened his mouth, but the beat of hooves that broke through the air cut off anything he was going to say.

Asa jumped to his feet, grabbing my bow in the process. He thrust it against my chest while shoving me toward the trees at my back. "You have to get out of here. There are more of us."

I looked behind him, back toward the men that had died at my hands. "My arrows."

"There's no time," Asa said, and then he pushed me again. Gently, but with enough force to send me back a couple steps. "They're on their way. Go, or they'll kill you."

"Thank you." I snatched my bow from him before spinning around and charging into the forest.

The pounding of hooves against the ground at my back chased me as I ran, followed a few beats later by the boom of male voices. They were loud and angry, but as I ran, they grew further away instead of closer. The hunters were not coming after me. I had no idea what Asa told them, but I had no doubt that he would be sure to lead them away from me.

He had saved me yet again.

Still, I ran, not slowing until I reached my cave. I barely pushed the branches aside before charging in, and the sharp sticks pricked at my skin as I squeezed through. Once inside, I collapsed on the cold floor, exhausted and out of breath, but thankful I had supplies hidden in the cave. It would be much too risky to head out into the woods when I had no idea what was going on, and the Fortis could be in the forest for hours searching for me, meaning I might be trapped here for the night.

Fall air that had just this week swooped in to engulf the wilds made the cave chilly. Once the sun went down, it would only get worse, and as soon as I caught my breath, I went to work making a fire. I needed it for warmth, but I had to keep it small in case the Fortis hunters did manage to make it this far west. The impending darkness would most likely cover any smoke that made it through the vents in the cave, but I wanted to play it safe. Thankfully, I also had the furs Bodhi had stored in the cave, as well as some jackets and other items I had taken from dead hunters over the last six months.

It was not until my stomach growled that I realized I had failed to get the game off the dead hunters. Three men had died and I had almost gotten killed myself, yet not a single rawlin had made it into my possession. Even worse, the Fortis would now know animals were not responsible for killing their men, which might make them wonder about all the other deaths in the forest. What would Asa tell them? I knew he would never implicate me, but who could he blame other than an Outlier? No one else lived in the wilds.

Even worse was the knowledge that the situation put my entire village in danger. *My* actions had done that. I had risked everyone with my impulsiveness. Would the Fortis slaughter them? Would they take out all the villages or just the nearest? The Trelite tribe was the closest one to where I now found myself, and even though it might save my tribe from the wrath of the Fortis, they should not be punished for something I had done. Of all the Outliers, they were the most peaceful, rarely even killing animals. They did not deserve to have the Fortis come down on them. None of us did.

My stomach growled a second time, and I cursed myself for not storing some kind of food in the cave. Dried fruit or nuts would have been nice, and as often as I came out into the woods, they would not have had time to go bad, only I had nothing.

There were animals living in these caves, though. The scratch of their claws against the stone as they scurried through the darkness had awoken me more than once when I was out here with Bodhi. Killing one of the creatures would be no problem, and neither would cooking it thanks to the fire I had already built. All I had to do was find one.

The main cave had always been a stopping point for me. Even back when Bodhi was alive, I had never bothered to explore the other tunnels. It was partly due to the warning he had given me the first time he brought me here, when I had asked him if he had ever explored the rest of the cave and how deep it went. He had told me it went far back where there was no light, which had discouraged him from exploring any more of the cavernous tunnels. I understood, knowing if his torch had burnt out he could have gotten lost and died in the darkness. The story had been enough to make me abandon any idea of going deeper into the cave myself, but I had also never needed to explore the area. Not like now. Now I had nowhere to go, and my stomach was begging for food. It seemed like the perfect time to take a risk.

I found the torch Bodhi had left behind and lit it, and then grabbed a knife before heading for the first opening. It was taller than the one that led outside, but narrower, only a little wider than shoulder width. It was tight, but turning sideways helped me squeeze through as I moved deeper into the passage, holding the torch out in front of me so I could see where I was going. Soon the tunnel widened and opened up into a room that was bigger than the first, deeper and taller because the floor sloped down.

The drip of water echoed through the darkness to my left, and I turned toward it. The light from the torch illuminated the area, revealing a small stream of water running down the wall and pooling on the floor. From there, it moved deeper into the cave. I followed it, picking my way carefully over the slick rocks and into the dark abyss beyond.

The stream led me to yet another tunnel, this one wider and taller than the first. Here it pooled again before moving further into the cave where it widened and grew deeper. From there, it moved much faster, and the sound of the rippling water bounced off the walls as I followed it into the depths of the cave.

I had been walking for a while when the first drop hit my forehead, and I looked up to find water dripping from the ceiling above me and running down the walls on both sides where it joined the stream, making it deeper and more violent. Another drop hit my torch, giving off a hissing sound, and Bodhi's warning rang in my ears. If my torch went out now, I would be plunged into darkness, making it difficult or impossible to find my way out. I needed to head back.

I had just made the decision and started to turn when another drop fell. It hit my torch again, this time dead on, and the fire went out with a puff that left me feeling cold.

Four

I WAS PLUNGED INTO DARKNESS SO THICK IT MADE me feel as if I had been dragged into the underworld. I froze, but was unsure if it was terror or shock that rooted me to the ground. The torch was still in my hand and I was shaking, and even though the thing was now useless, I could not bring myself to let it go. I just kept staring into the darkness where the fire had been only a moment ago, silently begging it to reappear even though it was pointless. It was gone, and now I was lost.

The thump of my heartbeat echoed in my ears, nearly drowning out the sounds of the stream, and I—

The stream!

That was my answer. I could follow the stream back. I had not walked far, and I was sure if I could just make it back to the second cave, the light from the fire I had made would be visible. It would be faint, but all I needed was enough light to tell me which direction to go.

I started walking, taking slow, even steps. The rocks were damp, though, and even my measured steps felt dangerous in the thick darkness that had engulfed me. So I kept my body low, hoping it would help me maintain my balance, praying things would get no worse than they already were.

The stream was to my right, and getting to the main cave was simply a matter of following it the whole way back. That was the thought going through my head when my right foot slipped out from under me. It slid on the damp rocks, and my other foot followed its lead only a moment later. I tried to catch myself on the wall to my left, but I still had the torch in my hand, and the effort was useless. I fell, but surrounded by darkness I had no clue where I would end up. When I hit the stone floor, the jolt from the impact vibrated through me, but that was only the beginning, because a moment later my entire body was plunged into the stream.

The icy water engulfed me. My head went under, and in an instant I was chilled to my very core. I pushed myself up and gasped, desperate to fill my lungs. Once I was sitting, the frozen depths still went up to my chest, and when I managed to drag myself to my feet, I discovered the water was all the way up to my knees. Much deeper than I had anticipated. I had to get out.

Due to the surrounding darkness, it took a moment to find the rocky edge of the stream. The stone floor seemed twice as slick now, and my feet slipped a few times as I tried to pull myself out of the water. Not wanting to fall again, I chose to stay down instead of getting to my feet, and instead crawled forward on my hands and knees.

Tremors started in my limbs the second I was free. The air in the caves had been cool before, but now it seemed to be coated in a layer of ice. I rolled onto my back for a moment, gasping as I shivered. My teeth chattered together and the tips of my fingers had lost all feeling. Every inch of my body was covered in bumps from the cold that I was certain would kill me if I didn't get warm soon. I had to move. I knew I did.

The stream was on my left now, so I turned as I pushed myself up on my hands and knees once again. But I had only crawled forward a few inches when I stopped, realizing I might have climbed out of the stream on the wrong side. Turning again, I felt around in the darkness as if the grooves in the rocks would tell me which way to go, but of course they did not. My sense of direction had been destroyed when I fell into the stream, and the cold water had pushed every thought out of my head except one—getting warm. I had paid no attention to which side I was climbing out on or which way I would need to go once I freed myself from the icy water, and now I had no idea where to go.

I sat on the damp floor of the cave, hugging my shivering body as I thought it through. No matter how hard I tried to recall what I had done, though, I could not. I was lost.

I hugged myself tighter and took a deep breath. My body was like ice, and getting colder with each passing moment. Staying here was not an option. I needed to move. If I went the wrong way, I could get lost in the cave forever, but at least it gave me a shot at making it out. Sitting here would accomplish nothing, and even worse, I would freeze for sure. I had to take a chance.

I pushed myself up, climbing to my feet with great care, and started moving through the darkness, the stream once again on my right. This time I walked slower, not just to prevent myself from falling again, but because I was shivering so much that my legs were unsteady.

There was no way for me to know how far I had gone when the first light zipped through the water, but the sight of it cutting through the blackness was shocking enough to freeze me in my tracks. By that point the shivers were twice as bad, and I found myself wondering if the cold had made me delirious, because it made no sense that something down here would be glowing.

I started walking again, hugging myself in a desperate and futile attempt to get warm, and only a few seconds later I caught sight of another light. This one was closer to where I currently stood, but just as brief as the first one had been. It zipped through the water, lighting the area up enough that it illuminated both sides of the stream, and even the rock the little creature disappeared under.

I blinked into the blackness where the light had been, sure I was seeing things. It did not reappear, but when I lifted my gaze, I found that what had looked like never-ending blackness only a few moments ago had changed. There were more lights in the distance, dozens of them. So many that the stream was clearly visible to me now.

I walked faster, not caring if I slipped on the rocks, and in no time I had reached yet another open area. I now knew I had gone the wrong way when I started walking, but I no longer cared. I was too awestruck by what I was seeing.

The room I now found myself in had a large pool in the center, and the glowing creatures were everywhere, not just in the water. They were on the walls, crawling across the rocks, and even hanging from the ceiling. Their pace was much slower on land than in water, which gave me a chance to get a better look at them. They were about the size of my hand and scaly like fish, but they had eight legs and front claws, and a tail that flipped up. It fanned out when I came near, emitting an even brighter light than before, and the little thing snapped its claws in my face as if trying to ward me off.

There were more than enough of them to light up the room, and I hugged myself as I looked around, getting a feel for where I was. It was smaller than the main room, and the stream had opened up here and doubled in size. It whooshed through and disappeared under the rocks, probably going outside, but before it did, it was joined by another stream, only this one came from a small pool on the other side of the room. I moved toward it, shivering and hugging myself, certain my eyes were playing tricks on me. There was no way steam was rising off the little pool. It made no sense.

But the closer I got, the more certain I became of what I was seeing, and then I was next to it and could actually *feel* the heat radiating from the water. After the cold stream, just being near this little pool was like slipping under a layer of fur after a snowstorm, but even more important, it meant I would not freeze to death.

I knelt down to test the water, afraid it might be too hot, but one touch was all it took to convince me that getting in would not melt the flesh from my body. I stripped my clothes off then once again tested the water with my toe before slipping inside.

The water warmed me almost immediately, and my brain function returned to normal. I was no longer lost because I could follow the stream back and make my way to the main room. Even better, if I could capture one — or more — of these creatures, I might be able to light my way as well.

I stayed in the pool just long enough to get warm before climbing out. After the hot water, my clothes were chilly against my skin, but it was not bad enough to kill me. As I dressed, I watched the little creatures for signs that they might be dangerous. They had no spikes or teeth that I could see, but there were pinchers. That could be a problem. Of course, it was possible they still glowed after death, which would make my task a lot easier. There was only one way to know for sure, though.

I pulled out my knife as I approached the nearest bug. It lifted its tail, and when it fanned out, the creature's glow intensified. The thing tried to run, but I was too fast, and I speared it through the middle with my knife before it had gone two steps. Blood that looked blue in the limited light sprayed across the rocks, and the bug twitched twice before going still. I barely had time to blink before the glow faded from its body and the thing went black.

"Crap," I muttered and tossed the bug aside.

The second its body hit the ground, a few of the nearby creatures scurried over and began devouring it, which gave me an idea.

I moved about the room, spearing bug after bug until I had a handful of the things, and then headed for the opening of the cave. I went as far as I could before the lights were too dim to see where I stepped, and then tossed one of the bodies I was carrying on the ground in front of me. The click of feet against stone as the creatures scurried forward echoed off the walls around me, and the tunnel grew bright again. I started walking before the things had even reached the body, moving as far as I could before once again tossing a dead bug on the ground. The creatures scurried after it, and I moved.

I glanced back to find dozens of the little bugs following me, with more of them crawling from the stream every few seconds. I dropped another body and more came, so I dropped another, and it happened again. I kept walking, dropping the bodies every few steps, spearing more of the bugs when I ran out, and the things followed me the whole way. Before long, the tunnel began to look familiar, and I realized I had reached the point where my torch had gone out. I tossed another body on the ground and walked faster.

By the time I reached the large room, there were so many bugs behind me that it was like day. They emerged from the tunnel and began scurrying up the walls, illuminating the room as they went. In the distance, I spotted more openings I knew would hold other wonders, but I also saw a few little rats digging in the crevices of the rocks. The sight of them made my stomach rumble, reminding me of why I had come into the cave to begin with.

I speared a rat easily, aided by the light the bugs gave off, and then cut it open, tossing the entrails on the ground. The glowing creatures swarmed them as I headed back into the main part of the cave.

My fire was low, so I added a couple more logs and settled in. Then I pierced the rat's body with a stick and cooked it over the fire.

It had to be dark outside by now, and I was in the middle of trying to decide if I should try to make it home or sleep in the cave when a boom of thunder broke through the silence, answering my question for me. I would sleep here and head out at first light. Not only would it prevent me from getting soaked, but it would also be safer that way. The Fortis hunters had no doubt headed back to their village, but I would rather not risk it.

FIVE

I MADE IT BACK TO THE VILLAGE JUST AFTER DAWN, giving me enough time to change and say a quick goodbye to my mother and Anja before heading out to meet Mira. The previous night in the cave had been warm thanks to the fire and fur, and comforting because it had made me feel like Bodhi was near, but on my trek back to the village my thoughts had once again turned to Asa. What had he told the other men last night, and what would he say to me when I saw him today? More importantly, what I would say to him?

He was different than the other Fortis. I knew that by now, but he was still one of them, and I had been killing his people. No matter how he felt about me, Asa would not be able to condone my actions, and I understood. If he were able to turn a blind eye to what I was doing, he would not be the man I thought he was.

Still, I could not tell him I would stop. He had to know why, had to understand what my people went through every day. It was part of the reason he had started helping me to begin with, but I was under no delusions about it. Asa would be angry with me.

"Why are you so quiet this morning?" Mira asked on our way to work.

I startled then shook my head as if the action would clear my thoughts, but it did nothing to help me sort through the emotions surging through me. "Tired. I got stuck out in the storm last night and had to sleep in the cave."

Mira's steps faltered, but she did not stop completely. "What cave?"

More than once I had told her about the time Bodhi and I spent together in the woods, but never about the cave. It had seemed wrong. It was something that belonged to my husband and me alone. Our special place. Even now that he was gone, I found I did not want to share it. I liked going there so I could feel close to him, and I did not want anyone, not even Mira, to take that away from me.

But I owed her some sort of explanation, so I said, "A place Bodhi and I used to go. That is all."

She nodded like she understood, and the fact that she asked no other questions confirmed it. She also did not speak again during the long walk to Sovereign City, almost as if she knew I needed this time to think.

The Fortis village was in an uproar when we reached it, and for the first time since they had begun construction on the quarters, the bang of hammers was not the loudest sound. People were shouting, angry, and it filled me with dread. I knew what this was about, but I tried to tell myself it would be okay. Asa had covered for me and there would be no angry mob of people waiting to rip me to shreds when I arrived.

"What do you think is happening?" Mira whispered as we approached the outskirts of the village.

"I do not know," I lied.

We had just crossed the threshold into the village when the door of the first house opened. A man stepped out, towering over us and close enough that it made me jump. I looked up, and to my shock came face to face with the very man I had spent the whole walk thinking about. The usual relief at Asa's presence was absent, though, and the expression in his brown eyes was like a burst of cold wind sweeping over me.

Before I had time to figure out what he was thinking, he had already looked away. My heart was pounding, nearly drowning out the angry voices surrounding us. I grabbed Mira's arm and pulled her with me, walking faster through the crowd in hopes of escaping not only Asa, but the rage throbbing through the air.

There were too many conversations going on at once for me to hear them all, but I caught enough to know the uproar was, in fact, about me. Just like I had thought, my arrow had given me away, and the Fortis now knew an animal was not responsible for their missing people. They were angry. Outraged. Out for blood.

They wanted revenge.

But the arrow, as damaging as it was, could not reveal my identity. Neither my name nor my tribe was identifiable by looking at it, and I tried to cling to that knowledge as Mira and I moved through the Fortis village, past angry words and violent threats against the person who had been slaughtering their people.

Asa was the only person who could identify me.

I ventured a look over my shoulder, but could not find him in the crowd. He had to be on his way into the city, though. He would not abandon me so quickly after my return to work, especially not after what had happened last time. Would he?

Doubt crept through me. He had saved me yet again last night, making it seem like he would still be on my side, but there was always the possibility he had had second thoughts. Maybe, after letting me go, he had changed his mind. Perhaps I had crossed a line that could not be forgiven. Perhaps I looked different to him now that he knew I was a killer.

Mira and I made it into the city without any real interaction with the Fortis, but we were both too shaken by the rage we had walked through to talk as we continued our journey through Sovereign City, headed for Saffron's house. Even though I was unsure whether I wanted to see him, I found myself looking over my shoulder every few seconds, searching the mass of people already crowded in the streets for Asa. Once I thought I caught sight of him, but when my heart skipped a beat, I quickly looked away. By the time I had gathered enough courage to look back, the crowd had once again swallowed him up.

I was jumpy and out of sorts all day, both waiting for and dreading the moment I would get a chance to talk to Asa. It was early afternoon before we finally came face to face. As usual, he found me in the hall leading to the servants' bathroom, only this time when he cornered me with his large body, it acted as a sudden reminder of how small I was and how, no matter how many Fortis hunters I had killed, I was still very much at the mercy of others inside these walls.

Asa looked down at me with menacing brown eyes, and for the first time since I had gotten to know him, fear shot through me. "It's time for you to tell me who you really are."

"What?" I had no idea what he meant, and for a moment all I could do was shake my head. Then I found my voice and said, "I am Indra of the Winta tribe. That is all. Just an Outlier."

Except that I was not just an Outlier, because I had been born within in these walls, to Sovereign parents. Only that was something I could not tell Asa.

He leaned closer, making me shrink away. "A girl who is *just* an Outlier doesn't kill more than fifty men and women all on her own. She doesn't turn a village upside down the way you have. My people know animals aren't responsible for killing our hunters. A person is. They're angry, Indra. They want blood. They want *your* blood."

My heart pounded against my ribcage and I gasped, "You told them it was me?"

Asa startled, and when he shook his head, his gaze softened, making him look more like the man I had gotten to know. "No. You know I wouldn't do that."

"Then what did you tell them?"

Asa exhaled, and in the process leaned further away from me, giving me space to breathe. He ran his hand over his head, and I found myself wondering how the short fibers of his hair would feel against my palm. Bodhi's hair had been long and wavy and soft, but I imagined that Asa's would be prickly to the touch.

"I told them I came upon a man, a man like none I had ever seen before," he said, his words drawing my gaze from his head and back to his face. "He had a bow in his hands and a bloody knife, and our men were dead. I told them the man ran when he saw me, and the rest of our group arrived before I could chase him."

"They believed you?"

"They believed me." We stood in silence for a moment before he said, "You've started down a very dangerous path, Indra. You have to know that. You've been lucky so far, but it can't last. Eventually, one of the men you attack will get the better of you, and then you'll get hurt."

Anger flared through me then, replacing the fear that had been swimming in me since Asa came upon me in the forest yesterday. He knew I had already been hurt, in so many ways. He had seen it with his own eyes, had told me that my pain had hurt him as well, yet he had the nerve to say this to me.

"*Hurt?*" I found myself spitting the word at him. "I am getting hurt every day, Asa. You have seen it. You have seen what these men have done to me, to the people I love, to my tribe, and to all the other Outliers working in the city. I stood by and let it happen for too long, but I will not do it anymore. I will not be the person who watches others get hurt and does nothing to stop it. Not anymore."

We stared at one another for a moment, each of us lost in our own pain, in the pain that was both for ourselves and for our people. I could see the battle raging in him, the one that pulled him in two different directions. Between me, a person he had come to care about, and his people. It was unfair to ask him to do this thing for me, to make a choice that went against who he was, but I could not turn back now, just as he could not change the fact that he had been born a Fortis. Those were his people, but I was an Outlier, and we had been fooling ourselves for too long. Our worlds were too different to mix. *We* were too different.

"I understand the things that have been done to you," he finally said. "I understand your anger. But I'm looking out for you, Indra."

"I know, but maybe it is time I learned to look out for myself," I replied.

"Are you saying you don't want my help anymore?" he asked, surprise and doubt clouding his vision.

I exhaled as the truth settled over me like a heavy weight. There was no way I could walk away from his help, not if I wanted to keep Mira safe.

"You know I cannot do that," I finally said, "but you must also know I cannot turn my back on my people either. I will leave it up to you to decide what you must do from here. If you cannot live with the things I have done, the things I plan to continue to do, I will understand." I stepped back, and it seemed as if a large canyon had opened up between us. I waved down at myself when I said, "This is who I am, Asa. That will not change."

His brown eyes swept over me, softening even more. "I know who you are, Indra, and even if I don't agree with it, I can't turn my back on you now."

For once, his assurances gave me no comfort. Asa and I were involved in an alliance which defied logic, and one which could not last. Eventually, something would happen that would cause him to turn his back on me, and when that time came, I was unsure of what would become of us. Of what I would be forced to do to not only save myself, but my people.

SIX

WEEKS WENT BY, AND THE WILDS WERE once again covered in snow. Things between Asa and me stayed the same, a silent partnership that defied our background and logic, but one we were both comfortable with. Before I knew it, I had been back at Saffron's house for more than two months, and God had smiled down on me during that time. I had not run into Lysander once. It was a situation that could not last, but one I was thankful for nonetheless.

With each passing day, I adjusted more and more to being back in the place where I had been brutalized, to being in the house of the woman who was responsible for my husband's death. I was no more comfortable than I had been on that first day back, but I was learning not to jump when someone came into the room behind me, and I began bracing myself for Lysander's appearance less and less whenever I walked into a room. I had almost convinced myself that I might be able to go forever without seeing him again, and no matter how foolish the thought was, it made my time in Saffron's house a little bit easier.

Then, one day, he was there.

I stepped from the kitchen and found Lysander standing in the middle of the dining room, his plump frame seeming to take up most of the open space. It was almost as if he had been waiting for me. As if he had known I would walk through the door at that exact moment.

He was already smiling, his round face sweaty and his skin yellower than it had been the last time I saw him, and when I froze, his expression morphed into something grotesque. A shudder wracked my body, shooting from the back of my neck all the way to my feet, and my stomach convulsed. I tried not to think about what had happened the last time I was alone with this man. Tried not to remember the sting of his hand hitting my face or how rough the wall had been against my cheek, but blocking it out was impossible. I could feel it, I could feel *him*, and it turned me into a mute. Made every part of my brain shut down until I was only able to do one thing: replay what had happened over and over again.

He stepped closer, practically waddling on his stubby legs, and stopped four feet away from me, but close enough that his body heat engulfed me. In one hand he held the electroprod, which he flipped on dramatically. The soft hum of the electricity filled the room, and my entire body jerked away from the blue glow it gave off. I had never experienced the shock of an electroprod, but I had witnessed enormous

Fortis men fall to their knees from it. Had witnessed the shrieks a full-grown man could give off from the slightest touch.

"Don't even think about trying to run this time," Lysander said in a low voice, his eyes darting down to the electroprod in his hand. Then his smile widened and he leaned even closer. "My mother told me you'd come back."

I swallowed, but could not muster even a sound. I felt wedged in, stuck between this man and the torture device he held in his hand, positive that he would not hesitate to use it on me if I so much as risked batting an eye.

"I was glad to hear it," he continued. "Your friend, the one you saved that day, she's been calling to me. For a long time, really, but I wanted to wait. I wanted it to be special." He cut the distance between us in half and lowered his voice until it sounded terrifyingly similar to the hiss a lygan let out just before it attacked. "I wanted you to be in the house. I wanted you to hear her cries. To be helpless. *Again.*"

The last word was even more sinister than a hiss. It was like a whisper from the underworld, something that came from the deepest depths, and standing there with Lysander so close, I wanted nothing more than to stab him and send him to the place where eternal fire would consume him. Where he would truly know what suffering was.

I could not, though, just as I could not move when Lysander leaned closer to me. It was as if he meant to kiss me, or maybe even bite me, and I managed to turn my face away. But I kept my eyes on him, not wanting or not able to let him out of my sight. His smile was an insult to the word. It was all evil, all threat. It seemed to wrap around my body in an attempt to pull me closer, and I had to put a lot of effort into staying where I was.

I had been strong since coming back here. I had not bent to Saffron's intimidation, had kept my head down while staying proud at the same time, but I was no match for Lysander. Not after what he had done to me. Not in the face of what he was threatening to do to Mira.

He reached out, and when his fingers ran down my arm, my entire body jerked. His distorted smile grew, and a tremble shook me from the inside out.

The door opened at my back, and footsteps entered the room, heavy and booming, but I could not look away from the man in front of me to see who it was.

"Sir." Even Asa's voice breaking through the quiet could not give me strength.

Lysander's eyes snapped up, moving past me to the Fortis guard who had interrupted him. "What is it?"

"I believe there is a message for you at the door."

Lysander let out a snarl, and his upper lip curled. He gave me one more look before flipping the electroprod off and turning away.

I watched him leave, watched him head across the room, still frozen. It was not until he disappeared that I was suddenly freed from my paralysis. My legs wobbled and I stumbled forward, nearly falling, but Asa was there to catch me, his strength once again holding me up when I was unable to keep myself on my feet.

A sob broke out of me, but no words. It was like my tongue had been ripped out.

"Indra," Asa said, and just the sound of my name on his lips was comfort.

How he was able to do that, I did not know, but it made me feel as if I were no longer alone. As if I had someone here who would back me up if I needed it. Asa had proven himself time and time again, and I knew he would die for me if it became necessary.

"I am okay," I managed to get out.

His hands were on my arms, gentle but firm. They were the only things holding me up, so I swallowed and forced the strength I had found within myself over the last few months to come out. I was the woman who had killed over sixty Fortis men and women. I had turned their village upside down. I could stand up to Lysander.

"I am okay," I said again, this time with more confidence, and then I wiggled out of Asa's grasp. "Thank you."

He nodded in response, and I suddenly felt like these were the only two things we ever did. Me telling him thank you, and him nodding in response.

Not that there could ever be more between us. We were from two different worlds, and at the end of the day, it did not matter if he thought he loved me or if I would feel indebted to him for the rest of my life for the things he had done to save me. When we left the gates, he went to his home in the Fortis village. A home that had walls provided by the Sovereign, where he ate food handed to him because he had been born in that village. In contrast, I had to walk through the borderland, with the rocky cliffs on my right where the lygan ruled, and the wastelands on my left where marsoapians roamed the desolate expanse, and the mammoth roaches lurked beneath the sand. Asa and I would never understand one another. Not completely.

"I have to go back to work," I said.

I turned away from him, mimicking the same dance we had done numerous times over the last year.

"I'll always be here to protect you," he called after me. "Even if you don't think you need it."

I stopped, but I did not look back. "No, you will not. That is what you do not understand, Asa. You cannot be. The distance between us is too great."

I started walking again, leaving him behind.

MY PLAN WAS TO KEEP A CLOSE EYE ON MIRA FOR the rest of the day. I did not tell her exactly what my conversation with Lysander had been about, only that she needed to watch her back and avoid the pantry at all costs. It should have been enough. It was, after all, the same thing we had been doing since the day she started work here.

In the end, though, it turned out there was nothing either of us could have done to stop the chain of events from taking place. Once again, we were powerless.

The kitchen was brimming with activity. All the housemaids were present, scrubbing pots and washing plates, cleaning up from the elaborate lunch the family had stuffed themselves with. It was in the middle of all this that Lysander stepped into the kitchen, stopping just inside, his bulk taking up the entire doorway. His gaze swept across the room and paused briefly on me, just long enough for the hair on my scalp to prickle, and then he was moving. Marching across the room with Mira in his sights, moving much faster than his short legs and chubby frame should have allowed him to.

"No," I whispered.

He made no effort to hide his intentions when he grabbed her arm, and even though he held the electroprod in his other hand, he did not even pause to turn it on. Mira let out a yelp that seemed to slam into me from across the room as Lysander pulled her toward the pantry, while all around the kitchen the rest of us stood frozen in place. Staring. Doing nothing. Letting it happen. Again.

The door slammed, and my body jerked. I still had not moved, and when the first sob penetrated the door, it felt like I was back on that stage about to watch Bodhi die. I was helpless and on the cusp of death. Useless. Nothing but a worthless Outlier.

But you are more than that, a voice in my head whispered. *You were born Sovereign. You are strong. You are a killer of Fortis hunters.*

Mira cried out a second time, and I moved. I did not think about what I was doing or what it would mean as I marched across the room. My focus was on the pantry door, but my gaze was moving around the room as I went, searching the counters I passed until I found what I needed.

I swiped the knife up on my way by, my gaze zeroed in on the door. My hold on it was crushing, but my free hand was steady when I reached for the knob. I yanked the door open and stood for a beat, taking the scene in. Lysander's back was to me, and he had Mira up against the wall. She was sobbing and fighting, but she would never win on her own, and she knew it. Just as I did.

I caught sight of the electroprod on the floor at his feet and made my move.

It happened so fast I did not register what I was doing until the blade had plunged into Lysander's back. He screamed, and I pulled it out, only to plunge it in a second time. Blood covered my hand, and he went down in a heap of whimpers, and in front of me stood Mira, panting and disheveled, but in one piece.

Only it would not stay that way for long. We had to run.

"Come on." I held my hand out. "We must go."

She took the hand I offered her, and together, we ran. Through the kitchen and past the other housemaids, all of whom were so shocked they had not moved from their original spots, and then we were in the mudroom and heading out the back door.

I was already panting when we made it outside, and it was then that I realized we had nowhere to go. Leaving the city through the front gate was impossible. Even if we did manage to make it there before Lysander's body was discovered, I was covered in his blood and still holding the knife. No. We needed another way out.

"Xandra." I gasped out the name of the woman who had led my husband to his death.

We had not spoken in months, not since the day she came to my hut to apologize. My anger had subsided as I was slowly able to acknowledge what she had said was true. Bodhi had followed her, and had she not led him to the tunnel behind the city, he would have died at the gates without ever setting foot inside. At least she had given him a chance, no matter how small. I only hoped she would be willing to give Mira and me the same chance.

"Come on," I said, pulling my friend with me as I ran down the alley and toward the back of the house, away from the main street.

The houses in Sovereign City had been constructed back to back, with the main streets that ran in front of them being wide enough for carts and people, while the roads that ran behind them were narrow and confining. They were so confining, in fact, that very few people used them unless absolutely necessary, which made it easier for Mira and me to travel unnoticed.

Still, I kept on the lookout as I moved, knowing people did use the road on occasion and not wanting to be taken by surprise. If another Outlier happened upon us, we would be okay. If a Fortis guard found us, I still had the knife.

I stayed close to Mira as we traveled, hoping she would block my bloodied hands and dress from sight in case anyone did pop up. I kept the knife close to my side, knowing I would use it again if necessary but praying it would not come to that.

The city was amazingly quiet, though, and the only thing I could attribute the silence to was the afternoon nap most of the Sovereign were in the habit of taking. I found myself whispering a prayer of thanks that the people living within these walls were so lazy.

We wove our way through the city until we reached the alley I had been searching for. Once there, I stopped and took a look around, surveying the area to make sure no one was in sight. The road in front of me was clear, but simply walking up to knock on the door was out of the question. I had no clue if everyone in the house was trustworthy. We were going to have to wait until someone—another Outlier—came out.

It seemed to take forever, and with each passing moment, my heart pounded harder. Mira was crouched behind me. She had not uttered a word since leaving Saffron's house, and the expression on her face told me she was in shock. A normal reaction, and one I probably would have experienced, too, had I not already worn so much blood on my hands.

When the door finally opened, it was a young Outlier girl who stepped out. Her shaved head told me she was from the Huni tribe, but she was still an Outlier, and I was certain even though our two tribes did not interact in the wilds, she would not turn her back on us inside the city.

I called out to the girl, and she froze but did not look scared. Not even when I revealed myself, bloody dress and all. "I need Xandra."

The girl's gaze moved over me only once before she turned and ran back inside.

When she was gone, I ducked back into my hiding place and took Mira's hand. "We are going to be okay. I promise."

"You killed him," Mira murmured.

"He got what he deserved."

When she looked at me, her eyes were wide. "I know. I just—" She swallowed. "You killed a man, Indra."

I wanted to tell her it was not the first time, that I had been hunting Fortis men and women for months, but it was not the right moment to reveal all my deepest and darkest secrets. Instead, I squeezed her hand and remained silent.

Xandra came out a few beats later, and I stood. She stopped in her tracks when she saw me, her dark eyes growing wide as they took in the blood staining my dress and the knife in my hand.

She stumbled forward two steps, but the small distance seemed to be all she could cross before gasping, "What have you done, Indra?"

"We need a way out of the city," I said instead of answering her question.

"What have you done?" she repeated, her eyes moving over me again as she ran her hand over her close-cropped hair.

"I killed a man," I said, "and I need to get out. Now, Xandra."

That snapped her out of it, and she barely looked over her shoulder before heading for the alley we had just come out of. When she waved for us to follow, I once again took Mira's hand, afraid she was still in too much shock to register what was happening, and hurried after Xandra.

The other woman was a head taller than I was, and her strides much longer. I practically had to run to keep up, but I was thankful because it made me feel like we were making real progress. Like it would only be a matter of minutes before we were outside the walls and safe. She took turns with no warning, twisting us deeper into the city and closer to the wall, but the massive structure was still a street away when she finally slowed.

"This is the place," Xandra said as she approached a door. "The tunnel is through here."

The house in front of us was larger than Saffron's and twice as grand, which I could not wrap my head around. Saffron was a very important woman in the city. Not a stateswoman like Paizlee, but a member of one of the original families. Few people had homes as large as hers, and those who did carried important titles. Did the Sovereign living in this house know about the tunnel? Could someone so important be trusted?

"Who lives here?" Mira asked in awe, as if all the thoughts that had just gone through my mind were going through hers as well.

"This is the House of Aralyn," Xandra replied.

I had worked in the city long enough to be familiar with the name, and I knew this woman was the leader of the minority party, the one that opposed Paizlee. Saffron had mentioned her before, saying Aralyn's ideas were radical, but I had never heard anyone indicate that she was sympathetic to Outliers. It made no sense that she would be. Why would anyone living inside these walls care about us? They barely had to lift a finger because we existed to serve them.

Xandra entered the house without knocking, and Mira and I followed her inside. We found ourselves in a mudroom much like the one in Saffron's house, but Xandra did not stop there. She moved into the kitchen without hesitation, and the women working there barely looked up from their work when we stepped in. No one asked what we were doing or who we were as we crossed through the room, and then through the dining room, finally stopping when Xandra reached a door. She pulled it open, and I peered inside, but it was only a closet. At least until she knelt and pried a panel up to reveal a hole in the floor and a ladder descending into darkness.

"In here," Xandra said, waving to the ladder. "Climb down and follow the wall until you reach a second ladder. I will talk to Aralyn after you are gone. I do not know if she would be willing to help, knowing you have killed a man."

"What will happen to you?" Mira asked.

Xandra waved to the tunnel more emphatically. "Just go. Do not worry about me. Aralyn is a reasonable woman." Her gaze went to me. "You should be worried about what you have brought down on our village, though. The Sovereign will retaliate, Indra. You must know that."

"What would you have me do?" I asked. "Stand by and listen as another one of my people is violated? Do nothing? You do not stand by and do nothing. How can you expect me to do the same?"

Xandra's expression softened, and she let out a sigh. "I do understand, but this thing you have done… It could be the end of everything you know and love, Indra."

"No more than when you led Bodhi into the city."

This time, the expression in Xandra's eyes turned sad. "That is always a risk. Now, you must go."

I did as I was told and moved toward the hole while my heart pounded at Xandra's warning. She was right. I had not considered the consequences. I had only thought of Mira and what was going to happen to her. Now, though, I was achingly aware of what could happen to our village. To my mother and sister.

We needed to get to them. Fast.

"What do we do once we find the ladder?" I asked.

"Climb. Above that, you will find another door. All you will have to do is push it open, and then you will be outside the city. Be very careful on the way back. The Fortis will most likely be looking for you."

I turned to climb down, but before I could make any progress, Xandra reached out and grabbed my hand. Her brown skin contrasted with mine, and it made me think of Asa and how there had been no chance to say goodbye to him. I was surprised when the thought caused an ache to spread through me.

"I will see you in the village," Xandra whispered, giving my hand a gentle squeeze.

"Thank you," I said before pulling my hand from hers and descending into the darkness.

SEVEN

THE DARKNESS IN THE TUNNEL SEEMED TO stretch on forever, and it sent me back to those first few moments in the caves after my torch had gone out and my sense of direction had been destroyed by the blackness that had engulfed me. The memory sent a shiver down my spine.

Only this time, I was not alone.

Mira was behind me, and I reached back into the darkness until I located her hand. She wrapped her fingers around mine and squeezed, and the contact gave me comfort, but also courage to keep moving. I would need it, because the black tunnel stretching out in front of us was only the beginning. After we climbed to the surface, we would have to find a way to make it back to our village without getting caught, and once we had arrived, there was no telling what we would face.

I ran my hand along the wall as I walked, feeling my way since my sight had been stolen from me. It was cold and rough like stone, but also full of grooves that told me blocks had been put down here to reinforce the tunnel. But by whom? That was the question that went through my mind over and over again as I moved. Who had built this tunnel, and what had their purpose been? Why had anyone ever needed a secret way in and out of the city?

When we reached the end, I stopped so quickly that Mira bumped into me. We had not spoken once, both of us too focused on getting out, but when I released her hand so I could feel around for the ladder, she let out a little whimper. Even surrounded by the blackness, it only took a second to locate, and then I was reaching back, searching the darkness for Mira once again. I found her arm and pulled her forward, putting her hand on the ladder so she was grounded.

"Hold on," I said, and then I started to climb.

It seemed longer than the ladder we had used to come down, and when I finally reached the top and pushed on the door, it opened as easily as Xandra had said it would. Sunlight burst in, making me turn my head away, and I looked down to find I had been right. The ladder was twice as long as the other one had been.

At the bottom stood Mira, squinting up at me through the sunlight pouring in through the opening. I waved for her to climb, and once I was sure she was on her way, I pulled myself out of the hole.

All around me, large boulders jutted up, perfectly shielding the tunnel entrance from view. Even though I could spy the top of the wall, which was a good distance away from where I now found myself, the large rocks prevented me from getting a clear idea of where we were. The ground beneath my feet was sandy and dry, meaning we had come up somewhere in the wastelands, possibly on the opposite side of the city from the borderland we usually traveled through. Not that it mattered. It would be impossible to take the same route if we wanted to avoid getting caught. No, we would have to find a different way home.

Mira pulled herself out of the tunnel at my back, and I turned to face her.

"It is going to take us a long time to get home."

She looked around, spotted the top of the wall that was just visible over the boulders, and frowned. "Are we in the wastelands?"

"We are." I paused, knowing she would not like what I was about to suggest but also knowing it was our only chance. "We are going to have to go through them if we want to make it home."

Her eyebrows jumped up, pushing the passage markings above them up as well. Despite the fear in her blue eyes, she did not argue. She knew as well as I did that traveling through the wastelands could be dangerous, but it was less risky than being spotted by the Fortis, who were most certainly looking for us by now.

"Can we make it?" she finally asked.

Her concern was understandable. As a Winta woman, she had spent her entire life being told that she could not take care of herself. A woman needed a man to protect her, or at least that was what I had always been taught. I now knew it was not true, but Mira had not yet reached that epiphany.

She had never hunted or fought a man off. She had never taken a life. I had, and despite the risk of traveling through the wastelands, I could do it.

I wanted her to be as confident in her ability to survive as I was, which meant baring the part of myself that I had kept secret from everyone other than Asa. Mira and I had been friends for as long as I could remember, but I had no idea how she would react to what I was about to tell her, to the knowledge that I had hunted and killed men, even the Fortis. It was a brutal reality to face, but we lived in a brutal world, and it was time Mira adjusted to that. Time she realized she had just as much power as a man did.

"We will be okay," I began, and then took a deep breath and held my hands out, my palms still stained with Lysander's blood. "This is not the first time I have had blood on my hands. For months, I have been going into the woods so I could hunt, only it is not animals I have been hunting. It has been men. Fortis men and women. I have killed them. I have shot them with arrows and watched as the blood poured from their bodies, have seen the life leave their eyes, and have witnessed the fear that I—a Winta woman and an Outlier—can evoke in a man. I am not afraid of a few marsoapians because they are no match for me. I, Indra of the Winta tribe, am a warrior, and I will get us home safely."

Mira said nothing. She stared at me as if I were a stranger, and I could not blame her. The Winta valued all life, even the lives of people as unworthy of the air they breathed as the Fortis, and it would take time for my friend to adjust. Only time was something we did not have at the moment.

"We should go." I pulled the cover back over the hole and stood, holding my hand out to Mira. "I want to be far away from the city by the time it gets dark. We will need a fire to keep us warm after the sun sets, and we cannot risk being seen."

Mira's eyes were still wide when she took my hand, and her gaze still told me that she was not sure who she was looking at, but she said nothing as I helped her stand.

Together, we climbed over the boulders, and once we were on the other side, I was able to get a better look around. In front of us stood the city, and to the left of that were the wastelands, stretching out as far as the eye could see. To the right of the wall stood the skeleton trees, but just beyond them, in the distance, the beginning of the forest was visible. Taking that route would be much faster and provide us with more of an opportunity for food, but it would also lead us past the Fortis village and Sovereign Lake, which was the main water source for both the village and the city. Going that way would put us at risk of running into patrols or hunting parties, neither of which I was equipped to deal with at the moment. No, we had to make our way through the wastelands. It was the safest route at the moment.

"What is that?" Mira said, pointing to something behind me.

I turned in the direction she indicated, and a blinding light in the distance made me squint. I shielded my eyes, trying to make it out, but it was so bright that it seemed to take forever for my eyes to adjust. Even when they did, I could not put a name to what I was seeing. There was a tower that stood as high as the city wall, and all around it mirrors fanned out in circles. Rows and rows of them, each reflecting the sun, making my head hurt and my eyes burn.

"I have no idea," I said. "It is unlike anything I have ever seen."

The mirrors had my curiosity piqued, but there were other things to worry about—namely getting home safely—so I turned back to the wall and studied the area. There was no one in sight, which was good, and I did not expect there to be. The gate was on the opposite side of the wall, which also happened to be where the Fortis lived. When they needed to expand, they moved toward the lake, not back this way. Back here there was nothing but sand and rocks, and dry ground that rejected most forms of life.

I glanced over my shoulder, back toward the mirrors. At least I had always been told there was nothing beyond the walls but the wastelands. This was the first time I had ever been on this side of the city, though.

The wastelands stretched on and on, leading to nothing but death. Decades ago, a group of Outliers had tried to escape the thumb of Sovereign City by heading out, hoping to find more fertile ground beyond the wastelands, but they had not gotten far. Most had died, either of thirst or exposure to the elements, or from the creatures that lived in the sandy landscape. Only a handful made it back to tell their tale, and the stories they had told about what lived in that desolate stretch of desert were enough to deter anyone else from trying. So we had stayed and continued to serve the Sovereign, believing there was nothing else out there for us.

Only there *was* something out there. What it was, I did not know, and I had no clue why no one had ever mentioned it before. Maybe it was nothing but ruins from the old world, like the city Bodhi and I had seen the first time he took me into the forest to hunt. Perhaps that was why the Outliers who had tried to make it across the desert had not brought it up.

A groan echoed across the silence, and I ducked behind a boulder on instinct, pulling Mira with me. I could not say what the noise was or where it had come from, but I had learned from months of hunting the Fortis not to take chances.

The wall was still visible from where we were crouched, and when a horse and cart emerged, I nearly stood back up. Where had it come from? I squinted, trying to get a better look at the wall through the blinding light of the sun's rays, and slowly what appeared to be a gate came into view. It was smaller than the one at the front of the city, barely big enough for the cart to fit through, which may have been why I had not spotted it at first.

"There is a gate back here," I whispered.

Mira sat up on her knees so she could see over the boulder as well. "There cannot be. The only way into the city is the front."

"There is," I responded.

We watched in stunned silence as the horse pulled the cart forward. The gate shut the moment they had passed through, and the horse walked faster, spurred forward by the two men driving it. They were Fortis. Their dark clothing gave them away, and the back of the cart was piled high with wooden crates and barrels. From where we sat, it was impossible to tell what they were carrying, but I instinctively knew where they were going. They were headed toward the mirrors and whatever was in that tower.

"As soon as they are out of range, we need to go," I said. "It will be impossible to make it home before dark, but I want to be far away from the city."

Mira and I stayed crouched until the cart had faded into the distance and was little more than a dot. Then I grabbed her hand and took off running. We needed to get away from the skeleton trees and lake, past the city. We needed to reach the wastelands that led to the wilds so we could get home.

Winter may have come to the wilds, but the scorched earth of the wastelands got no such break. The ground was dry and cracked under our feet as we ran, and every step kicked up more and more sand until it threatened to choke me. I covered my mouth and nose with my free hand, looking back at Mira to find that she had done the same. Even though I was no longer sucking in mouthfuls of sand, specks of dirt still pricked at my eyes, and before long they not only burned, but were watering as well. Moisture dripped from my eyes, but evaporated on my cheeks before it could get too far due to the scorching sun of the wastelands.

It seemed to take forever for us to pass the city. I had never taken the time, not even the first day I laid eyes on it, to think about how massive the walls were or how far they went. Dozens of houses and hundreds of people were sheltered within the city, and the walls surrounding them climbed high into the air, wrapping the privileged in its protective embrace the way a mother did a child.

We were both out of breath by the time we turned the corner and made it to the other side of the city. In front of us, the wastelands that would lead to the wilds stretched out, the dry earth only broken up by skeleton trees and boulders that looked as if they had forced their way through the cracks in the ground. I was still holding Mira's hand when I stopped behind the nearest skeleton tree, taking a moment so we could catch our breath and look around. We were on the side of the city now, and if we rounded the next corner, we would be on our way to the front gate. Running straight from here would take us right past the edge of the Fortis village, as well as the living quarters the Sovereign were building to enslave my people. Even from our current position, the occasional bang of a hammer could be heard.

"Will they be able to see us?" Mira asked, staring toward the Fortis village with wide eyes.

"We need to move away from the wall before we head into the wastelands. It will put distance between us and the Fortis village."

Mira's head bobbed in silent agreement, and then we were moving further from the wall, going from tree to tree in hopes that the sun-bleached bodies of the skeleton trees would hide us from view. The sun was hot despite the chill in the air, and before long my dress was sticking to my body. I wanted to rip it off, but I would need the fabric to keep me warm once the sun went down. The wastelands were scorching during the day, but at night, the cold felt as if it was trying to kill you. It seemed like everything in my world was this way, though. Out to get me. Hoping to kill me, or at the very least kill my spirit. The heat from the wastelands, the creatures living in them and in the cliffs, the Fortis, and the Sovereign. Only, today I had shown them that I would not allow anyone to kill my spirit, and no matter what happened from here on out, I needed to remember I had made the right decision. I had sworn I would no longer stand by and do nothing, that I would find a way to stand up for my people, and that was what I had done.

EIGHT

WHEN WE HAD MOVED FAR ENOUGH AWAY from the walled city and I was sure no one would notice us, Mira and I headed into the wastelands. Their existence was something I had grown up with, but never before had I ventured this far into them. The Lygan Cliffs were visible in the distance, and the wilds in front of us, but we were deep enough in the wastelands now that everything else looked unreachable in comparison. I was aware of the dangers lurking beneath the sand and rocks, and I was thankful for the knife I had taken from Saffron's house.

Grizzards were only one of the many species that thrived despite the harsh conditions in the wastelands. Marsoapians, large hairless rodents that burrowed into the ground during the day and came out to hunt at night, were a common threat, and then there were mammoth roaches. They could pick the bones of a dead animal clean in minutes if there were enough of them, but they did not always stick to the carcasses left behind by other animals. The roaches had been known to attack, and when they did, their hard exoskeleton made them difficult—if not impossible—to take down.

When the city had faded into the distance, I finally relaxed enough to realize that not once since fleeing Saffron's house had I asked Mira how she was.

I slowed so we were side by side, but did not stop completely. "Are you all right?"

Her blond hair was matted to her face with sweat, and when she shook her head, it barely moved. "Why did you do that, Indra?"

"What?" This time I did stop walking, not caring that the sun was beating down on me or that we were short on time. "I saved you."

"You— You put everyone at risk for *me*. Is that fair? Is it fair to save one person at the peril of everyone else?"

"We have no idea what is going to happen," I told her. "But you have to understand why I did it. You have to understand that I could not stand by and do nothing. Not anymore."

Mira swallowed, and before she spoke again, her gaze moved to the sandy ground at our feet. "I did nothing, Indra. When Lysander had you in the mudroom, I did nothing. I ran. I left you behind. Do you hate me for that?"

"Mira—" I reached out to her, but she jerked away. When she ventured a look up, the anguish in her blue eyes told me guilt had made her do it, not anger. "I could never hate you. I told you to run, and I am glad you listened."

"Then you should have done the same for me today. You must know I would not have blamed you if you had."

"But I would have blamed myself," I said gently.

Maybe he could not live knowing that he had done nothing.

The conversation Asa and I had the day my husband was killed came back to me, and I suddenly understood better than ever before why Bodhi had needed to go into the city. Why he had broken his promise to me. I had felt the same way standing in the kitchen today, listening to Mira's cries. I could not have lived with myself if I had done nothing, and my husband had been no different.

Tears streamed down Mira's cheeks, and I grabbed her and pulled her against me. My own tears joined hers, and together we stood in the wastelands, under the blazing sun, and cried. Cried for one another and for our people. Cried for what had and would happen to us.

"What will we do now?" Mira asked through her sobs.

I pulled away and wiped the tears from my cheeks. "We will go home to our village, pack our things, and flee into the wilds."

"Will they send people to the village?"

"I do not know," I said, but we both knew it was a lie. I had killed Lysander, and the Sovereign would not be able to overlook that. "We should keep walking."

The sun moved lower in the sky, and the air grew cooler and cooler until we were forced to stop so we could make a fire. I used branches that had fallen from a few nearby skeleton trees, and the long-dead wood was dry enough that it took no time at all to create a spark. As the fire caught, I found myself feeling more thankful than ever for the time Bodhi and I had spent in the forest. Not only had he taught me to hunt, but it had also made me proficient in building a fire.

Once the sun was down completely, the wastelands came alive. The scurry of feet echoed through the darkness, the sounds even louder than the crackle of our fire. Mira and I sat close to one another, close to the fire, both for comfort and for protection. The knife was in my hand, the blade still stained with Lysander's blood, and I was ready to defend us if need be, but I prayed the animals would leave us alone.

"There," Mira whispered, nodding toward a shape in the darkness.

"I see it."

It came closer, moving slowly. The light from the fire reflected off its eyes and made them glow. Its claws scratched against the ground as it shuffled forward almost hesitantly. I gripped my knife tighter, wishing for my bow. Even without being able to see the creature clearly, I knew it was a marsoapian, and a big one, too. Without my bow, the only way to take it down would be the knife, meaning I would have to get very close. It would be a struggle, and the creature's teeth and claws were sharp.

When I stood, Mira reached for me. "What are you doing?"

"Getting ready."

The thing moved closer until it was illuminated by the glow of the fire. Its nose twitched as if sniffing us out, and its hairless body appeared pinker than usual in the light of the fire. The animal was as long as I was tall, and plump from scavenging desert bugs, with a tail nearly as long as its body. I prayed the fire between us would be enough of a deterrent to keep the creature away, but then it shifted as if trying to move around the blaze. There would be no avoiding this fight.

"Get up, Mira," I said, stepping between her and the marsoapian. "Stay back."

Behind me, her feet shuffled as she scurried back, but I did not look away from the creature in front of me to see where she had gone. My eyes were on the marsoapian in front of me, and it seemed to be focused only on me as well. It opened its mouth and emitted a low hiss, revealing yellow teeth that looked square and unthreatening even though they were razor sharp. I tightened my hold on the knife and readied myself, making sure my feet were planted firmly on the ground. The marsoapian moved closer. It hissed again. My heart thumped harder with each passing second. I was ready when it lunged, but the creature jumped higher than I expected it to. It slammed into my stomach and knocked me to the ground despite my best efforts, and Mira let out a scream that echoed through the dark night as together the marsoapian and I went down.

Before my back had even hit the ground, I brought the knife around. The blade sank into the animal's side, and the thing hissed again, louder this time. It wiggled on top of me, its mouth open, and I shifted just in time to avoid its jaws from clamping down on my neck. Mira screamed again, but I was already pulling the blade from the creature's body. I slammed it back in, just as I had done with Lysander, and then did it a third and a fourth time until the creature finally stopped moving.

Its body was heavy against mine, weighing me down with its massive size, and I was covered in blood, but I was alive. Even better, we had dinner. I shoved the thing off me, and it rolled onto its back.

"Help me," I said, holding my hand out to Mira.

The hand she clamped over mine was trembling, but she did as I asked. Her eyes were wide when she looked me over, but dry. She was holding it together much better than I had expected.

"Are you hurt?" she asked.

"No." I jerked my head toward the creature. "And now we have food and a way to keep the desert roaches away."

I said a quick prayer over the animal, and then knelt next to it. Mira stood over me, watching as I sliced the marsoapian open and pulled out its guts. The darkness covering the wastelands was thick, and despite my now extensive experience with hunting, I had never killed one of these creatures before, so it took me longer than usual to clean the thing and free a decent chunk of meat. When I had, Mira held what would be our dinner while I dragged the rest of the carcass away.

The further I went from the fire, the cooler the air became. The effort it had taken to fight off the creature and butcher it had made my skin moist, and bumps pop up on my skin from the chill in the desert air.

I dragged the body as far as I could, and by the time I stopped I was surrounded by darkness and my arms were aching from the effort of pulling the large creature away. The area around me was black, but the scratch of feet against the sandy earth made the hair on my arms stand up. Already the desert roaches were moving in, anxious to clean the meat from the bones of my kill.

I dropped the marsoapian and hurried back toward the fire. Within two steps, the bugs had descended upon the carcass. The ripping of flesh as they tore into it echoed through the otherwise still night, followed by the click of their legs as more and more scurried out of the darkness.

Mira stood by the fire, her eyes wide as I approached.

"Are you okay?" I asked when I stopped in front of her.

She was looking past me, back to where I had dumped the body, and I glanced over my shoulder to find the darkness alive with black shapes.

When I looked back, her gaze was on me. "Who are you?"

"You know who I am," I said, taking the meat from her.

I speared it with a stick from one of the skeleton trees and crouched down so I could hold it over the fire.

Mira knelt at my side. "You have killed men?"

"I have," I told her.

I had expected this conversation and had even thought I was prepared for it, but with my best friend sitting next to me asking about the things I had done in the privacy of the forest, I found I was nervous. Nervous to find out what she would think of me, nervous that her opinion of me might change.

"Who are you, Indra?" she asked again.

I took a deep breath. "I am a Winta woman, an Outlier, but I am also Sovereign."

Mira gasped, but I did not give her time to speak before launching into the story my mother had told me about my origins. My friend listened in silence as the details came out of me. How I had gone into the woods to hunt animals, but how it had only taken one encounter with a Fortis hunting party for my focus to change. She said nothing when I recounted the dozens of men and women I had killed and how it had made me see myself in a different light.

"The Winta are wrong," I said when I had finished. "We have been told we are weak and that we need men to protect us, but that is not true. I have killed men much larger than me. I have brought in game and taken care of my family without the help of a husband or father. I love my people, but I do not love that they have worked so hard to make me feel weak when I am not. I am strong, Mira, and so are you. No matter what we find when we return to our village, we must remember that."

She nodded, but her silence told me that she did not know what to think about the things I had done. Still, there was no disgust in her eyes when she looked at me, no repulsion. Her expression was one of confusion, but there was awe as well.

We ate the meat when it was cooked, and even though I was anxious to know what my friend was thinking, I did not ask. She needed time to sort through her feelings, and I would give it to her.

It was not until we had settled down in hopes of getting a little rest that she finally spoke. "Is it wrong to take a life to save one?"

"I am not sure," I said with a sigh. "But I do know I feel no remorse for the people I have killed. Perhaps that makes me as evil as the Fortis, or maybe it means what I am doing is not wrong. I have no way of knowing for sure until I move into the afterlife and find out what ghosts have followed me, but either way, I refuse to stop. Not until our people are free."

"Is that something you can do?" Mira asked, the awe and hope in her voice thick now. "Do you think killing a few Fortis hunters in the woods can set us free?"

"No. It cannot. We must do more. What that is, I still do not know, but I will figure it out. When I do, I will make sure all the Outliers are set free."

Mira shifted so she was facing me, and the fire reflected in her blue eyes. "I am not sure if I have that kind of strength in me, Indra, but if I do, I want to find it. You are brave, braver than any man I have ever met. Think of what we could accomplish if more people had your courage. Think of what we could do if the Outliers chose to work as one instead of living as we do. Like we are separate."

She was right. Outliers outnumbered the Fortis and Sovereign put together, and if we could somehow find a way to join forces, we could accomplish so much more than what I had already done. But I was not sure if such a thing was possible. Centuries had passed since the Outliers had been one unified tribe, and since then we had interacted very little. I had doubts that the other tribes would even be willing to try.

Nine

As soon as the first rays of sunlight lit up the horizon, Mira and I were ready to resume our trek through the wastelands. By that point the fire was low enough that all I had to do was kick a little sand over the embers. It went out in a puff of smoke, and Mira watched it get carried away on the wind in silence. Like me, she was probably thinking about what we might find when we finally reached our village. About all the things we might have lost.

Impatience warred with dread inside me when we set out. I wanted to get home, to see my mother and sister and know I had not destroyed everything by saving Mira, but I also found it difficult to put one foot in front of the other. Found that my legs were heavy, as if weighed down by something huge and life altering, and it scared me more than anything I had ever faced before. More than the morning I woke to find Bodhi gone, more than sitting in a cell while I waited to watch my husband's murder. This was far bigger. I could sense it, and even though I was desperate to get home, I was sure that after today my life would never be the same.

It did not take long for the skeleton trees to become more common and closer together, and then we had reached the edge of the wilds. Smoke from the Huni village was visible to the west just above the trees, but Mira and I moved east to avoid them. Their village skirted the wastelands, right where the skeleton trees and wilds met, and they had settled there for a reason. The Huni were not friendly toward outsiders, even other Outlier tribes.

After the long trek through the wastelands, reaching our village should have been a relief. But it was not to be. We saw the smoke before the huts came into view. It wound its way through the trees, thicker and more spread out than usual, and even before we reached the clearing, I knew we were too late. Mira must have realized it as well, because she began walking faster just as I had come to this conclusion. I did the same, charging through the forest in an effort to keep up with her, my heart pounding with the beat of my footsteps against the ground.

The first hut we came to was little more than smoldering embers, the fire that had taken it down recent enough that smoke still wafted from the ruins. The next hut was the same, and each one after that, but worse than the sight of the burned huts were the bodies.

The snow dotting the ground had been dyed red by the blood of our people. Women had been stripped naked before they were killed, and children had been run through with swords. There were men who had been beheaded or tied to trees as if being forced to watch the slaughter before they too were sent into the afterlife.

As I walked, the lifeless eyes of my people stared up at me accusingly, asking why I had sacrificed all of them to save just one person. Asking me if it had been worth it. With Mira at my side, alive and well, I could not bring myself to think that it had not, but the ruins of my village contradicted every speck of resolve inside me until I thought I might vomit it out.

"They are all gone," Mira said, collapsing on her knees in the bloodstained snow. "The Fortis killed them all."

I did not fall down at her side, but instead moved deeper into the village, thinking only of Anja and my mother. Had they survived the massacre? Had anyone?

I reached our hut to find it, like all the others, had been reduced to ash. The outline of where our things had once stood was still visible—the table, a bowl that was charred from smoke now sitting on the ground, and the bed I had shared with Anja for most of my life. To my relief, it was empty, but the feeling was short-lived. Unlike the other one, my mother's bed held the charred remains of the woman who raised me. The woman who had been my strength and courage, who had loved me even though I had not come from her womb.

I dropped to the ground then, just as Mira had, falling to my hands and knees in the snow. My fingers groped at the ash that had been my childhood home while I stared at the bones of my mother. They looked impossibly small, and her body was twisted as if she had curled into a ball in an effort to protect herself from the smoke and flames.

This was my fault.

She was dead, and even though the Sovereign had ordered the Fortis hunters to kill her, my mother's blood was on my hands. I had brought this not only on her, but on my entire village as well. I had been arrogant and impulsive, and I had acted without considering the consequences, and as a result my people had been wiped out. My mother was dead, probably my sister, too, as well as Mira's family and Bodhi's, and everyone else I knew and loved.

The tears started without warning, but it was the sobs that immobilized me. They threatened to rub my throat raw with their violence, making it difficult to breathe, making my limbs shake until I had to lie on my stomach in the snow. I pressed my face against the ash, knowing I would be covered but not caring because the pain inside me was worse than anything I had ever experienced. It was impossible to imagine how I would ever be able to do anything but lie here on the ground. If only I had been in the hut. If only my body was spread out next to my mother's. At least then my suffering would finally be over.

My sobs grew worse until I could not breathe even a little, and I gasped, certain I was suffocating, suddenly desperate to fill my lungs even though only a second ago I had been sure I wanted nothing more than to die. When I finally managed to get a mouthful of air, a wail came out of me that sounded like a wounded animal. It rose, bouncing off the trees, and above me a group of rawlins flew from the branches, their feathers as bright red against the blue sky as the blood was against the snow.

"Indra."

Mira's hands pulled me up, and then I was in her arms and we were crying together. I held onto her like I was afraid she, too, would be ripped from my life, my body shaking and words impossible to get out in the midst of the wails coming out of me.

"This is my fault," I finally said. "I did this. I killed them."

"No. You saved me, Indra. The Fortis killed them, sent here by the Sovereign because you stood up to them." Mira pulled back so she could look me in the eye.

She had ash smeared across her face, probably from me, but trying to wipe it off would be pointless. My hands were painted black from the stuff.

"I have never heard of anyone standing up to the Sovereign the way you have," my friend continued. "No one. *You* are stronger than anyone I have ever known. You have killed Fortis hunters, men twice your size, and you defied the Sovereign. You told me that you did it because you could not stand back and do nothing anymore, and you were right. We must stop them from doing this, and you can do it. I do not know how, but I know you can."

"I cannot." I looked around at the destruction of my village, the slaughter of my people, and anguish filled me. "All I will do is bring more pain on everyone. Look at what I have done so far."

"Look at what you have done? Look at what *they* have done. *They* did this, Indra. Not you."

"I have lost everything, Mira." I looked back toward my mother's body. "I do not even know where Anja is, and I cannot make myself look. If I find her—" My voice broke and I could not finish.

Just thinking about the bodies of the women lying amongst the ruins of our village, naked and frozen from the cold night, made me sick. If that had been my sister's fate, I would never be able to live with myself. Knowing I had brought that horrific end down on her would crush me for good.

Mira hugged me again. "We will find her together, and then we will put her to rest. We will put them all to rest."

Mira and I searched the bodies together. The ruins of her hut held the bones of her own family, her mother and father, as well as her brother, already burned, as did the hut Ronan had lived in. Bodhi's family had met the same fate, along with so many others, but no matter how hard we looked, Anja was nowhere in sight.

As time stretched on, I began to hope that somehow my sister had escaped. I thought back on the day I had headed into the city after Bodhi, how I had worried the Sovereign would do this very thing—send the Fortis to destroy us. Before I left that day, I had told Anja to hide if she saw the Fortis coming. But that had been months ago. Was it possible she remembered? Could she be alive, maybe hiding in the forest? It seemed so far-fetched, but without her body in front of me, I found it impossible to give up hope.

Mira and I were still searching the bodies strewn across the village when the sound of someone calling my name bounced off the surrounding trees. "Indra!"

My head jerked toward the sound as I scanned the area. I had to be imagining my sister's voice. There was no way she was still out there. She—

"Indra!"

This time I turned, and Mira did as well. Like me, she was looking around, and we were both still searching the foliage that encircled the village when Anja burst through the brush.

"Anja," I gasped, rushing toward my sister.

She looked so young as she ran for me, her arms open wide. My sister was younger than I was by six years, but taller and lankier, all wiry muscles. With the sun shining down on her, shimmering against the tears on her cheeks, I was struck by how much she looked like our mother—they had the same deep brown skin, dark eyes, and black hair—and the pang that radiated through my body at the knowledge that I would never again see the older version of this girl nearly knocked me to the ground.

When we met in the middle of our ruined village, I threw my arms around her. The tears returned the second she was in my arms, only this time they were less crippling.

"I ran," my sister gasped between her own sobs. "Like you told me to. When I saw the Fortis coming, I got as many people out as I could. We went into the forest and hid."

"I am so glad. I am so happy to see you," I said between tears.

"How many of you are there?" Mira asked from behind me.

Anja pulled back so she could look at my friend, but I refused to let her go completely. "Around twenty. We hid, and later, after the Fortis left, Xandra showed up. She told me what happened in the city."

"Xandra is okay?" I said. "What about Isa? Who else made it out of the city with her?"

"Xandra said she knew there would be retaliation, so she tried to find as many of our people as she could before leaving. Instead of coming straight home, they hid in the Lygan Cliffs. She only managed to find Isa, Tris, Zadie, and Cera, though. She thinks everyone else from our village will be kept. That the Sovereign will make them move into the quarters."

"The building is almost complete," Mira said as if to confirm Xandra's suspicions.

"Indra," my sister said, turning her gaze one me, "I tried to get our mother out. She was so weak, and there was so much chaos." Anja's expression crumbled the way dead leaves did in the fall. "She could not walk, and I did not have the strength to carry her. She made me leave her."

"I know." I gave my sister's hand a squeeze, and the pain throbbing through me distorted the next words. "It is okay. You did a good job."

"Where is everyone?" Mira asked her.

"Still hiding. They are terrified. They refuse to come back here, Indra."

"They must." I turned away, still holding my sister's hand, and looked at our ruined village. "We must put our people to rest and gather as many supplies as we can. And soon. We should get out of here before the Fortis decide to make a second sweep."

"Where will we go?" Anja asked, the tremor in her voice matching the one in my legs.

"The caves."

I turned back to face my sister and my closest friend, my gaze moving over them slowly. Taking stock. We had not lost everything. Not yet. It would not be an easy adjustment, not for a group of Winta women, but we could make it if we were strong.

"But first," I said, "we must gather the bodies."

NONE OF THE MEN SURVIVED THE MASSACRE ON our village, meaning twenty-three women and children were all that remained of the Winta people. Even that small number was a miracle I could only attribute to Anja's quick thinking. I had not realized my little sister could be so strong, but as she led the remaining women back into the village, I saw right away that she was holding up better than most of the others.

I expected Xandra to greet me with bitterness, but when she stumbled from the woods, there were tears streaming down her cheeks but no malice in her eyes. She threw her arms around me just as Anja had.

"I am sorry," I said.

"You did what you thought was right, just as I did when I led Bodhi into the city," she replied. "You were right, Indra. We cannot stand by and watch our people suffer like this. Not anymore."

I looked around at the other women and children of the Winta tribe. "I am not sure we have much of a choice. There are so few of us left now."

"The strong have survived," Xandra assured me.

"I hope you are right," I said.

We worked together to gather the dead. Isa was not the only surviving member of her family. Emori had made it out as well, thanks to Anja, her baby—Lysander's baby—with her. Together, Emori and Isa gathered the remaining members of their family, their mother and two younger sisters, and burned them right on top of the ashes of their family hut. We did the same with anyone we could identify, burning families side by side so they could travel into the afterlife together, and those we could not identify we gathered in the center of the village and burned together.

Anja found Jax among the men, a spear still in his hand and a wound through his heart, and I helped her carry him to his own hut. That my sister had been so close to becoming the wife of this boy cut me in a way none of the other deaths had, not even my mother's, because it made me think of Bodhi and everything I had lost since the day he was ripped from my life.

Once we had finished burning the bodies, we searched the wreckage of our village for anything that might prove useful to us. Bowls, furs, knives, and herbs, as well as clothes or weapons. The only cart our village had was gone, along with the few horses, meaning we would be forced to carry everything ourselves. No one complained or said they could not do it, though, and to me it seemed like a sign that Xandra had been right. The strong had survived.

Before leaving for the forest, we assembled in the center of our ruined village, the twenty-three remaining members of the Winta tribe, and performed the remembrance ceremony. I wielded the tebori tool while Anja sat at my side, holding the bowl of dye. One by one the survivors knelt in front of me, the fire blazing at their backs as I marked them in the symbols of the people they had lost. After the devastation of the attack, most of them looked like different people when they stood, and I had to wipe enough tears and blood from their faces to fill all of Sovereign Lake.

When it was my turn, Xandra took the tebori. I had too many marks on my cheeks already. For the parents I had never known, the father I had lost too young, the husband who had come and gone faster than he should have, and now for my mother. Had I been a different person, I would have thought it unfair, but I was an Outlier, and for me life had never been fair.

I did not feel the pain when Xandra tapped the points into my skin, or when she rubbed dye into the dots she had marked me with, but when I had to repeat the process on my sister's face, it seemed like every press of the tebori against her skin was marking me all over. Her blood was my blood, her tears were my tears, and her pain was my pain.

TEN

THE GROUP WAS WORN AND DEJECTED BY the time we arrived at the cave, but having the comfort of the stone walls surrounding us seemed to lift our spirits. We had all spent the previous night without shelter, Mira and I in the wastelands, Xandra and the women she had saved from the city in the Lygan Cliffs, Anja and the rest of our group huddled together in the wilds. The cave was not home, but being surrounded by stone helped everyone relax, and thanks to the things I had stolen from the Fortis over the last several months, we had supplies in addition to the ones we had managed to find in the ruins of our village.

I made a fire while Xandra and Mira distributed furs and clothes. People settled in, and the food I had hidden in the cave was passed out, and I began to think we might be okay. We had lost a lot, but I knew from my own time in the caves that it had fresh water and animals for food, and even the warm pool in the very far cave that we could use to get clean. All hope was not lost. The women with me were scared, but I could show them we were capable of surviving without men. We were strong.

"The food we have will only last tonight," Xandra told me.

"I know," I said as I looked the group of women over. "We will have to hunt."

"But none of us has ever hunted," Emori replied.

The baby Lysander had forced upon her fussed, drawing my attention her way. The child's eyes were wide, and she had the face of her mother, but her eyes were those of her father. Big and gray despite her dark skin. Those eyes did not make her the monster her father had been. She was innocent of those sins, but I still could not find anything but disgust in my heart when I looked at her.

I looked away from the baby and focused on Emori instead. "I have hunted, and I will teach you."

"You expect us to go out into the woods and hunt for animals?" Tris asked.

The girl was young, only in her nineteenth year, and she had always had someone to look after her. Her parents at first, and then her husband, but after yesterday she was a widow, like me. If she wanted to survive, she would have to learn to take care of herself, something the women in my village had never done before.

"I know it can be scary," I said as I leaned down to scoop a couple knives up off the floor, "but it is necessary. Tonight we will not leave the cave. There are plenty of rats in the next chamber, and there is also water, as well as other creatures that will help us survive. But eventually, we will need the animals and vegetation the wilds provide if we want to survive. We no longer have our husbands and fathers to depend on. We must take care of ourselves."

No one spoke, and the wide eyes of Tris told me she was not yet ready to accept how much things had changed. She would do it, though, because if she did not, she would die. This was not the same as when I went into the forest to hunt. I had used hunting as a distraction, and so I could feel closer to Bodhi. Now, though, if we did not hunt, we did not live.

Still, they were in shock and needed time to register what had happened, so I chose not to press the issue. Instead, I grabbed a torch and lit it. "I will hunt by myself tonight."

No one moved except Mira, who grabbed a couple bowls off the ground and said, "If you show me where the water is, I can bring some back for us to drink."

I gave her a grateful smile before turning toward the tunnel leading into the larger chamber, and Mira followed behind.

I held the torch out in front of me to light the way. Weeks had passed since the night I ventured deeper into the caves, and I was not sure if the little bugs I had led from the furthest cavern would still be around. When I emerged from the tunnel, though, I was pleased to find dozens of the creatures. In fact, it seemed to me that there were even more present than the last time I had been here, and the light from their glowing bodies lit up nearly every corner of the room.

"What are they?" Mira asked when she stepped out of the tunnel behind me.

"They live here," I said.

Then, while she stood at my side staring at them in wonder, I told her about my first trip through the tunnels and how I had fallen in the water, and how I could have easily gotten lost forever without the little creatures.

"They are amazing," Mira said when I had finished.

"They will help us." I snuffed out the torch and set it aside. "There are tunnels everywhere, and the bugs will help us see so we can explore them. We could live here."

Mira moved deeper into the cave, toward the opening of a tunnel I had never ventured into. "There could be rooms. We could each have our own space."

"We will need lots of fur to keep us warm, but it could work."

She turned to face me, smiling for the first time since we left Sovereign City. "We could have a home here, Indra. We could start over and be safe from the Fortis."

"It will take a lot of effort," I said. "But you are right. We can make it work."

I turned from Mira and headed to the back of the cave where the sound of little feet scratching against rock was the loudest. The rodents living here were smaller versions of the ones in the wastelands, although not hairless. These were covered in black fur, which helped them blend into the darkness of the cave—almost as if they had evolved that way over time—but the scratching of their claws made them easy to find if you knew what you were looking for. They must have survived by eating the small bugs living in the crevices of the rocks, because they always seemed to be digging, and tonight was no exception.

Unaccustomed to people, the rodent I came upon did not try to run when I approached, but instead only paused to glance my way before going back to its digging. I speared it easily and then sliced the animal open and gutted it, tossing the entrails on the ground for the little bugs in hopes that the promise of food would keep them in the large chamber. Just like before, they swarmed the guts. One rodent was not large enough to feed all of us, so I speared three more and repeated the process as I quietly recited the prayer reserved for animals.

"May your death provide life to our people and sustain us through hard times."

The meat from four of the rodents would only make a dent in our hungry stomachs, but we had other food for tonight, and I was too exhausted to think about trying to rustle up more of the creatures.

When I turned to face Mira, I found her standing in the same place, watching me in silent awe.

"What is it?"

"You are so proficient in everything you do."

"I have had a lot of practice over the last few months," I said.

"You really believe we all have this strength in us? That the men in our village have been wrong to tell us we are too weak to take care of ourselves?"

"I do," I told her. "The men I have killed are proof of that."

"It will be hard to convince the other women."

"Then I will have to show them."

Mira and I went back to the main chamber where the women cowered, huddled together and totally silent, as if terrified to make even the smallest sound. Once there, I speared the dead rodents with sticks and passed them out to be cooked, talking the entire time about how I had killed them. Then I told them about the marsoapian in the wastelands, and the other animals I had hunted in the wilds over the last few months, before finally moving on to the men who had died at my hands.

I started slowly, easing the others into the idea that I had taken human life. No matter how I broached the subject, I knew I would be met with both shock and resistance. And I was right.

"You have killed Fortis hunters?" Xandra was the first to break the silence, and even in the shadows of the cave it looked as if her dark skin paled a little at the thought.

"I have." I did not look down, but instead held her gaze to show her I was not ashamed. "You must have heard the rumors in the city, about the Fortis men who have gone missing in the wilds. That was me. They died at my hands, from my bow and my knife. I have killed dozens of them, both men and women, and I do not plan to stop."

She said nothing, and I looked around, my gaze sweeping over what remained of my tribe. Their expressions ranged from shock to awe, and even a little fear, but I saw something else there, too. Hope. I saw it shimmering in Emori's eyes as she looked up at me, her baby in her arms and her sister at her side, the three of them the only remaining members of a family that just yesterday had numbered six. Xandra recovered from her shock quickly, and her expression was the same, only her eyes had more fire in them.

Anja, my little sister, was crying, but she stood tall and held her head high when she said, "Our mother told me you were stronger than the men gave you credit for. After you started hunting and the Head told her that you were putting yourself in danger, she would not listen. She said you could look after yourself. She said you were brave. She was right."

"It is not just me," I said, looking around again.

I took my sister's hand and focused on her. She was much younger than I was, and at times I found it difficult to imagine her as anything but a child. However, standing next to her now, I saw a fire in her that had not been there before. One that had sparked when our mother stood up to the Head, but had grown into an inferno when she led that group of women to safety. She was as strong as I was. They all were.

"We can do this together," I said, my voice rising, echoing off the walls of the cave. "I know none of this feels real right now. I know you are tired and hurting. But this is possible. All we have to do is work together."

I met Mira's gaze as the words she had spoken to me only the night before echoed through the room. Together we could do this.

Eleven

OVER THE NEXT FEW DAYS, AS THE SHOCK wore off and the women grew more accustomed to our new surroundings, as well as more sure of themselves, we moved deeper into the caves. We used the glowing bugs to explore different passages, finding that Mira had been right. There were dozens of little alcoves throughout the caverns, many of which were ideal for living spaces.

The first chamber was the only one vented for smoke, and we continued to use it for cooking, but otherwise we spent most of our time deeper in the recesses of the cave. It allowed people to not only relax, but it also helped them feel more secure. As if the caves would protect us from the Fortis or anything else the Sovereign might throw our way.

People began to claim their own spaces in the caves, and the fur we did have was split up, but it would not be enough to keep us comfortable on the rocky floor. We needed more, either through trading or hunting, and I was anxious to get out into the woods and teach the other women how to shoot.

"It is time to go out and hunt," I said to the group on our third morning in the caves.

Up until that point, I had stayed inside, killing the rats living in the shadows, but it could not last. They had become wise to us and were getting more and more scarce as the days passed. Plus, it took too many of the tiny creatures to feed our group. If we wanted to thrive, we needed the bigger game living in the wilds.

Most of the women stared up at me like they did not understand the words I had just uttered, so I said, "We need the fur and the meat."

Mira was the first to stand. "I want to learn."

"Good." I gave her a grateful look.

Anja, my baby sister, who until three days ago had still seemed so young in my eyes, stood next. "Me, too."

Around the room other women nodded, and it almost seemed as if they were slowly starting to wake up. The change filled me with more than relief. It filled me with hope and pride. We were strong, and even though getting the other women to acknowledge it would be difficult, this was a step in the right direction.

The first few groups to go out with me were small, consisting of only Mira, Emori, Anja, and Xandra. Despite the obvious desire in the other women's eyes, most of them were still too afraid. Or perhaps it was shock.

Whatever it was, they were used to being taken care of, and with no men around, it did not miss my attention that their gazes had turned to me. It was a burden I allowed for now, knowing it would take time for them to realize they were strong enough to take care of themselves, but also because I felt responsible. No matter what anyone said or who we cast the blame on, a part of me could not let myself off the hook for what had happened. It was my blade that had drawn Lysander's blood and sent the Fortis to our village. The deaths of our people were on my head, and I had no doubt it would follow me into the afterlife and drag me down to the underworld. But until then, I would do everything I could to save what was left of my people, even if it cursed me.

So I focused all my efforts on Mira, Anja, Emori, and Xandra, teaching them to shoot the bow the way Bodhi had taught me. Xandra was a natural who took to it quickly. Within a week she was able to go into the woods to hunt on her own while I worked to teach the others. It took longer for Mira, Anja, and Emori to pick it up, but in no time they, too, were able to hit the targets I had set up for them.

The rest of the women came around gradually, joining us one by one as their shock wore off and was replaced by anger. By the time the snow had melted and green had returned to the forest, every woman in the village was learning to shoot. Like me, they wanted not only to stop this from happening again, but also to find justice and make the Fortis pay. To make them feel the same pain we had felt when our village was burned to the ground.

We settled into a routine after that. It was different from our old ways, but comforting because we were working to make it on our own. We took turns hunting, as well as scavenging the forest for any edible plants—a time-consuming and often pointless venture, but one that was necessary since all our crops had been destroyed when our village was burned to the ground. At night we gathered around the fire to eat, and then retired to our alcoves. As the weeks passed, the number of furs we had grew, and we slowly became more comfortable. With that comfort came the knowledge that we were going to be okay. Our wounds had not healed, but we were surviving, and for the time being that was enough.

All of that changed the day Xandra returned to the caves wearing a Fortis jacket.

It was the first thing I noticed when she stepped into the large chamber. I was sitting with Anja, using the tall grass that grew in the clearing near our pond to weave a basket, and at the sight of Xandra, my fingers stopped moving. The jacket was long, going down to her thighs, and black, and made of a thick material we had no access to, but one I was familiar with because I had worked in the city.

"Where did you get that?" I asked after a moment of stunned silence.

She looked down, her gaze moving over the too-large jacket. It had clearly belonged to a Fortis hunter, and even though there could be no other explanation, for a moment I found it impossible to wrap my brain around what I was seeing.

"I took it off the man I killed," she said simply as she tossed her bow to the floor. "I have become a hunter of men. Just like you."

The light from the little bugs flickered over Xandra's face as she looked down at me. Her expression was fierce, and standing there, wearing the jacket of the man she had killed, it occurred to me for the first time just how many more of the Fortis hunters we could kill if we worked together. Until that moment, I had thought very little about having the other women join me in hunting the Fortis. Not only had I been too focused on our survival, on making sure the others knew how to hunt animals so we had enough food, but it had also seemed too risky. Almost like I would be dragging them to the underworld with me. But Xandra had made this decision all on her own, just as I had that first day I took a life, and I realized some of the others may actually *want* to hunt the men and women who had tried to wipe us out.

"What have you done?" Emori asked, her outrage ringing through the cave and making everyone else freeze in their tasks.

"I have stood up for myself. For my people," Xandra said, her gaze moving over us. "And I know I am not alone in wanting to do that."

"What are you saying?" I asked even though it was written all over her face.

"I want to hunt the Fortis," Xandra said calmly.

Murmurs filled the air, but no one joined in the conversation. Some of the women, like Emori and Tris, looked at Xandra as if she had left her mind behind in the forest. She ignored them and focused on me, her gaze holding mine, and even though she said nothing, I knew what she was asking.

I nodded, and a smile spread across her face.

Xandra and I went into the woods together the next day, heading away from the caves and toward the river leading into Fortis territory. It had been weeks since the last time I went looking for a hunting party, but nothing about their habits had changed, and it took only a few hours in the forest for Xandra and me to cross paths with a group.

There were three of them, a woman and two men. We spotted them from a distance, hidden by the thick brush the wilds provided, while we waited for them to get closer. At my side, Xandra's body seemed to hum with anticipation.

When they were in range, we lifted our bows, firing at exactly the same time, and the men hit the ground within a beat of one another.

The third hunter, a Fortis woman, had her sword out before either of us could fire again. The woman reeled her horse around, her gaze searching the forest for her attackers, but the surrounding bushes were too thick and concealed us too well.

"Come out!" she bellowed. "Show yourself!"

My bow was up, arrow notched, and without really thinking it through, I stepped through the brush.

The woman's eyes narrowed to points as sharp as her sword. "You will pay with your life, Outlier."

"No," I said calmly. "You will. For my village, which you burned to the ground, for my mother, who you killed, for my husband, who died at your hands, and for my people who have been violated by you over and over again. It is time for you to pay."

The woman let out a growl and banged her heels against her horse's flank, but it was too late. My arrow was already on its way. It found a home in her skull and her entire body jerked back, and then she fell from the horse, slamming into the ground beside her friends.

Xandra stepped from the cover of the forest and stood at my side, and together we stared down at the bodies. It had been weeks since my last kill, and the knowledge that we had taken three more Fortis from this earth was more rewarding than I had anticipated. I turned to look at Xandra, expecting a look of satisfaction, but she was frowning.

"This is not enough," she said.

"There will be more."

Thinking of the time Asa had discovered me in the woods and how I had been surprised by other Fortis hunters, I headed for the bodies. The sooner we searched them, the sooner we could be on our way.

"It will still not be enough," Xandra mumbled.

I remained where I was, kneeling beside the dead Fortis, but turned her way, unsure of what she was trying to say to me. "What would you have us do?"

"There should be more of us." Xandra turned her gaze on me. "All the women in the caves have suffered at the hands of the Fortis. They should all be here as well."

I stood, the bodies and their belongings forgotten. "You will have a hard time convincing some of them."

"So you think we should not try?"

"That is not what I said. But, Xandra, you are strong. You have been defying the Sovereign for a long time. Not everyone is as brave as you are. Not everyone is willing to risk their lives. Not even to take out the Fortis."

"You were. I had the other women in the underground to show me the way, but you did this all on your own, Indra. How? How did you find the courage?"

I thought about it for a moment, remembering the first day I shot a Fortis hunter. How I had done it on impulse, and how I held felt, both before and after I had taken that first life.

"I felt like I had nothing left to lose," I said. "I had been through the worst they could do to me already, and no matter what happened, the pain could not get any worse than it already was."

"Do you not think some of the other women feel the same? Do you not think they can be as strong as you are?"

"I know they can," I told her. "The problem will be convincing them."

"Then we must do everything we can to show them."

Xandra moved toward the bodies just as I knelt again, this time to say a prayer. It was something I had always done with my kills, whether they were animals or Fortis hunters, but when she stopped and looked at me with horrified eyes, I found myself questioning it for the first time.

"What are you doing?" she asked.

"Praying."

She took one step toward me, her hand outstretched as if wanting to pull me away, but stopped short of touching me. "You cannot be serious. You would pray for these people?"

"I would." Her gaze burned into me when I bowed my head, but I said the words out loud anyway. "May your death provide life to our people and sustain us through hard times."

When I lifted my head, I found Xandra still watching me, but her expression was less outraged than it had been. "That is the prayer for animals."

"It is." I stood. "Are they not animals? Will their death not provide our people with the sustenance we need?"

Slowly, as if getting a joke, Xandra's lips turned up into a smile. "Before our village was wiped out, we never had the opportunity to get to know one another, Indra, but I believe you and I view the world in a very similar way."

"Yes," I said, thinking about how we had both killed Fortis hunters with little thought despite being raised to believe human life was precious. "I think that is probably true."

This time, Xandra and I did not bother trying to cover our tracks. We took our arrows, but also as many belongings as we could carry. The way the bodies had been stripped clean would signal to the Fortis that their people were once again being hunted, but I no longer cared. I could not. Xandra was right. Three dead Fortis hunters were not enough. Not after they had burned our entire village and tried to wipe our people off the planet. We needed to do more.

There was some outrage when we returned to the caves with the stolen items. We were Winta, after all, and old habits died hard. Life was sacred. It was to be honored. Or so we had always been told. It was a noble idea, but one I could no longer cling to. There was nothing sacred about the lives most of the people in the Fortis village were living, nothing that was deserving of reverence. They were a black spot on the earth, and they needed to be wiped out.

"What have you done?" Tris asked.

Her eyes seemed to have grown in size over the last few weeks, but the expression in them changed from day to day. The fear that had at first lived in their brown depths had faded, but there was still a good deal of uncertainty in them. She had learned to shoot, had even gone hunting with Xandra and gotten a few forest rodents, but upon returning to the cave, she always acted like she had done something wrong. A battle raged inside her, and it was the same battle that raged in most of the women sitting in front of Xandra and me. They wanted to believe they could be strong and survive on their own, but they were fighting against a lifetime of being told they were weak. Without men to fall back on, it would only be a matter of time before they would have to give in to one of the arguments. Either join the fight I had started months ago, or join the rest of our tribe in the ashes of our village.

Xandra dropped the supplies she had stolen at Tris's feet. "I have done what I must, just as I always have. In the city I worked for the underground, as many of you know, and I am used to betraying the Sovereign. I know for most of you it is a scary thought, but I am here to tell you if we work together, we can do this."

"Do what?" Emori asked, outrage ringing in her voice. "What would you have us do?"

The child in her arms was asleep, its face serene and pretty, but I still could not look at her without feeling hatred in my heart.

"Finish what Indra has started," Xandra said.

"You mean kill the Fortis?" Mira sat on the floor with one of the children on her lap, a boy of six whose entire family had been killed when our village was attacked.

"That is what I mean," Xandra replied.

There was silence for a moment, but the lack of noise seemed to me a lack of argument as well, as if everyone wanted to agree but could not. As if all they needed was a little push. I looked around and found something in the eyes of the other women that had not been there before. Determination. These women were ready to fight, ready to stand up to the men who had tried to wipe us out.

All they needed was encouragement.

"The first time I killed two men, I was alone," I said slowly, my gaze moving around the room. "I did not think before I shot them, and when the reality of what I had done hit me, I felt an overwhelming sense of guilt." The silence grew heavier as everyone stared at me, waiting to hear what I could possibly say to justify the things I had done. "But then I saw the face of the man who killed my husband staring back at me. It was not him lying on the ground, not physically, but the man in front of me was no different. If he had been handed the sword that day, he would have cut Bodhi's head off without a second thought."

Mira closed her eyes as if whispering a silent prayer, and tears burned at my throat.

I swallowed them down so I could keep talking. "The truth is that most of the men and women in that village would have done it. We are nothing to them, and that will never change. Just as the Sovereign will never let us go. As long as they are in charge, we will be slaves. We cannot let the guilt of what we must do hold us back, because doing that is the same as sentencing our people to an eternity of slavery. We can stop it." I looked around, amazed at the change in the expressions of the women in front of me. Awed by their strength and determination. "Xandra and I were able to take three Fortis hunters out today with no problem. Imagine what we could do if we worked together. Imagine how much we could accomplish if there were ten of us. Fifteen. We could send the Fortis running. I know it."

My voice bounced off the stone walls for a beat after I stopped talking, but the echo had barely faded away before people were standing. Mira and Anja. Even Emori—who handed her child off to Isa—and then Tris. Others, too, each of them with expressions on their faces that said they were ready to fight. Like me, they no longer wanted to stand back and do nothing.

Xandra put her hand on my back, and I turned to find her smiling. "We are ready to follow you, Indra."

It was not until she said those words that I realized I had become the leader of an uprising. One that would either end with the freedom of my people, or with their total annihilation.

TWELVE

XANDRA AND I TOOK ONE EXTRA PERSON out to hunt with us at a time. Mira first, and then Anja and Emori. Others came later, and slowly our hunting parties grew until we had a group of ten or more. Sometimes we stayed together and searched the woods for large groups of Fortis hunters, but other times we split up in hopes of taking more than one hunting party by surprise. It was a successful venture, and even though the other women were all scared and timid in the beginning, we were able to ease them into it, and it was not long until, like Xandra, their fear began to slip away.

We had the advantage. Even if the Fortis spotted one of us before we saw them, they never thought of us as a threat. Not only were we Outliers, we were also women, and therefore no match for the men and women who had trained since birth. At least that was what they thought. We proved them wrong time and time again when we overtook them, and more than one Fortis hunter slipped into the afterlife with an expression of utter shock on their face.

For me, the time I spent in the woods became less relaxing than it had been. Where once the forest had been a tranquil place, a place where I was able to feel Bodhi's presence despite how much time had passed since he was taken from me, it seemed more like a battlefield now. Having people at my side helped, especially Anja or Mira, but it still felt as if my husband slipped away a little more with each day.

One of the few places left where I could still feel his presence was the cliff overlooking the ruined city, and I often found myself there when I had a little bit of free time. Being there, looking out over the wastelands, my mind often wandered to the first day Bodhi had brought me into the woods. How we had stood in that very spot, staring into the distance, and how he had asked me to leave with him. There was no way of knowing if things would have turned out differently if we had left together, but I liked to imagine they would have. Liked to think that Bodhi and I had made it across the wastelands, with Mira, Anja, his family, and my mother in tow, and found a new place. Another forest like the wilds, perhaps, where we could be happy and the Sovereign could not touch us. Where we would still be living. It was a silly dream, but one I could not push away no matter how hard I tried.

That was where I sat, watching the sun rise over the wastelands, when Xandra found me. She lowered herself to the ground at my side, saying nothing at first, and together we watched in silence as the sun climbed higher in the sky.

"Bodhi brought me here once," I said, not taking my eyes off the ruins. "He wanted to run away, but I would not. If I had gone with him, maybe he would have lived."

"You loved Bodhi very much," Xandra said with a sigh, "and there will always be a part of me that blames myself for how things turned out. For not thinking of a better way."

"There was no other way," I replied, tearing my gaze off the horizon so I could look at her. "When it first happened, I could not see that, but I know that now. Bodhi made his choices, and I now understand that he did what he felt he had to. He could not have lived with himself if he had done nothing."

Speaking the words out loud brought Asa to mind, and even though my thoughts were still focused on my husband, no guilt came. Weeks had passed since I had last thought about the man who had risked so much to help me, and I suddenly found myself wondering where he was and how he was doing. Wondering if he still thought of me from time to time. Wondering if I would ever see him again, and when I did, how it would feel.

"Why did you not marry?" I asked Xandra, and then immediately shook my head. "I am sorry. I should not have asked."

"It is okay, really." There was sadness in her dark eyes when she looked away from me, out over the ruins in the distance. "I have never found men desirable, not in the way you do, so I chose to stay with my mother." She did not turn her gaze on me, and the expression of sadness did not fade, but she smiled slightly before saying, "I had a friend in the village. Gaia. Do you know her?"

I remembered the woman, but only because she was also one of the few in our village who had not married. She was also quite a bit older than Xandra, ten years, perhaps.

"I know of her," I said. "I do not think we have ever spoken, though. She was much older than me."

"And me as well," Xandra said and then exhaled. "She worked in the city, and after leading you and Mira to the tunnel, I went to find her. She was not at her house, though, but was instead running errands for the mistress. I searched for her, but I did not have much time. I had to do everything I could to get more people out." Xandra shook her head and turned her gaze from the ruins to the ground beneath us. "If I had not searched for her for so long, I might have been able to save more people."

She said nothing else, and I studied her, trying to understand what she was saying and why she looked so sad over the loss of Gaia. I, of all people, understood risking everything for a friend, but the expression on Xandra's face was different. More like heartbreak.

"You love her," I said, realization dawning on me.

"I do." She looked my way out of the corner of her eye, but did not lift her head. "Does it make you think less of me?"

"No. I cannot because I know what it means to love, and I know that you often have no control over these things." I reached out to Xandra then, laying my hand on her arm. "You are not alone. You must know that. We have all heard stories about the Huni living this way."

Xandra kept her gaze down, plucking at a few blades of grass and ripping them to shreds before tossing them over the cliff. "I am not Huni, Indra. I am Winta."

"Not anymore. Now you are only Xandra." She finally turned her gaze on me when I gave her arm a squeeze. "We will get her back. I promise."

Xandra let out a deep breath, looking away when tears filled her eyes. She blinked, trying to hold them back, but the effort was useless. One escaped and slid down her cheek.

She wiped it away violently. "We do not even know if she is alive, and the only way to find out is to go to the city. But we cannot do that. It is too dangerous."

She was right. We had no way of knowing what was happening in Sovereign City, if our people were alive or dead, or even how many there were. But Xandra was also correct in saying we could not travel to the city. It was too dangerous to even consider.

Still, there had to be a way to find out what was happening.

"Most likely they are being held in the quarters."

I thought of Xandra and Gaia, as well as the Huni. For the first time, a thought occurred to me. One I had never considered before, but something that could benefit us in multiple ways.

"We could visit another tribe," I said. "Get information that way."

Xandra's brows furrowed as if thinking it through, but after a moment she shook her head. "You cannot mean the Huni? We have not been on good terms with them or the Mountari for generations."

"No, but we have an understanding with the Trelite. We have traded with them for years, have even considered them allies." I got to my feet and turned my back on the ruins.

"Where are you going?" Xandra called after me.

"To the caves. We need to talk about this."

I looked back long enough to confirm that she was behind me before heading down the hill.

We found most of the others in the first cave, eating the morning meal. Not everyone was gathered, but to me enough of us were present to at least start the conversation.

"We must visit the Trelite," I said when Xandra had stopped at my side.

The other women looked up at me with expressions ranging from shock to confusion.

"We need information," I said when no one said a word. "And they might also be willing to trade with us."

"They will not talk to us." Mira set her bowl down.

"She is right," Xandra said, drawing the gazes of the other women her way. "The Trelite are a highly patriarchal tribe. Winta men viewed women as weak and in need of protection, but the Trelite men see us as inferior. I worked with two Trelite women in Sovereign City. They were not permitted to walk to the city alone, and once the men from their village picked them up, they were not even allowed to speak unless spoken to first. The Trelite are very strict when it comes to these things."

"But you said so yourself, we need information about what is happening in the city," I argued even though the concern shimmering in her dark eyes gave me pause. "They are our allies, and even if they feel that way about women, I feel certain that they will not turn their backs on us when we need help."

Xandra pressed her lips together thoughtfully, but said nothing. I looked the other women over and saw the same doubt and concern shimmering in her eyes.

"It would be helpful if they could teach us a little about growing crops," Mira pointed out after a moment. "We have plenty of meat, but it will not be enough to keep us healthy forever. We need vegetables."

"Maybe they will trade with us," Tris said meekly, as if she were afraid to speak up. "We have furs."

She was looking at me, as was everyone else in the room, and it hit me, as it had more and more recently, that they were waiting for me to make the decision. It was a role the others had thrust upon me, but one I was not yet comfortable with. Still, there was no turning back, not after I had transformed them all into hunters of men, and whether or not I had planned it, this was my tribe now.

"We need their knowledge," I said, and then turned toward Xandra as if looking for reassurance that I was making the right choice.

This was another thing that had become common, a change I had not noticed at first and one I would not have expected. Mira had always been my closest friend, and that had not changed, but there was something about Xandra's experience and maturity that made me look to her more and more in moments like these. We had not elected a Head for our new village or even talked about it, but the feeling that I was in charge had grown with each passing day, and with

Xandra always on my side, it gave me the strength I needed to fake confidence, even if I did not always have it.

"What is the worst that can happen?" I asked, still looking at her. "They may turn us away, but they are not Huni or Mountari. The Trelite are not fighters. They rarely even hunt animals, so we do not need to worry about them attacking us."

"You are right." The other woman ran her hand over her head, smoothing down her short hair. "There is a good chance they will not talk to us, but the most they will do is turn us away. There is very little risk in going."

No one else argued, and I glanced around the room to find the other women nodding.

"We need to get a group together, but we also want to keep it small so we do not come across as a threat." I said, as I studied the group in front of me. "I will take Xandra, Mira, Anja, and Emori with me. Gather your things so we can go. You must arm yourselves, but do not take a lot of weapons. Keep it simple. Unthreatening."

Thirteen

OF THE FOUR OUTLIER TRIBES, THE TRELITE LIVED the furthest from Sovereign City. Their village was deep in the forest, close to where the wilds stopped and the wastelands began once again. Living in the caves, we were much closer to them than we had been back in our village, and it took us no more than an hour to reach.

They must have seen us coming, because before we had spotted a single sign that we were approaching our destination, a horn rang through the air as if announcing our arrival.

Behind me, Emori slowed. "Should we stop?"

"No," I replied as I surveyed the forest in front of us, trying to figure out where the sound had come from or at least get a glimpse of the village through the trees. There was nothing, though. "They will come out to meet us."

"How do you know?" Mira asked me.

"It is what we would have done," I replied.

At my side, Xandra was silent, but her confident nod said she agreed with me, and so we kept walking.

A small group emerged from the trees only a few beats after the horn had sounded. There were five of them, all men, and even though they were all wielding spears, nothing about the sight of the weapons had me worried. The Trelite may have been the most peaceful of all the tribes, but even they would defend themselves against intruders if necessary. We just had to convince them that we were not a threat.

"I am Indra of the Winta people," I said when we stopped in front of the men. "We have come to talk to the Head of the Trelite tribe."

"Where are your men?" the man at the front of the group asked.

He was twice my age and the oldest in the group standing before us. The Trelite were the only other tribe who used passage markings similar to ours, and it was not unusual for their people to be covered in lines by the time they died. Not just on their faces, but their arms and legs and backs as well. The more lines on a man, the higher his place in the village was, and the exposed skin of the man in front of us was nearly covered. His face was swirled with both wrinkles and passage markings, the lines dark against his tan skin, but they did not stop there. They went down his neck and covered his arms, his bare chest, and the way they curled around his shoulders told me his back was very likely covered as well. It was a good sign that they had sent someone so important to talk to us, but it also worried me. It was entirely possible he would refuse to deal with us because we were only women.

"They all died when the Fortis attacked our village," I told him. "Only twenty-three women and children escaped."

The man frowned, and his gaze moved past me to the other women from my tribe. "That is not good."

None of the men behind him spoke, and their neutral expressions made it impossible for me to figure out what they were thinking. They were all younger, their skin in various shades of tan and light brown, and although they all had faces as marked as the man at the head of the group, none of the others had nearly as many lines on their arms and chests.

"I am Zaire," the man said after a couple beats of tense silence. Then he turned to head back into the village. "You will follow me."

The group of men parted, giving us space to follow Zaire. When all five of us had passed through, the other men trailed behind us. It made it seem like they were surrounding us, and the urge to defend not just myself, but my friends as well, swept over me. I fought against it, though, clinging to the knowledge that the Trelite were peaceful. They had done nothing threatening so far, so I told myself there was nothing to worry about.

Even so, I was thankful to have my bow.

My steps faltered when we crossed the threshold of the village. I had known the Trelite lived in the trees, but seeing the huts hanging high above our heads, accessible only by ladders, was still shocking. On the ground they had animals and dozens of gardens, all overflowing with vegetation since they ate very little meat, especially in the summer when the forest was so green with life. How they managed to grow so much when the Winta had always struggled was something we had never figured out, but a trick I was hoping to learn. Assuming we could get the Trelite men to speak with us.

Zaire led us to the middle of the village where a large fire roared, and around it, dozens of men stood, each of them holding spears just like the five who had come out to greet us. The flames from the fire crackled into the air as if trying to reach the huts hovering high above it, connected to one another by walkways. Faces of women and children were visible in a few of the windows, but all the ladders had been pulled up at our approach, giving them no way to get down and no way for us to go up.

Zaire stopped on the opposite side of the fire and motioned to the ground. "Please sit. I will speak to the Head."

We did as requested, and even though his demeanor was still unthreatening, the gazes of some of the men standing before us were less amicable. They looked at us with suspicion, but it was not because we were from another tribe. It was because we were women.

The crowd in front of us shifted, allowing Zaire to step through, and he disappeared from sight. Leaving us alone.

At my side, Mira shifted and whispered, "They are not happy we have come."

"We knew it would be so," I replied, keeping my voice low.

Xandra turned her face toward me and in a low voice said, "It is an insult to them that we have come."

"Perhaps we would have had a better chance with the Mountari," Anja said from my other side.

"They are savage," Emori hissed.

"They are a people who take pride in strength," I countered, thinking Anja may have been right. Perhaps we should have gone to the Mountari.

Zaire was not gone long, and when he made his way back through the crowd, he was no longer alone. The man at his side wore a headdress made of sticks, indicating that he was the Head of the tribe, but he was much younger than Zaire. Probably only ten years older than I was. Somehow, though, his dark skin was covered in as many lines as the older man's. So many that they would be hard pressed to find skin bare enough to add more lines.

He looked us over as he walked, the expression in his eyes a mixture of the two greetings we had already received. How he had come to be Head at such a young age was impossible to know, but it did not escape my notice that his passage markings were intertwined with raised scars. They cut across his face, arms, and bare chest, making it look as if he had led a very violent life. Something that was not normal for a member of the Trelite tribe.

He stopped in front of us, but did not indicate that we should stand, so I stayed where I was, looking up at him from the ground. If I stood, these men might take it as a sign that I saw myself as an equal, and even though that was true, I did not want to risk anything that would terminate the good relations our two tribes had always had.

"Indra of the Winta tribe, I am Cruz, Head of the Trelite tribe."

"Cruz, thank you for agreeing to see us." I bowed my head slightly the way I had inside the city when dealing with the Sovereign and Fortis. "We have come with the hope that the good relations between our two tribes will be extended to us now that our men are gone."

"Zaire tells me that all your men were killed when the Fortis attacked your village."

"They were," I said.

"This is most disturbing news." Cruz's brown eyes clouded over. "It is not good for women to be alone, as I am sure your departed men would agree."

"They would," I said, agreeing with him while refusing to acknowledge I felt the same way.

It was true that the men in our village would have thought we were too weak to take care of ourselves, and even though we had proven that was not the case, I doubted it was something Cruz would want to hear.

He motioned for us to stand. "Come, Indra of the Winta tribe. We will discuss this by the fire."

He had already turned by the time the five of us were on our feet, but Zaire waited. He then led us across the village and through the large group of men who were gathered to watch. Their expressions of anger had lessened, but not disappeared completely. Many probably believed we should have thrown ourselves on the burial fires of our men rather than continue without them. It was a brutal custom that happened often in the Trelite village, but one I did not like to think about.

Cruz took his place on a chair carved from a tree stump, and I lowered myself to the ground in front of him, knowing this was what was expected of me. The other women did the same, and behind us the Trelite men began to disperse. A rope ladder was thrown down and women followed, as if the Head taking a seat indicated it was okay for them to descend.

"We heard about what happened to your village," Cruz began, "but we thought all of your people had been killed."

"I helped some of the women and children escape into the forest," Anja said. "And there were others who made it out of the city and hid in the Lygan Cliffs, thanks to Xandra."

Cruz looked my sister's way and frowned, and then focused on me once again. "We do not usually make deals with women."

"We understand your customs, but I know you are an honorable people, and I know you would not want helpless women and children to go hungry."

"No," Cruz said. "We would not."

A woman appeared at his side, holding a cup, and he took it without even glancing her way. She held one in her other hand as well, but made no move to give it to me, and she appeared uncertain about how to proceed, her large eyes seemingly magnified by the markings circling them as she looked me over.

"Give the cup to Indra of the Winta people," the Head said in a harsh tone.

The woman bowed her head and held it out to me.

I took it, whispering a quiet, "Thank you," as I did.

The frown on Cruz's face deepened. "You do not need to thank her. She is a woman, and it is her duty to make sure the men in the village are comfortable, and that comfort extends to our guests." He held his cup out. "Let us drink, and then we will discuss our terms for your survival."

I clinked my cup against his before tilting it toward my lips, my eyes on him the whole time, looking for cues as to how I should act. He watched me, too, taking in my careful attention as if sizing me up. I made sure I started drinking only a second after he did, and that I kept the cup to my lips the entire time he had his at his mouth so I was certain I did not offend him.

The liquid was sharp and bitter, stinging my throat when I swallowed it and making my eyes water. I did not stop drinking, though, but instead continued until every last drop was gone and Cruz had finally lowered his own cup. Then I coughed. It was impossible to hold in. The liquid scorched my throat the same way the sun had burnt the wastelands centuries ago.

Cruz's lips turned up into a smile. "Women do not usually drink spirit water, but you have done well."

"Thank you," I coughed out.

He held his cup out, not taking his eyes off me, and the woman appeared to take it from his hand. "What have you come to discuss with us, Indra of the Winta tribe?"

"We have come for information," I said as I held my own cup out to the woman. I wanted to look her way, to thank her as I had when she gave me the drink, but I focused on Cruz. We needed this man to work with us. Even if I did find his attitude repulsive. "We were hoping you would be willing to trade with us. We can give you furs in exchange for vegetables and knowledge of how to grow them."

"You plan to grow your own food?" The markings on Cruz's face danced as his eyebrows lifted and his mouth turned up.

Heat licked at my cheeks, but I worked hard to keep my expression neutral. Fortunately, due to my years of working in the city, I had lots of practice at hiding my emotions. "We do."

"And where will you get the fur you wish to give us?" His light brown eyes sparkled with amusement.

"We will hunt the animals."

Some of the laughter melted from his expression, and his eyebrows moved. "*You* will hunt?"

"My husband taught me to hunt before he died."

The Head paused at this bit of information, but only for a beat before asking, "He died when the village was attacked?"

"No," I said. "He died before that. He went to Sovereign City and was caught trying to kill a man. He was beheaded."

The pleasure sparkling in the Head's eyes faded, and was replaced by an expression I didn't quite understand. It almost looked reverent. "We have very few people working in the city because it is so far from us, but even we heard about this. It was a very brave thing your husband did, going to kill the man who dared touch his property. When we learned of his death at the hands of the Sovereign, we honored him."

I thought of Bodhi and how he would have reacted to this man referring to me as *property*. It could not have been further from the truth. My husband had taught me to shoot, and he had done it to ensure that I would be able to take care of myself. Unlike the man in front of me, Bodhi had respected me. Valued me.

I said none of this, though. Not only would it be impossible for Cruz to understand, but I also knew it would offend him, and we needed his help. Yes, we could take care of ourselves, but first we needed someone to teach us how to do it.

"He was a very good husband," I said, bowing my head.

"We also heard of the Winta woman who caused her village to be burned and her people to be slaughtered." I lifted my gaze from the ground when Cruz leaned forward, and his light brown eyes narrowed on me. "This was you?"

"She defended me," Mira bit out.

The Head's eyes snapped her way. "In my village, you do not speak unless spoken to."

"I stabbed a man in Sovereign City, and because of it, the Fortis were dispatched to destroy my people," I said, drawing Cruz's eyes back to me.

He was silent for a moment, staring at me, and my scalp tingled under his intense gaze. His eyes were pale brown, too pale for someone with such dark skin, and it made him look angry even when he was not.

"What is the information you seek?" he finally said, sitting back.

"We wish to know what is happening in Sovereign City. We still had people inside the walls when our village was burned, and we want to know if they are dead or being held."

"They are being held in the quarters the Fortis built," Cruz said. "We had only one person escape the city before the Outliers were taken prisoner, and since then none have returned."

"It is what we thought," I told him.

"Is that all?" When I nodded, Cruz mimicked the gesture. "Very well. You are undoubtedly strong, Indra of the Winta tribe, but you are still just a woman, and without men, you and your people will not survive long in the wilds. It is for this reason I have decided to invite you to join our tribe."

It was a response I had not expected, and one I found myself totally unprepared to respond to. I looked to my right, at Xandra and Emori, and then to my left where Mira and Anja sat. Not because I thought they would be any more open to the suggestion than I was, but because I was unsure how to respond without insulting the Head, and I wanted to buy myself some time. I needed his vegetables, but I did not need him or any of the other men in this tribe.

"That is a very gracious offer," I finally said.

Cruz stood like he thought the matter was settled. "We can unite the two tribes with marriage. I have four wives already, but I am willing to take you as my fifth, Indra. An offer you will be unlikely to find anywhere else. It is not often that a man is willing to take on a woman who does not know her role, but I am confident in my ability to help you see your place."

He stared down as if waiting for me to stand, but I did not move other than to curl my hands into fists. The idea that this man thought I should be grateful for such an offer was enough to make me want to charge out of the village and never look back, but I was no fool. Leaving now would mean turning my back on potential help, and I had too many people depending on me to do that.

"You misunderstand me." I bowed my head in hopes that it would ease my next words, and that it would hide the anger surging through me. "I am grateful for the offer, but we are very happy where we are. We have created a new home for ourselves, and we are doing quite well."

"But for how long?" Cruz once again lowered himself into the chair. "How will you defend yourselves if the Fortis attack again? Who will look after you?"

"We have done very well on our own so far," I said. "If you will help us learn to grow food, we will do even better."

Without lifting my head, I ventured a look up. He was frowning, and behind him, the other men were standing in groups, talking quietly. I had known before coming here that the Trelite men took multiple wives, and as I watched the men talk amongst themselves, I could not help wondering if they were already discussing who would take the other four women as wives. The thought made my stomach twist, and I clenched my hands tighter, digging my nails into my palms.

Cruz did not speak for a few beats, and the longer the silence stretched on, the more I began to doubt our decision to come here. These men would not attack or kill us, but I would not put it past them to try to detain us for what they believed was our own good. Women were little more than cattle to them, and it was possible they might actually view keeping us here as their duty.

Finally, Cruz exhaled. "You are not Trelite, so I cannot force you to join us, even if I know it is the best thing for you. I do know it will not be long before you realize how helpless you really are without your men. When that time comes, know we are here." He got to his feet. "In the meantime, we will help you. I will not teach you how to grow crops since it would be wasted effort on a woman, but we will be happy to trade vegetables with you."

The speech was so insulting that if we did not need this man's food, I would spit in his face and leave. As a member of the Winta tribe, I had always pictured the Trelite as more like myself, but no man in my own tribe had ever treated me like this. Even after Bodhi died and the Head spoke with my mother about my hunting, he had done it out of concern, not because he thought I was too stupid to make it back to the village without getting lost. It made me wish we had not come here at all.

Since the deal was already made, I stood and gave the Head a smile that I hoped looked grateful instead angry. "Thank you for your help."

He dipped his head once before saying, "Let us know when you are ready to join us." Cruz turned away then, waving to Zaire when he did. "See that these women are provided for."

"I DID NOT THINK HE WAS GOING TO HELP," Emori said after we had gotten a good distance from Zaire and the other men who had escorted us from the village.

"He only agreed because he thinks we will die otherwise." I uncurled my fingers and flexed them to relieve the tension. "They were insulting."

"I knew it would be so." Xandra shook her head as she shifted the basket of vegetables on her hip. "Imagine you marrying that man. It is absurd."

"It makes me think we should go to the other villages." Mira clutched her own basket tight against her breast as she looked the rest of us over. "They could help us fight the Fortis."

"What does that have to do with the Trelite helping us?" Anja asked, and I could tell she was as dumbfounded by the comment as I was.

In my eyes, the two things had nothing to do with one another. The Trelite and Winta had always cooperated, but the Mountari and Huni were as good as strangers to us.

"If we can convince the Trelite to work with a group of women," Mira said, "perhaps the other tribes will be more willing to work with us than we thought. Together, we would outnumber the Fortis."

"It would give us the numbers," Xandra agreed. "The Outliers outnumber not just the Fortis, but the Fortis and Sovereign combined. Even with the Winta gone."

They had a point, and it was not the first time Mira had brought this up to me, but I still did not think we could make it happen. The Outlier tribes had not worked together in centuries, and before our recent peace, we had been at war for decades, fighting amongst ourselves while we slaved away for the Sovereign. We were the same, but also different; our trip to the Trelite village had confirmed that. Our customs would never mix. The Trelite would not accept women as fighters, and the Head of the Huni was a woman. The Mountari, too, did not believe women were their equals, and women were all we had left.

"No," I said. "It cannot work. A group of Winta women cannot bring the Outliers together, not when the gap between them is so big."

No one argued with me, but as we continued our trek through the forest, I could tell a few of the others were less certain than I was. Mira, especially. Maybe she was right. I did not know for sure. I just knew the blood on my hands had barely dried, and I could not risk what remained of my people right now.

Fourteen

WE THRIVED IN THE FOREST. I HAD NEVER doubted we could do it, but the doubts the other women carried with them had been obvious, at times making it difficult for me to cling to my optimism. But with each passing week, things got better for us. My tribe became more confident, better hunters, and stronger than even I had imagined we could be, and with the added help of the vegetables from the Trelite, we were more than prepared for the cold when fall once again turned into winter. Outside, snow fell on the wilds, but we were tucked away in the caves, safe from both the weather and the Fortis who wanted to do us harm.

A year and a half had passed since Bodhi was killed, and nearly a year since the Fortis had burned our village to the ground. It seemed unreal that so much had changed in such a short amount of time. It had been difficult, but we had adjusted and grown. We had created our own tribe out of the remnants of the Winta with no help from men, and we had done well.

Either unable or unwilling to let go of the scars the Fortis had left behind, we continued to kill the men and women we came across in the woods, and with each passing day, we became more and more competent as both hunters and warriors.

Despite how well things were going for us, living in the caves could be stifling. Noise bounced off the stone walls and echoed much too loudly, making it difficult for me to think at times. In those moments, I found the forest always waiting, always ready to provide me with the much-needed break from the close quarters of the cave. The peacefulness of the wilds as I sat waiting for an animal to cross my path had been one of the few things that could comfort me after Bodhi's death, and despite how different everything now was, that had not changed. Even more important, when I was out by myself, it almost seemed like Bodhi was with me. Watching down on me, proud not just of what I had accomplished, but of who I had become.

I went out early that morning, while the caves were still silent and the sun was still trying to claw its way over the horizon. Winter was in full force, and the fine blanket of snow covering the forest sparkled in early morning sunlight. Steam rose in front of me with each breath I let out, and I watched it get carried away as I picked my way through the forest.

Suddenly, I was hit with the memory of how steam very similar to this had risen off the hot water in Saffron's house.

How being able to simply turn a knob to gain access to it had awed me so much when I first arrived there, and then later how it had infuriated me. It, like most things inside the walls, had morphed over time, changing from something that had seemed like magic to something that could only be described as an injustice. It had been one example in a long line of things illustrating how much more the Sovereign had.

I carried the memory with me as I searched for a tree and then climbed. My bow was slung over my shoulder, freeing my hands so I could hold onto the icy branches and pull myself up. Halfway to the top, I found a grooved branch and settled in. It was icy and unforgiving against my backside, but the silence was peaceful. I let out a deep breath and watched as steam once again rose, and when it was carried away by a gust of wintry wind, I imagined it took my thoughts of Sovereign City and Saffron with it. Out here I wanted to be able to embrace the tranquility, not dwell on the horrors of that world.

Winter made animals more scarce, so it was no surprise that hours passed with little more than the squawk of a rawlin. But like all the times before, the stillness of the Wilds wrapped around me, making the time welcome.

The sun was high above my head by the time the snap of twigs broke through the quiet. I turned toward the sound, my bow already up and my arrow notched. Holding my breath, I listened, waiting for whatever was headed my way to make another sound and give its location away.

At first nothing happened, and I began to think the animal had retreated. Then, with no warning, the man emerged from the forest, his movements slow, almost hesitant. Whether he sensed my presence or there was another reason for his hesitation, I did not know. Nor did I care.

I shifted my bow and took aim. My fingers twitched and my shoulders ached from the effort of holding the string back, but I found it suddenly impossible to release my arrow. A year had gone by since I had hesitated, but for a reason I could not comprehend, I found myself doing it now. The man's back was to me, but there was something about him that gave me pause. Something familiar.

Only a moment after stepping into the clearing, he turned my way, and when I saw his face, all the air left my lungs in a whoosh of steam that disappeared in a blink. Asa. I had not seen him in months, not since my last day in Sovereign City, but I had thought about him often. Had even wondered from time to time if I would ever see him again. And now he was here, standing in front of me.

"Asa," I whispered to myself as I lowered my bow.

He seemed to be alone, and as far as I could tell, he had not come out here to hunt. He had no game, and even though his sword was out, it was not raised. What else could he be doing this deep in the wilds? Was he looking for *me*? Despite the chill in the air, a flush spread across my cheeks at the thought.

Asa crept further into the clearing, so quietly it impressed me, still unaware of my presence. His eyes never stopped moving, though, never stopped scanning the area as he went. It would not be long before he noticed me, but I kept quiet, watching him from the tree, needing the time to recover from my surprise, as well as sort through the strange mix of feelings swirling through me. Excitement at seeing him, curiosity about why he had come, as well as a tingle that was impossible to name.

Asa stopped moving when he spotted my footprints in the snow. I held my breath as his gaze followed them across the ground to the tree, and then up to where I sat crouched. His eyes met mine and he visibly started, and I half expected him to run. But he stayed where he was. Unmoving, his eyes locked on mine for what felt like years.

"Come down," he finally said, his words just loud enough for me to hear.

The sound of his voice transported me back in time, back to Sovereign City and Saffron's house. Only the feelings and memories that came with the sensation were not unpleasant the way I would have expected them to be. Instead, they brought to mind how caring Asa had always been, how he had scooped me into his arms when I needed help, and how he had held my hand when I needed comfort. It woke the part of my heart he had managed to capture more than a year ago, and the feeling took my breath away, making it impossible to speak. I nodded instead, mimicking the gesture I had seen him make dozens of times in the past. Then I threw my bow over my shoulder and twisted so I could climb down.

It only took a few beats, and my back was to Asa when my feet hit the ground. He was as silent as he had always been, but somehow I could tell he had moved closer. When I turned to face him, I found he was near enough to touch.

He was silent as his brown eyes took me in, holding mine for a moment before sweeping over my face. They lingered on my new passage markings — the ones for my mother — before moving lower. Standing in front of him just then, I felt exactly as I had dozens of times before, small and oddly overwhelmed by his magnitude. Not because he scared me, but because I had a feeling that if I let him, he would wrap me in his size and keep me safe forever.

He said nothing, instead seemingly content to stare at me, but I found it impossible to stay silent. "What are you doing here?"

"I came looking for you."

"For me?" Even though I had suspected as much, I found it unbelievable. A year had passed since the last time we saw one another, and yet Asa had been unable to let me go. "Why? What exactly do you want from me, Asa?"

"I came to warn you."

"I am not your responsibility," I said gently. "You saved me, and for that I will always be grateful, but that was a long time ago. I am a different person now. I am stronger."

"Yes, I've noticed." Something flashed in his eyes, wiping away the softness that had been there. "You've made quite the mark on the city."

The expression in his eyes made him look colder, more like the man who had confronted in me in Saffron's house after learning I was killing Fortis hunters. It reminded me of who was standing in front of me. A man who had helped me, yes, but also a Fortis. I could not forget that. Could not let my guard down simply because he had worked his way into my heart.

"What is that supposed to mean?" I snapped at him.

"Everything has changed since you stabbed Lysander. The Sovereign have become stricter than ever before, and the Outliers who work in the city are slaves. They live in the quarters. Did you know the building was finished?" Asa shook his head, almost angrily. "Well, not finished, but good enough for Outliers."

I straightened my back, lifted my chin, and held his gaze as I said, "I do not regret the things I have done, so if you came here to make me feel bad, you have wasted your time. I stood up for my people. I saved my friend. Lysander deserved to die and much more. He—"

"He's alive, Indra."

Asa's words were like a dagger in my heart, and I stumbled back one step at the impact. "You lie," I hissed, even though I knew he was speaking the truth. No matter how confused and out of sorts Asa made me feel, he was not a liar.

"He was badly hurt, but their doctor managed to save him."

"Then I do have something to be sorry for," I said.

Asa was quiet for a moment, looking me over again, and his stare warmed just as it had back in Saffron's house. His gaze had softened again, and the emotion in his brown eyes was raw, unyielding. After all this time, after months and months apart, I thought Asa might have moved on. That he would have forgotten me. But he had not, it was clear now. He was still in love with me.

"I thought you were dead," he finally said, and just like that all the hardness in his expression was gone. "The Fortis were dispatched to your village, and when they came back, they said they had slaughtered everyone. The things they bragged about..." He looked away when pain flashed in his brown eyes. "I was sure you were gone for good."

"I was not there. Mira and I had to make our way through the wastelands, and by the time we arrived home, our village had been burned to the ground. My sister managed to get a few people out, but not all. And she could not save our mother."

Asa lifted his gaze to meet mine once again, and this time I could read the expression in his eyes clearly. Sorrow. "Your mother died?"

"She was too sick." My hand went to the dots on my right cheek, tracing them. "Your people burnt our village down, including my hut. She was in it."

"I'm sorry," he whispered.

He watched me trace the dots, emotion swimming in his gaze. It seemed to wrap around us, to overwhelm me, bringing to mind the past. The times I had let my guard down and allowed Asa close to me. When he held my hand after Bodhi was captured, when he carried me into Saffron's house, when he saved me from the grizzard attack, and I admitted something to myself for the first time. The man standing in front of me had the potential to make me love him. It made no sense because of who we were, but it was true.

I looked away before he saw the truth in my eyes, because I had no clue what to do with the feelings swirling through me. "You should go."

"I haven't told you what I came to say."

I keep my gaze averted, afraid of what would happen if I looked at him right now. "Asa, I—"

"Indra!"

The sound of my name rang through the air and we both turned. I had just enough time to glimpse Emori through the bushes before she loosed her arrow. A cry ripped its way out of me and I reached for Asa, but I was too late. He went down, his body hitting the snowy ground with a thump that sent a throb of pain through my body.

FIFTEEN

"NO!" I gasped, dropping to my knees at his side. "No, Asa. Asa!"

The arrow had struck his arm, and beneath him the snow had been painted red. Asa's face was contorted in pain, but he shook his head and managed to mutter, "I'm okay."

"Indra." Emori ran up, stopping at my side. "Are you okay?"

"He is a friend. He helped Mira and me when we worked in the city. He came to tell me something," I said without looking up.

I urged Asa to sit, and he obeyed, grunting with each move he made. The injury would not have worried me so much considering where it was if there had not been so much blood, but the snow beneath us was coated in it. Only he was wearing too many layers, making it impossible for me to see how bad it was. I could not strip him down here. It was too cold. Too out in the open. I needed to get him to the cave.

I pulled on his arm again, this time trying to urge him to his feet. "Help me," I said to Emori. "I need to get him inside."

She did not move, did not say a word, but it did not matter. Asa was able to get to his feet on his own, and once he was up, I turned to face Emori. The expression in her eyes was icier than the surrounding forest.

"We cannot take him there, Indra. He is a Fortis. We cannot show him where we are living."

She was right, but I could not send him home with an arrow in his arm. He could bleed to death and die on the way.

"We will blindfold him," I said.

I removed the strip of animal hide I had around my waist and stood on my toes. "Lean down," I ordered when I realized Asa was too tall.

He obeyed, dipping his head so I could tie the strip around his head, covering his eyes. I took a moment to arrange it, ensuring that his vision was completely blocked. When I was sure he could see nothing, I took hold of his uninjured arm and began leading him through the forest.

"This is not good," Emori called before hurrying after us.

I pushed past snow-covered branches, holding onto Asa with one hand and my bow with the other. "I know, but what choice do I have?" I did not look back at Emori, knowing her glare would be even more brutal than before. "He saved Mira and me many times. I cannot let him die after everything he has done for us. It would be wrong."

Emori was silent for only a beat before saying, "Are you sure there is no other reason?"

This time, I was unable to keep my gaze off her. The accusations in her eyes were loud and clear, but I said nothing, fully aware that Asa was listening and very likely wondering the same thing. Just as I was.

When we reached the cave, I paused long enough to push aside the branches covering the opening, and then urged Asa to duck so he did not hit his head on the low hanging rocks. Then we stepped inside.

I had anticipated the uproar that followed his entrance, but I was unprepared for its magnitude. A cry rang out and all around the room women moved for their weapons. Xandra actually drew a sword, while Isa rushed to shield Emori's baby.

"It is okay," I called before anything got out of hand. "He is a friend."

No one lowered their weapons. At least not until Mira pushed her way through the crowd and said, "Asa? What happened?"

The atmosphere in the room relaxed, but only a little. It was to be expected. Mira and I knew Asa, and we knew he could be trusted, but no one else did. He was a Fortis, and we had spent the last year hunting men just like him.

"Emori shot him," I told my friend, and then to Asa said, "Sit."

He did as he was told, and I pulled the blindfold from his eyes, giving him his first look around. Most of the women had begun to retreat into different tunnels, but the few who had stayed behind were holding weapons and openly glaring at Asa. Xandra among them.

"He will not hurt us," Mira said as she knelt beside me.

Xandra looked at me, and then at Asa, and I could feel the questions in her gaze as surely as she had felt them in mine that day we spoke to one another on the hill. I would owe her an explanation, but first I needed to tend to Asa. And figure out what the feelings inside me meant.

"We need to get his clothes off," I said, keeping my focus on Mira so I did not have to look Asa in the eye. The idea of stripping him down made heat flood my cheeks, but I had no desire for him to know it.

I had to break the arrow, which made Asa grunt in pain, but once it was shorter, I was able to get his jacket off and then the shirt underneath, leaving him bare from the waist up. Blood was streaked down his arm and across his chest. A chest that was crisscrossed with passage markings and broader than any I had ever set eyes on. Being so close to him, feeling his massive presence and heat, was distracting, and I had to concentrate so my mind did not wander from his injury. It was an impossible task.

I had never seen a man like Asa before. The men in our village had been strong, but not like this. The Fortis were naturally large people, but this was a man who had trained since childhood, who had worked hard to grow his muscle. This was a man who could crush me with one hand if he wanted to, and yet he had only used those hands to comfort me. It was a reality I still could not wrap my brain around.

"It does not look bad," I said when I had finally managed to survey the damage. "I need to get the arrow out, but I think the injury will be minor."

"I will get fresh water for the wound," Mira said, standing.

I watched her walk away, realizing for the first time that every other woman in the room had fled while I was focused on Asa. Which meant when Mira disappeared through the tunnel, he and I were alone.

My hand was on his arm, just below the wound, and he placed his over mine. When I looked up, I found him watching me.

"I've wanted you to touch me for so long."

"Do not do this, Asa. Please."

It found it impossible to look away from the desire burning in his brown eyes. It was not the first time I had seen that expression, but it was the first time I found myself alone with him like this. Asa half naked, us sitting so close to one another that it seemed like we were the only two people in the world. His hand on mine, and his skin warming me in a way that was as intimate as a caress.

"I have to," he whispered. "I didn't tell you how I really felt before, and then I thought you were dead. Do you understand the regret that comes with that feeling?"

"You know I do," I replied.

"Then you know I have to say this. I love you, Indra. I don't know how it happened, but it did, and it isn't going away."

I did not move my hand from under his, and the warmth of his touch had begun to seep into me, but I still whispered, "This cannot happen."

"Maybe not. Maybe I'll leave here today and we'll never see each other again. I don't know what the future holds, but I know I can't keep this inside any longer."

Then he kissed me.

It happened so suddenly that I found it impossible to react. Not when his mouth moved over mine, not when his tongue brushed my lips, and not even after he had pulled away. I was motionless, my body filled with warmth and uncertainty, staring at him as if I were made of stone.

I still had not moved by the time Mira returned, but her reappearance jolted me out of my stupor. If she noticed anything, she did not mention it, and together we worked to remove the arrow from Asa's arm. The silence was a combination of concentration and total bewilderment on my part. I had no idea what I would have done if I had been given time to react to Asa's kiss, but I did know I would not be able to forget how his lips had felt on mine any time soon. Maybe not ever.

When his wound was cleaned and bandaged, Mira sat back. "It is late. You should stay the night."

"I should go," Asa replied.

He was not looking at me, but I did not know if it was a result of regret or embarrassment, or if he was simply afraid of what he might see in my eyes. Since I was as uncertain as he was, I could not blame him for wanting to avoid it.

"You will not make it back before dark," Mira argued.

"She is right," I found myself saying. "It would be dangerous and unwise."

Asa finally lifted his gaze to meet mine, and his brown eyes were searching. Hopeful. "If you think I should stay, then I will."

Mira climbed to her feet. "No one will be very happy about it, but it is the right thing to do."

I stood, too, and Asa followed. He winced, and even though it was small, I found myself reaching out to touch his arm. He chest was still bare, and the heat from his skin was twice as intense as before.

"Does it hurt much?" I whispered.

"It'll be fine." He looked around, his eyes moving to the small tunnel that led into the bigger chamber. "Is this where you go to sleep?"

Heat licked at my face, but I nodded anyway. "The biggest living space is back this way, and I have claimed one of the small caves as my own."

"Where will I sleep?" he asked, his gaze still on the tunnel as if he were afraid to look at me.

I glanced toward Mira, but she was not looking our way. Instead, she was busying herself with cleaning up the blood that had splashed across the rocks.

There had been many moments over the last few years when I had acted without thinking. When I shot that very first Fortis hunter, and then later when I had grabbed the knife off the kitchen counter and stabbed Lysander in the back. I had regretted neither of those things, and as the next words came out of my mouth, I found myself praying I would not come to regret this decision either.

"You will stay with me."

Asa's brown eyes finally moved to me, holding my gaze as the heat between us grew, but his head only bobbed in response.

SIXTEEN

EVERYONE STARED AT ASA IN SUSPICION WHEN I led him into the large chamber, even Xandra and my sister. It was their looks that gave me pause, but knowing Mira had set things up so I could make this choice if I wanted to gave me confidence. She knew Asa, but the other women did not.

I kept my head held high as I moved through the room, positive he would not harm us, either physically or by leading others to the cave. Thankfully, he seemed not to notice the hostility directed at him, because he was too focused on his surroundings. His gaze moved across the room, past the little stream that led deeper into the caves, as well as the other openings, finally stopping on the glowing creatures that dotted the walls and ceiling. I had become so used to them that I sometimes forgot they existed, but the sight of them froze Asa in place.

"What is this?"

"They live here," I told him. "That is all I know. I have never seen them anywhere else, but because of them, we are able to live in the cave. Without these creatures, we would not be able to see."

"I've never seen anything like this," he whispered, awe ringing in his voice.

I said nothing, instead taking his arm once again and urging him forward. The eyes of the other women followed us, but I did not meet anyone's gazes. I did not need to look at them to know what they were thinking and the questions going through their minds. I was all too aware of how big Asa was compared to me. Of what I was risking. Despite what the others thought, it was not my life on the line, but my heart.

The opening into my little cave was low, forcing Asa to duck so he could fit through. Once inside, though, the ceiling towered above us, allowing him to stand straight. With him in my little alcove, the space was cramped, making it impossible for me to put space between us like I had done in the past when his size overwhelmed me. With nowhere else to go, however, I found I did not want space. If anything, I wanted to be closer to him.

"Rest," I said, nodding to the bundle of fur on the floor.

He lowered himself to the floor, saying nothing as he did, and it made me smile. I had not forgotten how silent he could be, and being around it again was comforting in a way I had not expected.

Asa's gaze followed me as I moved about the small area, removing my bow and setting my arrows aside. My fingers moved to the leather strap around my waist just as they did every night, but I hesitated. I knew where this could lead, and despite the heat between us, I still was not sure I wanted to give in to the feelings I had for this man.

Suddenly, as if someone in the beyond had whispered in my ear, it hit me that I was doing the exact same thing with Asa that I had done with Bodhi. I was running from him. I knew Asa wanted to catch me as much as my husband had, and the regret I had felt after Bodhi's death was still vivid in my mind. More than once I wondered why I had resisted being caught for so long. Why I had not given in sooner. It would have given us more time together, given me more memories to cling to after he was gone.

With that thought in my mind, I pulled the leather strap free and stepped out of my pants.

Asa watched in silence as I moved toward him, settling onto the fur next to him. It had been a year and a half since I had known the comfort of a masculine form at my side, and I was surprised by how welcome the feeling was. There was comfort in his nearness, as well as in the heat his body gave off.

There were only two of the glowing creatures in the room, high up on the ceiling, but they gave off more than enough light to allow us to see one another clearly. The expression swimming in his eyes was the same one I had seen dozens of times before. They were searching as they looked me over, and full of something I understood even while it filled me with confusion.

"What are you thinking when you stare at me like that?" I asked.

"That I don't understand the feelings inside me or why I'm so drawn to you." His gaze moved over me, down the fur covering the upper half of my body, and then to my bare legs, stretched out beside his. "That you are beautiful."

"You are beautiful, too, Asa," I whispered.

I traced his bare chest with my gaze, wishing I could use my hands instead, but holding back. It was too big of a step to take. If I touched him now, it would be an invitation, one I would not be able to take back. Not when my body was so aware of his and the feel of his mouth on mine still lingered on my lips. I wanted more. I wanted him.

These were the thoughts running through my mind when Asa reached out and touched my face. He ran the tip of his finger over the passage markings on my right cheek, and a shiver moved down my spine. His touch was feather light. Soft and gentle, and in perfect contrast with his hulking size. His finger moved from the markings on my right cheek to the symbols on my left, and then he ran his fingers up the side of my face to my temple. I had known for so long that he wanted to do this very thing, but it was not until this moment that I realized I had longed for it as much as he had.

"Every time I see you, there are more." His voice was low, but in the tight space it seemed to vibrate through my body. "What do they all mean?"

Bumps popped up on my arms from the warmth of his touch, and my throat threatened to close. I swallowed, and somehow managed to find my voice. "The ones on my cheeks are for the people I have lost," I whispered, pausing for a moment when he ran his finger over the marks on my temple. Once again, my throat tightened, and I had to take a deep breath to force the emotion down. "Those were given to me at the age of twenty, when my mother became too sick to work and I took her place as the head of the family."

Asa's fingers moved up again, this time to the dots above my eyebrows. "And these?"

"They are given at birth, or in my case, when I was brought to my mother. They signify what family I belong to. Anja has the same markings, as did my father, but my mother wore the markings of her father."

His fingers moved up again, this time to the symbols on my forehead. He traced them longer, taking his time, the tip of his finger moving over each dot and line as if he were trying to wipe them away. In front of him, I sat perfectly still, totally mesmerized by the expression on his face and how close he was to me.

When he looked down, his gaze captured mine, holding it as he said, "And these are for your husband."

"We were both given them on our wedding day."

I whispered this part, as if I found speaking of that day difficult or inappropriate with this man sitting in front of me. Only I was not sure if it was true, especially when I could not make myself even pretend I wanted him to leave. Not when he was so close and so beautiful, and not with the warmth of his skin calling to me the way the songbirds called out to one another in spring.

"And if you marry again?" Asa said after only a beat of silence. "Will the markings change?"

For the first time since I lay down at his side, I was filled with uncertainty. "I will not marry again, Asa," I said, my voice softer than a whisper. "We do not mix with other villages, and all the men from my tribe have been wiped out. I am a ghost now."

He nodded as he always did, saying nothing while his gaze once again focused on my face. His fingers moved down to my left temple and then my cheek, tracing the lines on them before cupping my face. He did not meet my gaze again at first, but instead looked me over, his eyes focusing on every dot and line and circle, taking it all in like I was the most beautiful thing he had ever seen. My heart thumped in my chest, harder and harder with each passing second, and by the time his eyes were once again focused on mine, I was holding my breath, waiting to find out what he was going to do. And how I was going to respond.

"And there is no one else you would consider?"

The air I had been holding in whooshed from my lungs. I had expected him to kiss me again, not to say this. Not to ask about something that could never happen.

"Would you marry outside your people?" I said instead of answering his question.

"I don't think there are any women in my village who would have me." His hand fell away from my face, and I was instantly sorry for the loss.

Asa looked away for the first time since stepping into my alcove, and something about it made my heart beat faster. Had something happened to him? If so, it no doubt had to do with me. Had I caused trouble in his life?

"Why?" I asked him. "What has happened?"

"Greer has spread stories about me. He's told the entire village about my relationship with you, the girl who tried to kill Lysander. The other Fortis look at me like I'm a traitor now. Thankfully, word hasn't reached the Sovereign." His brown eyes darted my way, but only for a moment before once again moving to the glowing creatures on the ceiling. "We both know what would happen if it did."

Fear gripped me at the thought of Asa having to face the wrath of the Sovereign, and with it came guilt because it was my fault.

"Helping me has destroyed your life."

"If it has, I haven't learned my lesson." When he shifted his gaze to my face again, the warmth had returned to his brown eyes. "I'm here now, ready to help you yet again."

"How are you going to help me, Asa? What have you come to tell me?"

"I came to warn you that Lysander hasn't forgotten about you. He wants to make sure you're dead."

"He will have a difficult time killing me from inside the city."

Despite my confidence, my heart beat faster. I wanted Lysander to come find me, I realized. I wanted to kill him for real this time, to make sure he could never hurt another person.

"He'll send the Fortis," Asa said.

"Let him." I lifted my chin so I was looking down at the man next to me. "I am ready for it."

Asa let out a sigh, and a wall went up between us. He looked away again, making it impossible for me to read his expression. "You're talking about my people, Indra."

"I am talking about people who have done unspeakable things to me, to the people I love. Just as you know you will get wet if you step into the river, you must know your people have committed acts of violence against Outliers for centuries."

Asa's head bobbed. He kept his eyes on the ceiling, but this time I could read his thoughts. He was ashamed. Ashamed both by what his people had done, as well as the fact that he could say nothing to defend them.

"I know," he finally said.

"Then you must understand why."

Asa did not respond and he did not look at me. I wanted to give him space, so I mimicked his position by rolling onto my back and staring up at the ceiling, at the glowing creatures above. As if sensing I was watching it, one of the bugs lifted its tail, and the light it gave off intensified.

I was still looking at the little bug when Asa's fingers brushed my arm. I turned my head his way and found him propped up on his one good arm, staring down at me. All the shame and hurt from a few seconds ago was gone, and the expression I had seen in his eyes a hundred times before was back. Only, in the tight space, it seemed so much more intense than it ever had before.

He was close enough that I imagined I could hear the beat of his heart, and I found myself reaching out to touch him. With my hand flat against his chest, his heart thumped against my palm. His body heat was more intense than the sun burning down on the wastelands, only instead of wishing it would go away, I wanted to let it engulf me.

"Indra," he whispered, and I moved my gaze up to meet his once again. "I want to be with you."

"I know," I said.

He paused for a moment as if waiting for me to say more. When I remained quiet, he said, "Do you want me?"

I swallowed, already knowing how I was going to respond, but unsure of the complications it would bring to my life. Unsure of what the consequences would be.

"In my village, people do not lay together unless they are married," I began, saying it for my own benefit as much as for his, "but my village is gone now, and I have started a new tribe. We have brought some of our old ways with us, like the passage markings, but we have had to adopt new ways as well. Before my tribe was wiped out, women needed men to protect them, to take care of them, but we have no men now, and so we must be strong on our own."

I moved my hand up his chest to the back of his neck, and pulled him down until his lips were on mine, doing what I had not done earlier. Kissing him. Letting myself really *feel* the kiss, opening my mouth to his prompting, and allowing his tongue to trace mine.

The longer it went on, the more forceful it became, and soon I found myself pulling him closer, kissing him deeper. His hand moved over my body, pushing the fur aside so I was bare to him. Heat flared through me, and with it came a need I had not felt in more than a year.

I pulled back, gasping, but I only broke the kiss long enough to say, "My tribe is gone now, and so are the old ways."

When Asa's mouth covered mine again, his hands were already pushing the rest of the fur from my body. I helped him, freeing my flesh so I could give it to him. When he ran his hands over me, the feeling was familiar, and yet so different at the same time. Asa's hands were larger, stronger, and more calloused, but his touch was gentle and almost hesitant.

"You will not hurt me," I whispered between kisses.

"I don't want to scare you."

I pulled away so I could look into his eyes again, marveling at the softness in them. At how different he was from the rest of his people. "You could not scare me, Asa, because you make me feel safer. I want this. I want *you*."

He was still staring at me when I moved my hands down his body. My fingers undid the button on his pants, and I worked to push them off. Asa helped me then, kissing me as we worked together to remove his clothes.

Then he was free of them and his bare skin was against mine. He was all hard muscle, his body huge compared to mine, but having him against me was not overwhelming or scary. It was freeing. Like I was letting some of the pain from the last year and a half go. Like I was looking toward the future. It made it seem like there was happiness and a future within my grasp, and even though I was not yet ready to acknowledge exactly what my feelings for this man were, I loved this moment with him. Loved that he was helping me feel more whole, and stronger.

AFTERWARD, WE STAYED IN MY LITTLE ALCOVE, naked and stretched out next to each other. The floor was hard, but the pile of furs helped cushion us from the rocks. Between the fur underneath me and the man at my side, I found a comfort I had not known since before Bodhi was killed and my world fell apart. It was more welcome than I could have thought possible.

Asa was as silent as ever, content to simply stare at me as he ran his fingers up and down my arm. The intensity of his gaze took me back to Saffron's house, to the weeks following our first interaction. I had stumbled and almost fallen, and Asa, a Fortis guard who by all rights should have hated me, had reached out as if trying to stop my fall. Before that day, I had barely known he existed, but afterward it had seemed like he never stopped watching me. It was not until much later that I realized he had been aware of me long before I noticed him.

"When did you first notice me?" I asked him.

Asa's fingers stopped moving, and I twisted my body until I was on my side, facing him. For a moment he said nothing while his brown eyes swept down over my naked body before moving back up to my face.

"On your first day," he finally said. "I noticed you right away."

"Why?" I asked. "What made you notice me more than all the other Outliers working in Saffron's house?"

His mouth twitched like he was holding back a smile. "Because you're beautiful."

A laugh I could not hold in popped out of me. Of all the things I had expected him to say, this had not been one.

He smiled, a real smile that lit up his eyes. "What's so funny?"

"You claim you love me, but you did not fall in love with my beauty."

"No." He was still smiling when he pulled his gaze from mine so he could watch his hand as it once again began moving up and down my arm. "I noticed your strength. How you always put others before yourself. Mira, especially." The grin faded, and he shook his head like he was trying to push something from his mind. "I know what happens in the city, and I know what you've sacrificed. I saw you protect Mira. I saw you take the girl under your wing—Isa?" His eyes flitted up to mine as if for confirmation, and I nodded. "When she started her job, you worked hard to help her. Then there was the boy whose hand was cut off. You were totally focused on him during his first day, desperate to make sure he did everything right."

I looked down when sadness gripped me. "It did no good, but I tried."

"You tried. That's the important part." He paused for a moment before saying, "What happened to him?"

"He died when our village was burned down. Just like almost everyone else."

"I'm sorry," Asa whispered.

He leaned forward and pressed his lips against my forehead, and I closed my eyes. For a moment, he did not move away, and when he finally took hold of my shoulder and urged me to turn over, I complied, moving so I was on my stomach, my heart beating faster and my eyes still closed. I knew what Asa was looking at, and I had no desire to see his expression when he did. I had never seen the scars decorating my back with my own eyes, but I had felt them. They would not be pretty, but that wasn't what made me avoid looking at Asa. I did not want to see the pain that would most definitely be shimmering in his eyes.

After I was whipped, my back had been in ruins, but that had not been the worst part. The injuries had healed much faster than my heart had, and at the time there had been a part of me that was sure it never would. Not completely. With Asa at my side now, I found I no longer believed that.

He said nothing, and I kept my eyes closed as he ran his hand down my back, over the scars. It was not long before he urged me to move again, only this time onto my back. My eyes were still closed when his lips covered mine, and the intensity of the kiss nearly took my breath away. Anxious to feel him, to have him closer, I shoved the furs away.

It was not until he was on top of me that I finally opened my eyes. "Why do you love me?"

Asa's gaze held mine as his body hovered over me. "I ask myself that every day. The only answer I've been able to come up with is that you're the best thing I've ever seen. In a world where I'm surrounded by darkness and anger and hatred, you're something that shouldn't exist. You're good and pure. You're everything the world should be."

The words rang in my ears as he moved closer, kissing me while his body covered mine, and in that moment I acknowledged a truth to myself. Asa was the only thing that could heal the remaining cracks in my heart. More importantly, I could not help thinking he had been made for that exact purpose.

EARLY THE NEXT MORNING, WHILE MOST OF MY people were still safely tucked away in their private spaces, I escorted Asa through the caves. The few women who were up watched him with weary eyes, but I did not lower my head in shame, and I felt none about what had happened between us. In my old tribe, what I had done would have been wrong even if it had been with a Winta man, but this was not my old tribe, and Fortis or not, I wanted Asa.

I was not a fool, though, and there was no doubt in my mind that I would have to answer for what had happened here. Xandra watched us pass in silence, her eyes burning with questions. She had trusted me with her secrets, and I would do the same with her. Before the day was out, she and I would talk about Asa.

We came from two very different worlds, something I was well aware of, but I also knew that the future held no certainty for either of us. A year had gone by between our last meeting and this one, and with the war looming between his people and mine, even more time could pass before we met again. There was also a very good chance the goodbye we shared today would be our last. The thought pained me, but it was reality. Nothing was certain in this world.

Asa and I stopped in the main chamber where he leaned down, allowing me to once again blindfold him. I wrapped the strip of leather around his head and tied it tight, then ran my hands down his face, stopping on his cheeks. He was still bent, and all I had to do was lift myself up on the tips of my toes. The kiss was gentle and sad, and filled with the uncertainty our futures held, but we did not mention any of that.

When I finally broke the kiss, I ran my hand down his arm, entwining my fingers with his before leading him outside.

No more snow had fallen during the night, which I was grateful for. Each time it did, we were forced to leave fresh footprints in the snow, making it more and more likely that someone would be able to follow us back to the caves.

I kept a firm grip on Asa's hand as I led him through the woods, winding around the area for much longer than necessary before finally taking the blindfold off. We were at the edge of the river by then, more than a mile from the caves, and from here he would easily be able to find his way back to his own village. Back to his own people and his own world, and possibly away from me forever.

"Thank you for coming to warn me," I said as we stood facing one another.

Pain filled his eyes, and even before he spoke, I knew what he was going to say. "I want to see you again."

"It is too dangerous," I said gently, even though inside my heart was aching with the desire to tell him we could make it work. "You must know I cannot risk it."

Asa took my hand in his, and I stared down at our entwined fingers. My skin was pale against his, snowy where his was dark and warm, and looking at the contrast made it seem impossible that we should fit together the way we had last night, but we had. We had fit together so perfectly that even if I never saw him again, I would never be able to forget the feeling.

"Is this goodbye, then?" he finally said.

I tore my gaze away from our hands so I could look up into his brown eyes, and the emotion in them made my breath catch in my throat.

"For now," I somehow managed to whisper.

He pulled me forward, and when he took me in his arms and kissed me, I was able to return the kiss with no shame and no remorse. No matter what happened, I would never regret the night Asa and I had spent together.

After only a moment, he pulled back. "Until we meet again," he said quietly, his lips close enough that they brushed mine.

"Until we meet again," I whispered in response.

Asa released me and stepped back. He stared at me for only a beat before turning away, and then he disappeared into the forest, and I was left standing alone. Again.

SEVENTEEN

IT WAS NOT A SURPRISE TO FIND XANDRA WAITING for me when I returned. She stood just outside the cave opening—bundled in the black jacket of one of the Fortis hunters she had killed—her dark eyes watching me as I approached, but there was very little judgment in them. Only curiosity.

"I thought we had gotten to know one another so well," she said when I stopped in front of her, "but you have surprised me once again, Indra. A Fortis guard?" She shook her head, but again there was nothing about her body language to indicate she was angry. "I never would have guessed it."

My fingers tightened around my bow, which was slung over my shoulder. "He is trustworthy."

"I believe you." Xandra tilted her head to the side, studying me. "This is the same man who helped you home after your punishment?"

"It is."

"I heard about it, of course, but at the time no one knew what to make of the situation." She pulled the jacket tighter around her body. "Having that man lead you into the village, then carry you to your mother's hut, caused quite an uproar. Mira was with you and she vouched for him, but people still talked."

It was something I had never thought about, not really. When I awoke in my mother's hut after being whipped, I had asked after Asa, but there were too many other things to focus on for me to even consider how the village had reacted. It had never occurred to me that people had whispered about the Fortis guard who helped me, or what they had thought about it. It should have, though.

"What did they say?"

"That this was the man Bodhi had gone into the city to kill. That you and this Fortis were having relations." Xandra shrugged as if the words meant nothing. "Foolish things. Or at least I thought so."

Pain throbbed through me, and it was quickly followed by rage that seemed to warm my blood despite the cold day. My own people believed I had betrayed my husband, a man I had loved with every fiber of my being. I could not fathom it, and yet I had no reason to think Xandra was lying.

"It is not true," I said, the words coming out harsh, but desperate as well. Even if no one else would, I needed *her* to believe me.

She nodded once, and then shrugged again. Either she did not believe me, or she did not care, only I was unsure which it was.

"I have never been one to listen to idle chatter." Her gaze moved past me to the forest like she was searching for Asa. "Although, I cannot lie. Seeing him come into the cave gave me pause." Her brown eyes moved back to me, but she was quiet for a moment longer before whispering, "Especially when I saw how he looked at you."

"I knew he cared for me a great deal." I looked down at the snow, my eyes focusing suddenly on a footprint that was much larger than the others. Asa's. I swallowed and lifted my gaze so it was once again on Xandra. "I never thought of him like that. Not when Bodhi was still alive."

"I believe you never did anything to betray Bodhi, Indra. I saw how devastated you were over his death. I will never forget it." Pain flashed in her eyes, and she hugged herself again, tighter. Only, this time, I did not think it had anything to do with the cold.

The expression in her eyes made my anger melt away the way snow did when it fell in the wastelands, and I let out a deep breath. When the rage was gone, all I was left with was weariness.

"Will he come back?" Xandra asked.

"No." Snow began to fall in fat flakes, and I looked up like the sky would tell me how much it was going to drop on us. "It is too difficult. Too dangerous. Asa and I do not belong together."

"Do not let anyone tell you who to love, Indra." I looked back to find Xandra watching me with a sad smile on her face.

"I do not love him," I said, but the words had no force. They were like the leaves that fell from the trees in fall, brittle.

"If you say so." A shiver shook Xandra's body, and she turned toward the cave entrance. "It is cold, and I know I am not the only one who will have something to say about this. Come inside so we can get this over with."

Knowing she was right, I followed her into the cave where we found the main chamber alive with activity. Now that Asa had gone, it seemed like things had returned to normal, and everyone had gathered for the morning meal. While most of the women barely glanced my direction, a few looked at me with suspicion, and even hostility, when I walked in. Emori was the only one with enough courage to address me about it directly, though.

She stood as soon as I entered, drawing the attention of everyone in the room. "You cannot bring him back here again." Her voice rang through the room, much louder than necessary. "He is a Fortis, Indra."

"I did what I had to do," I said, working to keep my voice low and calm. It was not easy. Not when the anger I had just managed to push away had returned. "He was injured, and if I had done nothing, he could have died."

"Why do we care about one dead Fortis?" she spit back. "How many have we killed over the last year? How many more do we plan to kill? One more is nothing compared to what we want to bring down on them."

"Asa is not like the others. He helped me, more than once. He saved my life."

"He is still—"

"I will vouch for him as well." Mira emerged from the shadows at the back of the cave, pushing her way through the crowd until she was closer to Emori. "Asa protected me even after Indra left the city."

Emori glared at Mira, but it was only a moment before her fiery gaze snapped back to me. "And what of your husband? What of Bodhi? How do you think he would feel knowing you were *with* one of the men who killed him? That you allowed him to defile you in that way!"

Heat shot through me like a bolt of lightning and I took a step closer to her. "Bodhi—" My voice trembled, as did my body, and I had to curl my hands into fists. "—is gone. He is dead, and—"

"At the hands of the Fortis!" Emori shot back, raising her voice until it bounced off the surrounding walls.

Her child started crying, pulling my gaze her way. As always, all I could see when I looked at the little girl was Lysander. It took me back to Sovereign City. Back to the humiliation I had endured there. At Lysander's hands.

Emori was wrong. I had been defiled, but not by Asa. He was different, and no matter what, I refused to back down from this fight. I refused to allow people to treat him like he was no better than the other Fortis guards when that was not true.

I focused on Emori when I said, "Asa did not defile me, and he did not kill my husband. The Sovereign did both of those things. A Fortis guard may have swung the blade, but he was not responsible for Bodhi's death. The Sovereign gave the order. The Sovereign provided the sword. The Sovereign put my husband in the position where he felt he had to defend me or die trying." I paused and inhaled, realizing I had said all this in one breath. "The Fortis are not faultless, and we must still work to take them out, but it is not enough. The Sovereign must pay, too."

Behind Emori, some of the other women nodded, Mira among them, and I remembered what we had talked about after leaving the Trelite village. She had wanted to take our fight to the other tribes weeks ago, had wanted us to find a way for us to work together so we could do more. Only, I had refused because I did not trust them. I had not believed we could work together when we were so different. Yet I had trusted Asa enough to bring him here and risk everyone I had left.

The other tribes were Outliers, too, and just like us, the people inside the city had abused them. They worked as servants just as we had, and their people were now imprisoned just like the Winta who had not escaped the city with Xandra. We had a common enemy, and even though we had never worked together before, it benefited all of us to learn how to do it now.

My gaze was focused on Mira when I said, "We must take our fight to the other tribes."

Emori scoffed at me. "You cannot be serious. We do not mix with the likes of them. We are Winta."

"We are not." Mira pushed past Emori so she could join me, taking her place at my side. "Winta did not allow women to hunt. Winta did not teach us to be strong."

"What are you saying?" Emori looked between Mira and me, her brown eyes wide. Disbelieving. "You think we should forget our people? That we should stomp on the memory of the Winta who died only a year ago?"

"No." I lowered my voice, hoping a soothing tone would calm Emori and help her understand what I was trying to say. "But we are different now. We must hold on to tradition, but it is time for us to form a new tribe. Time for us to declare that we are stronger than the Winta told us we were. We keep the parts of our past that matter the most, but work together to create a new tribe. A tribe we are proud of."

Emori lifted her chin. "I am proud to be Winta."

"I am not," Xandra said.

Since reentering the cave with me, she had stood at my side, listening quietly. When I turned to face her now, though, I found her eyes blazing with an emotion I had never seen in them before.

Emori turned on the other woman with wide, angry eyes. "How dare—"

"Let me talk." Xandra held up her hand. "Give me a chance to explain."

Emori did not argue, but her fiery glare remained. She looked around, perhaps looking for someone to back her up, but around the room the other women were silent. And their gazes were fixed on Xandra.

"Inside the city," she began, "the house I worked in was very different from most. The mistress was sympathetic to our people, as her family had been for decades. She was working toward change even though she knew most of the Sovereign would reject it. She was not alone either. The tunnel out of the city was in the House of Aralyn, and she was the one who helped us get away that last day. She also helped other Sovereign who refused to obey the laws, and she was instrumental in getting babies to safety when they were in danger. Her strength helped me see just how weak the Winta women were. I saw it before the Fortis attacked, but even more when I arrived in our village and found it burned to the ground.

"Our tribe would have fared better if the women had not been taught to cower behind men. If they had known they could pick up a sword and defend themselves, more of them might have survived. Our people were good and moral, and I will always mourn the Winta, but they are dead. We are not Winta, not anymore, and I agree with Indra. It is time to choose a new Head, and start a new tribe. One that helps us all find our strength."

"I agree," Mira said.

Before I had even had time to look my friend's way, Tris called out, "So do I."

One by one the women in the room stood and gave their assent until Emori alone was left seething. Even her sister, Isa, who had worked by my side in Saffron's house, got to her feet. In her arms, the child that was half Lysander and half Emori had calmed, but when the girl's large eyes focused on me, a shiver moved down my spine.

Emori said nothing, but her expression told me she had not changed her mind. Not that it mattered when everyone was against her.

"It is decided." I looked the other women over. The firelight flickering across their faces made them appear fierce. Brave and strong. "How do we choose a Head?"

Xandra took my hand, and when I met her gaze this time, I found her eyes burning with pride. "You are the one who brought us here, who taught us to hunt and to be strong. You should be Head."

It seemed wrong, not because I was a woman, but because I was much too young for such an honor. Xandra was the eldest, and a part of me had always hoped she might one day take the lead. Now, though, I realized that all this time she had had other ideas. Ideas that had me leading a new tribe into battle against the Fortis.

"If this is what you want for our people."

The cave was silent except the crackling of the fire and the scratching of rodents. When I looked the other women over, the only resistance I was met with was Emori's. It burned in her eyes, a distrust that was forming into something bigger. Hate. She remained silent, though, perhaps choosing to say nothing because she knew she could not win. Not when everyone was against her.

When I was certain no one was going to speak up, I took a deep breath and said, "I accept the position as Head of our people."

"We need a name for our new tribe." The pride shining in Xandra's eyes grew as she looked around the room. "Something that will honor Winta, but signify that we are not the same."

"Windhi," I whispered the word almost reverently. "It is a name that will honor both the Winta people and Bodhi. His death was the beginning of everything. It brought us where we are now. It changed me. It changed all of us."

"It is a good name," Anja agreed.

Mira nodded, her blond hair bouncing while the light from the fire flickered over it, making it appear orange. "It is."

All around the cave, the other women murmured their agreement.

"Indra." Xandra, still holding my hand, lifted both of ours into the air as the sound of my name bounced off the walls of the cave. "Head of the Windhi people."

She smiled at me, and something about the expression in her eyes told me she had been expecting this for a long time now. I had not. Even though it had entered my mind a few times that we needed to appoint a new Head, I had never pictured myself in the role. Until last night, I had never even considered forming a new tribe.

"I will get the tebori." Xandra lowered our hands, releasing mine in the process. "You must have new markings. Something that will signify that you are Head."

My sister crossed the room and took my hands in hers. She had said nothing to me about Asa's visit, but she had to be wondering what he meant to me. After the things Xandra had told me about the rumors that had followed Bodhi's death, I felt like I needed to make time to talk to my sister. To tell her this was a new thing, and I had never betrayed my husband.

"You will be a good Head," Anja said, smiling down at me as tears shimmered in her eyes. "Our mother would be proud."

Emotion clogged my throat, like something large was lodged in it, and I had to swallow. "Do you think she would be surprised to see what we have become?"

"No, because she knew how strong you were even before you did."

"I miss her." A tear slid down my cheek, but I did not wipe it away. "Sometimes I do not feel like I am the right person for this role. I wish I could talk to her about it."

"You are the right person," Anja said. "You are stronger than anyone I have ever known."

I squeezed her hand as Xandra returned carrying a bowl of dye and the tebori.

My hand was still in hers when Anja turned away. "We must all get passage markings that signify we are one united people," she said to Xandra. "Markings that establish us as a new tribe."

"Yes," Xandra knelt in front of the fire, nodding for me to do the same. "But first, Indra."

The last time Xandra carved markings into my skin, it had been to signify the loss of my mother, and the loss of my tribe. I had cried then, just as I did now. Only these were happy tears. Tears of pride and hope. They ran down my cheeks as Xandra made a line down my nose, starting between my eyes, followed by two more, one on each side of the first.

As the tool tapped against my skin, my mind wandered from how much trust these women were putting in me, to Asa. Once again, I would have new markings the next time I saw him. How would he react? I imagined him running his fingers over these just as he had with my other markings, his touch light and tender. Just like he was. The thought made me smile.

When Xandra finished the markings that signified I was Head of our tribe, she moved the tebori to my chin, this time starting the design that each and every member of the Windhi tribe would receive. I paid little attention to it, my mind still so focused on Asa that I barely registered what she had drawn until my turn was over and Tris had taken my place.

Xandra copied the design she had just done on me, drawing a line across Tris's chin that swirled up on each side like a smile. Then she made nine more, each of the lines cutting through the first one. The result was fierce. A marking that would unify us, but one that would also signal to others that we were a tribe of warriors.

That was what we were now, after all. We had been transformed from Outliers, nothing more than Winta women and servants, into warriors and hunters. We were strong, and if things went as planned and we were able to unify the other tribes, we would only grow stronger.

EIGHTEEN

There was a time, centuries ago, when the four Outlier tribes were one unified group. Back then, constant discord had plagued the tribe until eventually it fractured, splitting into four separate groups. The first decade following the divide was nothing but war as the Outliers fought for control of the wilds and the meager water they provided.

If things had continued that way, the Outliers might have succeeded in killing themselves off. Luckily, it did not take long for our ancestors to come to this conclusion, and a treaty was made. The land was split evenly, with access to the pond being granted to everyone, and we agreed to never again fight one another. Since then, peace had been the rule of the wilds and it made sense. After all, the Fortis and Sovereign worked hard enough to destroy us without the tribes helping them.

Still, the four tribes did not work together. We did not intermarry, and even trade was not common among the different tribes. The Huni and Mountari women I had worked with in Saffron's house had been civil to me, but even within the walls we had done our best to remain separate. It would need to change if we were going to take out the Fortis, though, and eventually the Sovereign.

Once we had made up our minds to approach the other tribes, deciding where to go first was an easy decision. The Huni were not only known for being great hunters, but they were also the only tribe that spent equal time training their men and women to hunt. If they agreed to join our fight, it would not only give us numbers, but would also work as an incentive when we approached the other tribes.

At least that was what we hoped, anyway. I was under no delusions that the Trelite would be easily convinced. They were neither hunters nor fighters, and they did not view women as valuable. The hope, however, was that if we visited their village last, after we had reached an agreement with the other two tribes, we might be able to persuade them it was a worthy cause.

The next morning, when the sun was still low in the sky, I set out with a small group. The Huni village was the furthest from the caves, all the way on the other side of the wilds where the brown of the wastelands met the green of the forest, and when the trees of the wilds grew farther apart and the skeleton trees became more visible in the distance, I knew we were getting close. Here the barren earth melted the snow before it could collect, and the ground beneath our feet remained naked and cracked, dry despite the precipitation winter brought.

Men and women came into view, along with the huts that signified we had reached the Huni village. People turned at our approach, and I tensed, but as far as I could tell, no one moved for a weapon. It was a good sign.

I had elected to take only the four women who had accompanied me to the Trelite tribe, but the looks the Huni people shot our way made me wonder if keeping our group so small had been the wrong move. We did not have enough people with us to come across as threatening, but we also did not have the numbers to defend ourselves if the Huni decided to attack.

We had not yet crossed the threshold into the village when I spotted a woman I recognized from Saffron's house and paused. She had been working the day I attacked Lysander, had probably even been in the kitchen when it happened. Did this mean the Outliers working in the city were not really being held prisoner? Had Asa lied to me?

"Rekha," I called. "How is it that you are here? We were told all the Outliers are now locked in the quarters outside Sovereign City."

The woman had never seemed friendly, but when she narrowed her gray eyes on me now, they shone with malice I had not been expecting. "I fled after you attacked the mistress's son. I knew the Sovereign would retaliate, and I was afraid of what they would do to me. It saved me."

"Then it is true?" Emori asked her. "The Outliers are now slaves?"

"They are," Rekha said, her eyes still on me. "Because of you."

Mira pushed past me so she was standing in front of the Huni woman. "Indra saved me. You know it. You were there."

"She brought death to her people and slavery to mine."

Rekha's mouth scrunched up, giving me warning, but I was still unprepared when she spit at my feet. I had not expected her anger to go that deep. Had not imagined she would think I was to blame for what the Sovereign had done.

Around me, my people shifted as if moving for their weapons.

"No." I lifted my hand before they could do anything rash. "I am sorry for your pain. I did what I felt I had to, and I did not think about how it would affect anyone else. But you cannot blame me for the things other people have done. Is it my fault the Sovereign do not think we are people?" I scanned the other Huni men and women gathered around before once again focusing on Rekah. "It is not my fault, but if it helps ease your pain to put the blame on my shoulders, I will accept it."

The other woman said nothing.

When the hatred in her expression did not ease, I turned my gaze from her, once again scanning the other people. "We wish to see your Head."

The crowd shuffled, but only a moment passed before a man stepped forward. He was as tall as one of the Fortis, but thin like the skeleton trees, making it seem as if a strong wind would blow him away. Dozens of teeth and claws were pierced through his skin, trophies from the animals he had killed, telling me that he was a great hunter and therefore much tougher than his scrawny frame made him appear.

"I will take you," he said, his voice deep for someone so gaunt.

The crowd parted when the thin man turned, allowing him to lead us to the center of the village and toward a blazing fire. The Huni men and women we passed watched us in silence, but other than Rekah, we were met with no real hostility. Only wariness, as if they were unsure what kind of omen our visit would bring.

Just past the huts, which were made of wood and mud and much like the ones we had lived in before the Fortis burned our village to the ground, sat the skeleton trees that signified the beginning of the wastelands. They were intermingled with others that were currently bare thanks to winter, but not pale and lifeless like the ones in the wastelands. In the distance, the barren land stretched out as far as the eye could see, the sandy ground flat except where it was broken up by rocks or long dead trees.

A woman ducked out of a nearby hut, and it took only one look at her to know she was Head of the Huni people. A crown of rawlin feathers sat atop her head, their plumes bright red against the dark skin of her shaved scalp, and piercings decorated her face and ears. Claws from birds had been stuck through her earlobes, while the teeth of forest cats ran in a line across her forehead.

"I am Ontari, Head of the Huni people." When she stopped in front of us, her gaze moved over my face, stopping on the new passage marking on my chin. "You are Winta?"

"We were Winta. Now we are Windhi." I waved behind me, to the other members of my tribe. "I am Indra, Head of the Windhi tribe. I have come for an audience with you and your people."

Ontari did not blink, as if the knowledge that we had created a new tribe and I, a woman of the former Winta people, was Head did not surprise her. She did, however, look hesitant when she glanced behind me toward the rest of her tribe.

After a pause, her gaze moved back to me. "What is it you want from us?"

"We have come to ask you to join us." I raised my voice to ensure that the people gathered around would also be able to hear me. "We want to wage war on the Fortis. We want to destroy them as they have tried to destroy us, and we want to free our people."

"Impossible," the Head muttered. Then louder she said, "We are not warriors. Not like they are. Even together, the Outliers are no match for the Fortis."

"You are great hunters." I waved at her to acknowledge the many teeth and claws piercing her skin.

"Of animals," Ontari corrected me.

"It is no different."

I kept my gaze on the Head as I held my hand out to Mira, and she passed me the bag we had carried with us across the wilds. I did not blink, did not look away from Ontari as I reached inside, doing my best not to react when my fingers wrapped around the damp hair. When I pulled out the severed head of the Fortis hunter I had killed only the night before, a gasp moved through the crowd.

Ontari took a step back, outraged. "What is this?"

"This is a Fortis hunter who died at my hands." I dropped the head, and when it landed on the ground at her feet, the thud was loud amidst the silence that had spread through the village. "He is only one out of hundreds. All of them dead because of us. My tribe has been hunting the Fortis since they destroyed our village, and I have been killing them for even longer than that. The first time I killed one, I was alone in the woods. I took him down with my bow." I raised the weapon over my head, turning so I could look the Huni villagers over. "He fell to the ground and bled and died, and as I watched it happen, I discovered a warrior had been hidden inside me my whole life. One who will no longer do nothing while her people suffer." I turned back to face the Head. "So I killed another, and then another. They sent parties out to search for me, but they could not find me. I have taught my people—" I waved my bow toward the women at my back, "—to kill as well, but we want to do more. We want to take the fight to the Fortis, to destroy them so we can finally free ourselves from the Sovereign. But we cannot do it alone." My gaze was focused on Ontari when I lowered the bow to my side. "Inside the city we work together, but out here we are strangers. It makes us weak. If we work together, we can do this. We can save our people. We may not be warriors like the Fortis, we may not train from birth, but we have the advantage because we are Outliers. We have had to fight and struggle to survive in the wilds. We do not depend on anyone the way the Fortis do."

My voice rang through the village, echoing off the trees and coming back to me. The Huni gathered around were silent, but they did not seem frightened at the prospect of fighting, and neither did Ontari.

"Have you spoken to the other tribes?" she asked once the echo of my voice had faded to nothing.

"You were the first," I told her, "but we plan to visit the Mountari today, and the Trelite tomorrow. The other tribes know what great hunters you are. If I tell them you are already with us, they will be more likely to join the fight."

The Head looked around, studying her people. Whether she was gauging their reactions or trying to decide if they were as strong as I claimed they were, I did not know. Their expressions ranged from determined to terrified, but no one spoke up to say they did not want to join the fight. If anything, it seemed like they *wanted* Ontari to agree.

"It has been many decades since the Outliers worked together," she said after a prolonged silence. "Do you really believe we can do this?"

"We are not at war, and we have not been for a long time. Plus, we have a common enemy. A common problem. Inside Sovereign City, they do not look at us and see Huni or Mountari. The Fortis and Sovereign see us as one. We are only Outliers to them, nothing else. If we want to stop them, we must act as one."

"She is right," said the slender Huni man who had greeted us when we first came into the village.

Ontari did not act like she thought he was talking out of turn when she turned to look at him. "You believe we can do this, Arkin?"

"I do," the man said, and then tilted his head toward me. "Indra speaks the truth. We are hunters, and it should not matter if what we are hunting is a man or a beast. They both bleed when they are cut." He lifted the spear in his hand. "They can both be taken out by a spear."

Ontari's gaze moved across her people. Many of them were nodding in agreement, and this time when I studied them, the determination on most of their faces was stark. They wanted this as much as my tribe did. They wanted to be free of the Fortis and the Sovereign.

The Head saw it, too, and when she turned her gaze back on me, I knew she was going to agree before she had even opened her mouth. "We will join you, Indra of the Windhi people. We will fight the Fortis with you, and when they are gone, we will take the Sovereign out as well."

A cry rose up among the crowd, and the sound filled me with a sense of relief. Even to myself, I had not admitted my concerns over how the Huni would react, but now that they had agreed to our proposition, I realized the depths of my worry. Without them, it would have been pointless to go to the Mountari or Trelite for help. The Huni not only had the most hunters, since the number included both the men and the women, but they were also the largest of the Outlier tribes. They did not marry or even believe in monogamous relationships, and the number of lovers a person had during their lifetime was almost as important to them as the number of animals they killed. Because of this, they procreated more than the rest of us, with some of the women having their first child when they were still in their teens. Just children by Winta standards.

As we followed Ontari and Arkin through the village, I saw evidence of this everywhere I looked. We passed teen girls whose bellies were swollen with child or had a baby to their breast, as well as toddlers and small children in the dozens tottering across the barren ground. Everywhere I looked I was met with proof of how different our two tribes' values were. This was why the Winta had always kept their distance. It was an uncomfortable reminder, because it made me doubt the very alliance we had just created, and I could tell by the expression on the faces of the women with me that they were feeling the same things.

Not all of them, though. Xandra studied the people we passed with interest, reminding me of the love she had embraced and how it never would have been accepted in our old tribe. It also reminded me of what she had said to me after Asa left the caves. She had told me not to let anyone tell me who to love. While I still could not say whether I loved the Fortis man I had shared my bed with, the very fact that I had done it told me that I was in no position to judge how these people chose to live. We all had a right to live our lives, which was exactly what we were fighting the Sovereign for.

We were more than halfway through the village when I caught sight of a young boy, no more than five years old. He held a stick like a cane, dragging his left leg behind him as he walked, and on closer inspection I noticed it was because he had no foot. The foot had not been cut off, though. It was rounded like a club, almost as if all the bones had been balled up while he was still forming in his mother's womb.

We reached the center of the village, and my attention was drawn away from the boy when Ontari sat, motioning for us to follow. Arkin knelt at her side so he could fill cups with a light brown liquid, passing them out to those of us gathered around.

Once we all had one, Ontari lifted hers in the air. "To our treaty."

I raised my own cup before taking a drink. The liquid was bitter to the taste, reminding me of the drink the Trelite had given me when we first visited them. Thankfully, unlike when I was in the other village, I did not feel compelled to drink the whole thing.

Arkin stayed close to Ontari's side, and the way they interacted made it clear they were intimately familiar with one another—a relationship that no doubt elevated his position within the tribe. When he reached out and fondled Ontari right in front of us, heat licked at my cheeks and I had to look away. Like me, the other women in my tribe averted their eyes, with the exception of Emori, whose face scrunched up in disgust.

Ontari's eyebrows lifted and the line of teeth on her forehead rose with them. "We live so close to one another, and yet we come from very different worlds."

"You must forgive Emori," I said, in hopes of smoothing things over. "She was unmarried when our tribe was wiped out, but not unaware of the ways of men and women. A Sovereign man introduced her to those, as he did with me."

"She is not alone in that. We are no strangers to the brutality of their people." Ontari waved Arkin away as she turned her gaze on Emori. "I have great admiration for people who choose to harness their primal natures, but it is not something we do here in our village. It is a shame not everyone can enjoy the flesh as we do, but I wish for us to exist in peace and have no desire to make you uncomfortable. Out of respect for your position, I will do my best to rein in my thirst while you are around."

"I appreciate your consideration," Emori said, but the hardness in her eyes told a different story.

She had not been easy to live with since Asa's visit, and I feared it would not be long before her hostility boiled over. Xandra and I had even discussed leaving Emori behind today, but we worried it would only push her closer to the edge. Now, though, I found myself wishing we had left her back in the caves.

If Ontari noticed the hostility, there was nothing in her demeanor that said she took offense to it. She simply took another drink from her cup, her gaze moving over us as she did.

"We feel that we should select a common place in the forest where the Heads of all the tribes can meet," I said, hoping to keep the focus on the alliance and off Emori. "Something that is neutral and non-threatening."

Ontari lowered her cup. "It is a good idea. Did you have a place in mind?"

"The clearing at the pond."

The Head nodded, and the crown of feathers that sat atop her head bobbed, somehow managing to remain in place despite her smooth scalp. "That will be sufficient for us."

She lifted her cup again, tipping it in my direction, and I copied the gesture. I had no desire to drink more of the bitter liquid, but I did anyway. Like Ontari, I wanted our tribes to get along.

The Head smiled as she took a sip as if aware of what I was thinking, and the expression softened her features. It made her look younger. More attractive.

"Indra." Xandra touched my knee. "We must head out soon if we want to make it to the Mountari village."

"Yes." I put the cup down, grateful to have a legitimate reason not to drink more of the liquid, and turned to Ontari. "We will plan a meeting tomorrow evening. At sunset. For now, we must take our leave."

Ontari stood, as did Arkin, and the feathers on her head bobbed again. "We will be there, Indra of the Windhi."

As we were leaving the Huni village, I noticed yet another child with an odd deformity. This time it was a hand that was shriveled and useless, and half the size of the other. When I tore my gaze from her, I saw another girl who bore a hole where her mouth and nose should have met, and another child whose head was misshapen. I had never seen anything like this before, but since the Huni slept with one another unabashedly, paying little attention to bloodlines, I attributed the deformities to that. It was yet another reason why the Winta valued marriage and had chosen to live with one partner their whole lives.

Nineteen

THE MOUNTARI VILLAGE SAT AT THE EDGE OF the Lygan Cliffs, right where the black rocks met the wilds, and like the Huni, they were hunters. Only their efforts were more for sport than food, which in my mind made them twice as intimidating as the tribe we had just left.

We had not yet reached the outskirts of their village when we happened upon a group of four Mountari women in the process of carrying lygan skins full of water back from the pond. They ranged in age from a girl of around fourteen to a woman I guessed to be past her fiftieth year, and all four of them were dressed in lygan skins. The bright red and purple scales of the creatures contrasted with the snowy forest, while at the same time shimmering under the afternoon sun.

The women paused when they spotted us, and I prepared myself for another hostile greeting, but they seemed neither wary, nor angry at finding us so close to their village. Only surprised.

When we were still a good distance away, the oldest woman called out, "You are Winta." She watched us approach with gray eyes that were nearly the same shade as her hair, which was a mess of tangled curls that went down to the middle of her back. Her expression was curious, but unguarded. "We thought you were all dead."

"We were Winta," I said when we had stopped in front of her. "But we have formed a new tribe. I am Indra, Head of the Windhi people, and I have come to seek council with your Head."

The woman's eyebrows lifted in surprise. "A woman Head?" She pressed her lips together as she shifted the bulging lygan skin in her hand, her gaze sweeping over me but giving away nothing about what she was thinking. "I am Zuri, wife of Roan, Head of our tribe."

It was a stroke of luck to run into someone so important before we had even made it to the village, and even better that she did not seem upset by our presence. Hopefully, it was also a sign that the Mountari were friendlier than we had always thought they were.

"Will your husband talk to a woman?" I asked.

When Zuri smiled, the creases at the corner of her eyes deepened, accentuating her age. "We are not Trelite. Roan will talk to a woman or he will hear from me."

It was my turn to smile, and the expression was laced with relief. When I looked back at my friends, it was clear they were feeling it, too. The Mountari were an intimidating tribe, and even more than the Huni, we had been concerned we would be met with hostility. It was nice to find out we had been wrong.

"You may follow me." Zuri nodded toward the forest before turning.

She and the other women led the way into their village, and as we entered, people turned to stare. Our marked faces identified us both as outsiders and Winta, but like Zuri, the expressions of the people we passed seemed more surprised than angry. It helped ease my worry even more. Though people rarely said it out loud, the Winta had long thought of the Mountari as savages. Perhaps we had been wrong. It would not have been the first time.

Here the homes had been built on stilts that raised them high off the ground so that they towered over my head, and I could only assume it had something to do with how close the village was to the lygan infested cliffs. The bones, skins, and teeth of the scaly creatures were everywhere. Their skulls lined up outside huts like trophies, while the Mountari seemed to use the animals' scaly hides for nearly everything—clothes and water skins, as well as bags to carry things. They had even been sewn together and stretched across the roofs of huts to keep the weather out. It made the village bright and colorful, even surrounded by the drabness of winter.

Zuri stopped outside a hut before turning to face us. "Wait here while I speak to Roan."

"Thank you," I said.

She nodded once before climbing the ladder in front of her, and only a beat later she disappeared into the hut, leaving us alone. I turned to face my people and found them looking around. Like me, curiosity shone in their eyes, and even a little bit of awe. Around us, the Mountari had mostly gone back to their work, as if their surprise at seeing us had already worn off, and the total indifference they showed us was almost welcoming.

"They are much more friendly than the other tribes," Xandra said.

"It is a good sign," I replied.

"I did not expect it," Mira whispered. "We had always been told they were savage."

"Can you blame us for thinking that?" Emori alone did not work to lower her voice as she looked toward the lygan skulls lined up in front of us.

I did not want to give her the satisfaction of agreeing, but silently, I did. Going by appearances alone, the Mountari did look savage.

They were the only Outlier tribe that did not mark their faces, and the women we passed bore no passage markings at all. In the Mountari village, a boy did not become a man until he had killed his first lygan, and it was their custom to pierce the two sharpest fangs of each kill through the man's skin. Every lygan that met its end at the hands of a Mountari man elevated his position in the village, and the arms and chest of the greatest hunters were usually covered in piercings.

Despite the cold day, many of the men in front of us wore no shirts, openly displaying their fang-pierced skin for all to see. The man closest to me had a line of them on each arm, going from his wrist to his shoulders and across his chest. There the two lines met just below his collarbones before moving down to his belly button. He had even more teeth on his chest, in swooping lines that mirrored one another, and the sheer number of them was difficult to comprehend. I had only seen a handful of lygan in my life, and the idea that this man had killed so many made me wonder if he was the greatest hunter in the village. I could not imagine anyone having killed more than this.

My attention was dragged away from the display of fangs when Zuri reappeared, followed by a man who was quite a bit younger. His face was unlined, and the dark hair under his headdress did not have even a streak of gray in it, and the broad muscles of his shoulders reminded me of the Fortis men I had gotten so used to seeing in Sovereign City.

Together they climbed down, first Zuri and then the man. He did not smile, but there was nothing about him that said we were unwelcome, and at his side, Zuri stood wearing the same friendly expression as before.

"I am Roan," the man said when he had stopped in front of us, "Head of the Mountari."

A lygan skull that had been fashioned into a headdress sat upon his head, and just like the other men in the village, Roan wore no shirt despite the cold day. The sheer number of fangs piercing his flesh was staggering, at least twice as many as the man I had just been studying. The teeth were stark white against Roan's dark skin, and two rows moved up each of his arms while so many decorated his chest that he almost looked like he wore a shirt made of fangs. Every time he moved, the skin pulled tight, making it seem as if the teeth were shifting positions, and I found myself wondering how he ever got comfortable. It seemed like every move would hurt.

I had to work hard to meet his gaze and not stare at the fangs decorating his skin. "I am Indra, Head of the Windhi."

Roan's eyebrows lifted in surprise just as his wife's had. "You have formed a new tribe."

"We have," I said even though it was not a question. "A tribe of hunters, and we have come here today to ask you to join us in our fight."

"Your fight against who?" Roan asked, but the way his head tilted to the side told me he knew, or at least suspected, what I was about to say.

"The Fortis."

"We have heard whispers that Fortis hunters who come into the wilds often do not make it out alive," Roan said, and just like I had suspected, he seemed unsurprised by the declaration. "Is this your doing?"

"It is," I told him. "I have been hunting and killing the Fortis for over a year now. After they burned our tribe to the ground, I taught others to hunt as well. Together we have taken out hundreds. We wish to finish the job, to go into the Fortis village and wipe them out for good. We do not have the numbers to do it alone, but if we unify the tribes, we will. That is why we are here, to ask the Mountari to join us in taking out the Fortis."

"What you ask is a lot." Roan's mouth turned down in one corner. "If we fail, the Fortis will unleash vengeance on us. They will destroy us all."

Unlike the Huni, Roan did not tell me that his people were no match for the Fortis, and it made me like him. It also made me wonder if these people might be even greater allies than the Huni.

"There is a lot to risk," I acknowledged, "but there is also a lot to gain. We would be free, and it would leave the Sovereign vulnerable. Without the Fortis, they can do nothing."

I scanned the people standing around, trying to gauge their reactions. They did not seem opposed to the idea, and a few even wore an excited gleam in their eyes, as if the idea of fighting the Fortis was no more risky than hunting a lygan. Roan was one of those men, which was no surprise. The number of fangs pierced through his skin illustrated how much he enjoyed the hunt. Still, though, he said nothing, but instead seemed to be thinking it through.

"The Huni have already agreed to join us," Xandra said when the silence had stretched out too long.

For the first time, Roan's eyes widened in surprise. "The Huni are not known for being welcoming."

"They were hesitant at first," I told him, "but their Head is a reasonable woman, and like us they are tired of being slaves to the Sovereign. Their numbers will give us a great advantage, but if we can get you to join our fight, your men and women both, we will have no problem destroying the Fortis. They are strong and they are warriors, but we outnumber them."

Roan looked toward Zuri. "Will your women fight?"

I had been wondering the same thing. I was under no illusion that the Trelite would allow their women to join us in the fight, but the Mountari were different. At least I hoped so.

Zuri smiled, an expression she seemed used to and one I had not expected to find so readily on the faces of the

Mountari. "We spend our lives fighting. How many times have I fought for the right to remain in your bed?"

Roan was the one who smiled now. "Many times, my wife."

The Mountari were more committed than the Huni—although their relationships could sometimes be short lived—but unlike the Winta, they did not choose a mate for life. Here, the greatest hunters were the most sought after mates, and the women of the Mountari tribe fought one another for the privilege of being a man's wife, even leaving their current mate because he had fewer kills. No weapons were involved in the battles, just shear force of will, and the last woman standing won her mate. Mountari women were tough, and I had no doubt that having them in the fight would be a huge advantage.

"I have not given up fighting yet, and I do not intend to. This includes the Fortis." When Zuri looked toward me, there was determination in her eyes, but something else as well. Pain. Anger. "I have a daughter in the city, held prisoner by the Sovereign."

"I am sorry," I said. "We have people there as well. How many, we do not know. There are so few of us left because of the Fortis, and I refuse to stand by and do nothing while our people suffer. Not anymore."

Roan nodded, as did Zuri, and then the Head said, "I must speak to the elders of the tribe before I make a decision, but I would like to join your fight, Indra of the Windhi. We have been told we are weaker than the Fortis because they train as warriors, but I am not weak." He waved to the fangs decorating his chest. "I proved that at the age of twelve when

I killed my first lygan, and then at twenty when I took my place as Head. For twelve years, I have maintained my position as the greatest hunter in our village, and killing the beasts is no longer a challenge for me. The Fortis will be no different."

At his side, Zuri stood tall, her back as straight as a spear. She wore her pride at being the wife of the greatest warrior the same way Roan wore the fangs of the lygan he had killed. The age difference between them had to be at least two decades, something I could not comprehend, but the way they consulted one another as they spoke told me they were well suited. Even if he had not had a say in their relationship.

Roan left to gather the elders while Zuri led us across the village toward the fire where a pot sat poised above the flames, steam rising from it. Using a bowl, the Head's wife scooped up some of the stew before passing it to me, repeating the process until each of us had been served, and then we lifted the bowls to our lips at the same time.

The stew was earthy, but good, and I had no doubt that the chunks of meat floating in the broth were lygan. I had never tasted the creatures before—the couple times Mira and I had killed one on the way back from Sovereign City, I had turned the carcass over to the village—but I was not one to turn my nose up at food, and I had no interest in insulting the woman in front of me.

"I am sorry to hear about your daughter," Xandra said after she had lowered her bowl. "How old is she?"

Zuri's mouth turned down for the first time since we met her, her own steaming bowl suddenly forgotten. "She is seventeen. Her position in Sovereign City came from her father's family, passed down from her grandmother. Her father was a great hunter before he was killed by a lygan. Roan had only been Head for three years when my husband died, and his wife was young. Too young to be married to the Head. I challenged her. I was not the first, not even that day, but I was the strongest." She smiled like she found the memory of the fight amusing. "There were five of us, and I was the oldest. I do not think anyone believed I could win, but I did. I took the Head's wife out first, and then the other three one by one until I was the last woman standing." Zuri lifted her chin. "Roan and I have been together for nine years now, and no woman has been able to defeat me."

"Will the men in your village agree to let you fight with us?" I asked.

"They will have to." Zuri lifted her chin. "I have no desire to stay behind, and I know I am not alone in that. The women in our village may not hunt lygan, but we are strong."

"Yes," I said. "I can see that."

It did not take long for Roan to return, followed by four other men. All I needed was one look at their expressions to know they had decided to join us, and the knowledge that we would soon be waging war on the Fortis had my heart pounding like the beat of a drum.

"We will join the Huni and Windhi people in taking out the Fortis," Roan said when he had stopped in front of us.

"Thank you." I bowed my head slightly, first at him, and then toward the elders who stood at his back. "We have one more stop, the Trelite, but we wish to have the Heads of all the tribes meet tomorrow at sunset, in the clearing by the pond. It is a neutral area, and it will help our good relations if we meet on common ground."

"You are wise, Indra of the Windhi, but do you think the Trelite will agree to such an arrangement? We have never had a woman Head, but that does not mean I do not value them." Appreciation shone in his eyes when Roan looked toward Zuri. "I know firsthand how much a good woman is worth. But the Trelite do not see it that way."

"We know it will be difficult to get them to agree, but we must try. They are as much a part of this as the rest of us."

Roan's head bobbed as he pressed his lips together. "I do not wish to overstep, but if you think it will help, I would be willing to offer my assistance. I could go with you to speak to the Trelite."

I glanced toward Xandra as I had a habit of doing, and found her already looking my way. "What do you think?"

"It might be useful," she said. "The last time we were there he only offered to help so we did not die. He may see our return as a sign that you are ready to accept his marriage proposal."

Roan chuckled, and when I tore my gaze from Xandra, the Head held his hands up. "I am sorry."

Zuri's smile disappeared as she looked from her husband to me. "What is so funny?"

"The thought that the Trelite Head believes he is what this woman needs." Roan gave me an appraising look. "You seem very capable to me, Indra."

"Yes, but you are not Trelite," I told him. "I could fight the Head to the ground and hold a knife to his throat and he would still think I am weak."

"That is very true," Roan conceded.

"Which is why I will accept your offer. It may help pave the way with the Trelite more than anything I could ever do. We plan to head out at first light. Will you meet us by the pond?"

"I will," Roan said. "I will come alone so they do not feel threatened."

"Then we will see you tomorrow."

Twenty

True to his word, Roan was waiting for us when we arrived in the clearing the next morning. Since the presence of women was already going to be a stressful point for the Trelite, Xandra and I had elected to go to the village alone this time, and it was a relief not to have Emori with us when we headed out.

"You will not think I am disparaging you if I take over the negotiations when we arrive?" Roan asked as we wound our way through the forest, the snow crunching beneath our feet with every step.

Although we had established a decent rapport with the tribe, I was not a fool. Even if they had learned to tolerate us, they would respond much better to a man. Even a Mountari man.

"I will not." After our meeting the previous night, I had spent hours in the forest searching the wilds for a Fortis hunting party, and I motioned to the bag I carried. "Even with you taking over things, I know it will be difficult for the Trelite to believe we are capable. That is why I have brought the head of a Fortis hunter. So they can see with their own eyes."

"It is a good idea." Roan looked me over, admiration shining in his eyes, and I suddenly found myself wishing we had not agreed to let him come with us. "I very much admire the things you have done for your people, Indra. If you were Mountari, I would ask you to challenge Zuri."

On the other side of Roan, Xandra's eyebrows jumped up in surprise. "That is something your people do?"

Roan glanced her way for only a beat before turning his gaze back on me. "It does not happen often, but if a hunter finds another woman more desirable than his current mate, he can ask her to fight for him."

The Head's gaze was still on me when Xandra asked, "Did you do that with Zuri?"

"I did not." Roan looked away, focusing on the wintry forest in front of us. "I value Zuri very much, but she is a great deal older than me, and I was satisfied with my previous mate. She was not as sharp as Zuri, but she was pleasant company and a good fighter. I do not think anyone else would have been able to defeat her, just as no one else has been able to defeat Zuri."

Xandra and I exchanged a look, but we chose not to respond. Like me, she probably had no idea what to say. Roan did not seem angry that Zuri had overthrown his mate, and he seemed to care for her, but he admitted he had not wanted it to happen. Even that he would have been open to someone overthrowing his current wife. It was a sad state, having someone you were comfortable with replaced just because they were not as strong.

We walked the rest of the way in silence, but the forest around us was not quiet. Branches concealed by the snow snapped under our feet, and the trees above us were alive with the call of rawlins. Here and there I spotted a forest rodent scurry from sight, and even though I longed to notch an arrow, I did not. Having my weapon ready when we were so close to the Trelite village was not a good idea.

Just like on our last visit, our presence was announced by a horn before the Trelite huts had come into view. Xandra and I fell back, allowing Roan to take the lead, and only a few beats passed before the same men who had greeted us before appeared, Zaire leading the pack.

"Indra of the Winta," he called out even as his gaze focused on Roan. "We did not expect you back so soon."

Before I had a chance to respond, Roan took a step forward. "I am Roan, Head of the Mountari, and I have come to speak to your Head."

Zaire looked from the other man to me. "Have you decided to join the Mountari tribe?"

"We have not." While I wanted to keep my explanation brief, I was compelled to let Zaire—as well as the rest of the Trelite—know we would not be joining his or any other tribe. "We have formed a new tribe. The Windhi."

"A tribe of women." Zaire gave a slight shake of his head. "It is unthinkable."

Roan stepped forward, putting himself between me and the Trelite man. "It is true, and the Windhi have created a treaty as well, with both the Mountari and the Huni. We have come to ask the Trelite to join us."

Zaire's eyebrows jumped up, causing the passage markings as well as the deep lines on his face to shift. "A treaty? It has been many decades since a new treaty was needed. How did this one come about? Has there been an altercation we are not aware of?"

"There has not," Roan said. "We have joined together with the plan to take the Fortis out."

The men from the Trelite tribe said nothing, not even Zaire, but their shock and doubt rang through the air so loudly that it seemed like they were screaming.

Roan paused, waiting for the men in front of him to react, when they did not he said, "Can I discuss our plan with your Head?"

Zaire nodded once before shaking his head, almost like he did not know what to think or how to respond. "This is most surprising."

He turned and headed back toward the village without asking us to follow, but Roan was not a timid man, and he went after Zaire anyway. Xandra and I did as well, but the second Roan had made it through the crowd of Trelite men, they blocked our way, leaving us to walk behind them.

"They will not join us," Xandra whispered as we followed the men into the village.

"Perhaps not," I replied, "but I think bringing Roan was the right choice."

"I agree." She arched her eyebrows at me, and the corner of her mouth twitched like she was holding in a smile. "Even if he tried to proposition you."

I rolled my eyes but made no reply. There was nothing to say, not when she had witnessed it firsthand.

Xandra gave me an appraising look as her mouth stretched into a real grin. "Both the Trelite and Mountari Heads have shown interest in you. Perhaps Ontari will be the next to try and win your hand? Or maybe I will try my luck?"

"I would not dare take you away from Gaia." This time when I rolled my eyes, I also found myself smiling.

Xandra let out a small laugh that was coated in pain. "It will be a relief when she is with me again."

"For all of us," I said, putting a hand on my friend's arm. "Because it will mean our people are free."

Just like the last time we were here, the group in front of us stopped when we had reached the center of the village. Once again all the men had gathered with spears, and the ladders that led into the trees had been pulled up. The Trelite men were no less hostile than they had been before, only this time their angry gazes were focused on Roan instead of Xandra and me.

Even when Zaire went off to find Cruz, Xandra and I stayed behind the Mountari Head. He did not look back or acknowledge us in any way, and had I not met Roan in his own tribe, I would have assumed by his cool exterior that he found us as beneath him as the Trelite did. Since I knew better, I did my best not to take offense at his attitude. It was not an easy task, not after all these months of proving my strength.

By the time Cruz appeared, it felt as if the hostility would set the whole forest aflame. He looked past Roan to where Xandra and I stood before focusing his gaze on the Mountari Head. Even though the Trelite were not hunters, the look Cruz gave the other man told me he was considering his odds. They were not good, at least in my opinion.

"I am Cruz, Head of the Trelite," he said when he had stopped in front of Roan.

"Thank you for seeing me. I am Roan, Head of the Mountari, and I have come with Indra, Head of the Windhi, to ask you to join our cause."

Cruz nodded my way. He barely focused his eyes on me when he did it, but I took it as a sign to step forward anyway. Knowing who I was dealing with, though, I chose to stay a step behind Roan.

"Zaire tells me you have formed a new tribe and you plan to fight the Fortis?" Cruz frowned, pulling the many markings and scars on his face down. "Was this your idea, Indra of the Windhi?"

"It was," I said.

Last time we were here, the Trelite had made a point of telling us that women should only speak when spoken to, and even though Cruz had addressed me directly, I chose to keep my answer short. There was no point in pushing my luck.

"What arrogance and foolishness your husband instilled in you before he died." Cruz's eyes were filled with disgust when he shook his head. "He would have done well to teach you your place."

"Her place is beneath the Fortis and the Sovereign," Roan said, his voice only slightly louder than necessary. "Just as mine is. Just as yours is. It is something we want to change, and it is what we have come here to discuss."

Cruz narrowed his gaze on the other man. "You have encouraged this? Do you want the blood of these women on your hands?"

"It is not my hands that will be stained if they die." Roan waved behind him, toward Xandra and me. "It is the hands of the Sovereign and the Fortis. *They* have done this. *They* have killed all the men of Indra's tribe and forced her to take the position she now finds herself in."

Cruz's frown did not ease, but his mouth did tighten like he was considering Roan's words. "You speak the truth, but you cannot possibly think we are any match for the Fortis. We are not warriors."

"You are not." Roan paused so he could pull his shirt over his head, revealing the dozens of lygan teeth pierced through his skin. "But we are."

High above our heads, the Trelite women and children peeked through windows and doors, fighting for a chance to get a glimpse of the Mountari Head. He was a sight to look at, especially for the Trelite who lived so far into the wilds and had so few people working in Sovereign City. They were secluded out here, many of them having never ventured even as far as the pond—the women, especially—and the teeth piercing Roan's skin was something very few of them had ever seen.

"The Huni, who have also agreed to join the fight, are hunters as well." Roan tipped his head toward Xandra and me. "And the Windhi have spent their days in the wilds killing every Fortis hunter they come across."

Cruz focused his disgusted gaze on me for the first time since we had arrived. "I do not believe it. A group of women cannot take Fortis hunters down."

"You are secluded out here." Roan kept his eyes on Cruz as he held his hand out to me. "You have not heard the rumors, but in the Mountari village, we have heard about the many Fortis men and women who have come into the wilds only to meet their ends."

My gaze was focused on Cruz when I pulled the head from the bag and passed it to Roan. He grasped it by the hair, lifting it high into the air so everyone could see. The men in front of us murmured to one another as their expressions changed from hostile to shocked, while in the trees the women and children ducked away from the sight.

"This is what the Windhi have done," Roan called, his voice ringing through the village. "All three of our tribes have experience as hunters, and we can teach your people as well. Once we have joined together, we can take the Fortis down." He tossed the head on the ground, and it rolled a few times before landing face up, the lifeless eyes seemingly focused on Cruz. "When they are gone, we will be free to live the rest of our lives as we choose."

Silence followed the speech. Birds squawked as somewhere nearby one took off, and the beat of its wings seemed deafening amidst the sudden quiet. Cruz stared down at the head on the ground before looking up to study me, and the hair on my scalp prickled under his intense gaze. It was like he was looking me over for flaws. Like he was desperate to find them. Either he did not believe I had done the things Roan claimed, or he did not want to believe them.

Cruz said nothing to me before turning his gaze to Roan, studying both the other Head and the teeth that pierced his chest.

Finally, the Trelite Head spoke. "I do not know if we can join in this fight."

He looked toward Zaire, who was standing at his side just as he had last time we were here, and the older man frowned. All around the village the other men seemed as uncertain as the two in front of us did, and I felt their numbers slipping through my fingers the way water did when I tried to scoop a handful from the pond. We could do it without them, and they were the least experienced of all the tribes, but having the Trelite on our side would give us twice as many warriors as the Fortis. It would give us a much greater advantage.

Almost as if Roan could also feel their numbers slipping away, he said, "You will not have to deal with any of the women. My men will teach you the moves you need to fight the Fortis."

Cruz's head bobbed as he considered this, and at his side, Zaire leaned closer to him.

"We have people in the city," he said in a low voice. "They are prisoners."

Cruz turned to face the older man. "I am well aware of the people we have lost. But do we risk everyone else to get them back? Are the lives of the many worth the freedom of the few?"

"Doing this will give freedom to the many," I said, suddenly finding it impossible to stay quiet. "You will be setting your children and your children's children free."

Cruz spun back to face me, his hand lashing out and catching me completely off guard. The crack of his palm against my left cheek echoed through the forest, and I stumbled back.

"You do not address me unless spoken to." The words pushed their way through Cruz's teeth.

I cupped my cheek as I stared at the man in front of me, all the while the weight of the knife on my hip seemed to grow. The urge to pull it out made my fingers tingle, but I fought against it. We were outnumbered. We needed these men to join us. We should work together to fight the Fortis.

The urge did not lessen.

Roan stepped between Cruz and me. "That will be the last time you raise a hand to another Outlier. Our fight is with the Fortis and Sovereign, not with each other. We wish for you to join us, but if you do, you will be agreeing to a treaty. That treaty does not force you to associate with any of the women, but it does mean that you will agree to exist in peace with them."

"Peace?" Cruz spit out the word like Roan had asked him to do the most detestable thing he had ever heard of. "You mean pretending she is as good as a man? As good as *me*?"

Roan's back straightened even more, a feat I had not thought possible considering he already seemed to be standing so tall. "I mean you will not strike or lash out at any member of another tribe. Man or woman."

"These are not unfair terms," Zaire said, still speaking low as if he thought it would be able to keep us from hearing him. "And the Mountari Head is right. We outnumber the Fortis. We can win."

Cruz turned to face him completely, signaling that the discussion was private. "Do you really believe that?"

"I do," Zaire replied.

The Trelite Head exhaled and turned his eyes to the ground. A moment of silence passed while I held my breath.

Then he lifted his gaze and focused on Roan. "We will join your treaty, but we will not associate with the women of the other tribes, the Huni Head included."

My face stung where Cruz had struck me, but we still needed him, as much as it pained me to admit it, and speaking out of turn would only make things worse, so I touched Roan's arm. When he looked back at me, fury simmered in his eyes.

I gave my head a slight shake, letting him know I was okay, and then whispered, "The meeting at the pond."

Roan's head barely bobbed before he turned back to Cruz. "We will have to meet on occasion, the Heads of all four tribes. Will you join us for the meeting? It will be tonight in the clearing by the pond."

Cruz's upper lip curled even as he said, "I will join you."

"Then we will take our leave," Roan said.

He stepped back, urging Xandra and me to do the same. No one stopped us as we turned, not that I had expected them to, and silence followed us as we left the village behind and headed into the forest.

Roan pulled his shirt back on as we walked. "He is lucky he was not in my village when he struck you. I would have cut his throat."

"It is okay." I was still carrying the empty bag, and I tightened my grip on it. "I knew before going in that I should keep quiet."

"There is no reason to keep quiet when you are right, Indra. Remember that."

Roan's gaze held mine as we walked, his eyes swimming with appreciation for me. It was different than when Asa looked at me, though. This was something else. A man who is used to having the best and strongest women fight over him. I had a hard time imagining I fit that description, even after all this time, but it seemed as if Roan saw me that way.

THAT NIGHT, WE MET BY THE POND AS PLANNED. Xandra and Mira accompanied me, and we stepped into the clearing to find Ontari already waiting for us, with Arkin at her side. Thankfully, their greeting was much more cordial than it had been the first time we met.

"Indra," Ontari said, and the nod she gave me was solid and welcoming. "Were you able to get the other tribes to agree to your proposition?"

"I was. Or at least I was able to get the Mountari to agree. Roan, Head of the Mountari, spoke with the Trelite Head for me. He has agreed to join us under the terms that his men will not have to train with any women."

Ontari's mouth turned down. "And you have agreed to these terms?"

"I have no desire to change their way of life, even if I think they are fools."

Her frown gave way to a smile, the second one since we met. Once again, I was struck by how much it softened her looks, something I had not thought possible considering how fierce her shaved head and pierced face made her seem.

"I would think," she said, "that simply meeting you would change their opinions."

"I am not sure anything could change the way they view women," I replied while at my side, Xandra smirked. Which I chose to ignore.

The crunch of footsteps put our conversation to an end, and I tensed as I waited for whoever was approaching to reveal themselves. If it was Roan, there would be no problem, but if Cruz arrived before the other man, we might have an issue continuing with the treaty. The sting of his hand against my cheek had not faded completely. When this was all over, the Trelite Head had better pray we did not meet in the forest, because I would have no problem teaching him a lesson in just how strong a woman could be.

To my relief, Roan broke through the trees only a second later. He nodded to me, as well as to Xandra and Mira, and then I made the proper introductions. Just like when we had first arrived in her village, Ontari was cold toward the other Head when we began discussing strategy, but Roan treated the rest of us like equals, and in no time she began to thaw.

When Cruz finally arrived, Zaire was with him. I had expected as much, just as I had expected him to address only Roan and barely even glance at Ontari. With Arkin at her side, she was invisible to the Trelite Head, a situation I could tell made the slender man uncomfortable.

Nothing could be done about it, though. This was the way of the Trelite people, and I had spoken honestly when I told Ontari that I had no desire to change the Trelite's views on women, just as I had no wish to make the Huni see sex in a different light. We were all different, but the same in that our customs were sacred to us, and that was something I would not interfere with. Even if Cruz disgusted me.

The other women and I stood back, allowing Roan to speak for us. The Huni Head was more frustrated by the situation than I was. The planning took very little time and did not involve us anyway since Cruz would only accept the help of Roan's men, and it was not long before the Trelite men took their leave.

After they disappeared into the forest, Roan turned to Ontari. "I am sorry. This was the agreement we made with the Trelite, but know I do not share their opinion. The Mountari have no issue with a female Head and welcome your expertise. We know you are great hunters."

"As are you." Ontari nodded to the fangs peeking out from beneath Roan's shirt.

"It is a wonder we have not met before," Roan said.

"Perhaps this will be the beginning of a new era for the Outliers," I said. "We have been separate so long, but who is to say we cannot work together?"

"I agree," Ontari replied. "Although I do not see the Trelite changing their ways."

"No. Their treaty with us will end as soon as we have defeated the Fortis and the Sovereign," Roan agreed.

"When will that happen?" Ontari's gaze moved to me.

"We must wait for warmer weather." I lifted my face to the sky like it might tell when spring would arrive. "We do not want to wait too long, though. If we can hit the Fortis before summer, it will make the Sovereign even more vulnerable going into the warm months. They rely on their guards during grizzard attacks, which are more frequent during summer."

"Your knowledge of the city will be helpful," Roan said thoughtfully. "What else can you tell us about Sovereign City and the people who live there?"

"The Sovereign's numbers are small. Perhaps only a couple hundred."

"Why do the Fortis not rebel?" Ontari asked. "It is something I have always wondered. To me it seems like they would want to free themselves from the thumb they live under as much as we do."

"The Fortis have no experience with technology, meaning they would have no idea how to use the very items inside the city that make their lives so easy. Plus, there are maybe twice as many Fortis as Sovereign. The city is much too small for them. Even worse, if they were to lose the war, they would be cast out. The only place for them to go then would be the wilds, and they have no knowledge of how to survive on their own because they have never had to do it before."

"They have been made dependent," Ontari ran her hand over her smooth scalp, "and now they are useless except for their brawn."

"Centuries of conditioning," Mira said. "Like us. We have been told we were nothing for so long that it never occurred to us to try."

"Until Indra," Xandra said.

My friend's eyes were on me, as were the gazes of everyone else in the clearing. Their admiration made me shift. Not just because Roan was once again looking at me with obvious appreciation, but because everyone else was as well. Yes, I had been the one to start this war, but I had not done it alone. Mira had suggested uniting the tribes, and Xandra had been at my side, leading with me for months. This was not just my doing. We had done this together.

"We are not nothing," I said, hoping to break the silence. "Together we are an army."

"Yes," Roan said, finally pulling his gaze from me. "What about the Fortis and Sovereign? Combined, how big can we expect their army to be? Four hundred?"

"Around that." I looked back at Xandra, and she nodded in agreement. "Because of us, the Fortis numbers have gone down greatly over the last year."

"That is good," Ontari said, and then asked, "What will our numbers be? Do you know?"

"Unfortunately, the Windhi will not be able to contribute much," I said sadly. "There are only seventeen of us capable of fighting."

"Seventeen women have brought down hundreds of Fortis?" Roan looked my way, but I avoided his gaze so I did not have to acknowledge the appreciation in his eyes. "That is impressive."

"It was survival," I clarified. "Nothing else."

"You have brought us together. That is a contribution," Roan assured me. "With all able-bodied men and women fighting, there should be around four hundred Mountari."

"We have nearly six hundred," Ontari said.

"The Trelite will only have men," I said, "so I would put their numbers closer to two hundred."

"Even without their women," Roan said, shaking his head like he could not believe what he was about to say, "we will have three times as many fighters as the Fortis do."

We fell silent. It was unbelievable. I had always known we outnumbered the Sovereign and Fortis combined, but faced with the numbers, I felt like a fool for not listening to Mira months ago when she first brought up the idea of uniting the Outlier tribes. It was wasted time, another wasted opportunity.

Ontari was the one to finally break the silence. "I still cannot believe no one ever considered this before."

"We did not work together," I pointed out even though I agreed with her. "We have always been too focused on surviving to think about knocking the Sovereign off their throne."

Even to my own ears, the excuses sounded trivial.

Twenty-One

WITH THE WORRY OF UNIFYING THE TRIBES NOW behind us, we switched our focus to training. Roan sent men to the Trelite tribe so they could learn to shoot a bow and wield a sword, while the rest of us met in the clearing to train. My own tribe was small, meaning all the Windhi warriors were able to attend, but with hundreds of Huni and Mountari fighters, it was impossible for them all to come at once. I knew, however, that they were busy training in their own villages. Each time I met with the other Heads, I respected them more, and they would no doubt put everything they had into preparing their people for battle.

The first time we met in the clearing, we started by demonstrating our skills. My tribe was practiced with the bow, and while the other tribes also used bows, I soon learned it was not often their weapons of choice.

The clearing was crowded with warriors as Ontari approached the front of the group, a spear in her hand. She lifted her weapon, but paused before throwing it so she could look back over her shoulder, her eyes focused on me.

When she smiled, her teeth were starkly white against her dark skin. "This is how I take out any marsoapians that wander into our village."

She turned back, pausing just long enough to aim before hurling the spear and sending it sailing through the air. The point stuck in a nearby tree with a thud that echoed through the forest, which was quickly followed by the squawk of a rawlin.

The bird burst from the tree the spear had just hit, and I pulled an arrow from my sheath as it flew in circles above us, screeching. I took aim, focusing on the red bird, and released my arrow only a moment later. It hit the mark, sinking into the bird's body and sending a burst of red feathers through the air.

When the animal had dropped to the ground, Ontari turned to face me, eyebrows raised. "I see why so few Fortis hunters make it out of the wilds alive."

"They are even easier to kill than the bird." I waved my bow toward the carcass. "Not only are the Fortis bigger targets, but they are also fools who think they are invincible."

"They will not think that for long," she said, smiling.

Like Ontari, all the members of the Huni tribe proved to be efficient hunters. Spears were typically their weapons of choice since they often went up against the large creatures inhabiting the wastelands, but they were also experienced with bows and knives. But while the Huni were undeniably tough, they had never had to fight another person. Which was what made the Mountari shine.

Lygan were wily creatures and more difficult to kill than the animals in the wastelands, and most of the Mountari men preferred knives—enjoying the closeness that came with the kill—meaning they were much better at dodging an attacker than the Huni were. Still, it was the Mountari women who really stood out. Since they regularly fought one another to claim a mate, their skills in hand-to-hand combat were impressive, something Zuri demonstrated on our first day of training. She may have been twice my age, but watching her go head to head with another Mountari woman made me understand how she had won the right to become Roan's mate, and why no one had been able to defeat her since then.

For our part, the Windhi were useful in giving the other tribes insight into what to expect from the Fortis. We had gone up against them more times than I could count, and were by now used to fighting. It seemed that the members could not get enough of the stories I told about my exploits in the forest. Roan especially never tired of asking me questions about the Fortis men and women I had killed. His wife, to her credit, watched all of this with an amused smile on her face.

Training continued as the snow began to melt and winter faded. Soon the wilds grew warmer, and with each passing day and each practice session we held in the clearing, I became more confident in our ability to win. With the four tribes now united, we outnumbered the Fortis by the hundreds, but we also had the advantage of surprise. They had no idea the tribes had joined forces or that we knew how to fight, and if we snuck into the village at night while they slept, we would be able to take them completely by surprise.

My only real worry was for Asa. He did not deserve the wrath we were about to bring down on his people, but he would be in the line of fire just like all the other men and women in the Fortis village. It seemed wrong. More than wrong. He saved me when he discovered me in the forest, surrounded by the bodies of his men, and he had come into the woods, risking his own life, to warn me about Lysander. I could not turn my back on Asa now.

My worry multiplied as the day of the battle grew closer until I found it impossible to ignore, and only three days before we were set to attack, I could wait no longer. I needed to warn Asa.

Telling no one of my plans, I left the caves just as the sun was setting and traveled by way of the river so I did not need to worry about carrying a torch. The moon was high by the time I reached the outskirts of the village, but the night was not quiet. The Fortis were loud and rowdy despite the late hour, and it would be a while still before they turned in for the night, but waiting was not an option.

Their voices echoed off the houses and kept me on edge as I moved through the darkness. I was small, and I worried that if I were spotted it would be immediately evident that I did not belong in the village.

The fear did not stop me, but it did keep me on alert. I stuck to the shadows as much as possible, doing my best to avoid large groups of Fortis men and women who were busy drinking. I had seen Asa come out of his house only one time, but I was confident I remembered which one it was. It was impossible to forget that day, or the cold way he had looked at me.

When I reached the building, I paused before circling around to the front, taking a deep breath as I concentrated on the voices echoing through the dark night. Asa's house was right on the main road, so close to the open square in the middle of the village that I was certain when I turned the corner there would be a large group standing right in front of me. Only it sounded as if the laughter was coming from further away. Closer to the wall.

I slinked to the corner and poked my head around, my hand on my knife. If I were caught, I would not stand a chance against an entire village of Fortis men and women, but I needed to be ready just in case. After everything I had been through, I refused to allow them to take me down without a fight. Even if I died trying.

Light flickered through the village from the fire burning in the square, distorting the shadows and making it difficult to see at first. After a moment, the picture came into focus and I let out a deep breath. There were men and women on the main street, but further down, on the other side of the square, past the fire. They were talking, laughing, and drinking, and they were so far away that I was confident I would not be spotted.

I turned the corner, stepping out into the open, and gave the house a quick glance. There was no doubt in my mind that this was the building I had seen Asa come out of all those months ago, and so I only hesitated for a beat before opening the door and slipping inside.

He was awake, sitting with his back to me and his shirt off. Light from the lantern flickered across his muscles and the passage markings decorating his dark skin, and memories from our last time together flashed through my mind. This was not why I had come here, but I could not stop from thinking about letting Asa strip my clothes off and carry me to his bed. About being with him one more time before everything changed yet again.

I took a small step forward, and he jerked. In a blink, he was on his feet, spinning around. His dark eyes widened, but he did not move, almost as if he thought he was dreaming and any movement would make me disappear. When his gaze swept over me, the look was like a caress. Like his fingers were traveling over my bare skin.

"Indra, what are you doing here?" He looked past me to the door, before focusing on me again. "If they see you, they'll kill you."

"No one saw me," I whispered, suddenly finding it difficult to speak.

I swallowed, hoping my brain would focus, but it did not help. I had come here for a reason, one that had nothing to do with Asa and the feelings we had for one another, but suddenly that was all I could think about. My brain was all Asa. There was no city, no Sovereign, no Fortis or even Outliers. It was just the two of us.

He took a hesitant step forward, and something about it seemed to help me focus. I had come to warn him, to tell him to leave and hopefully save his life in the process.

"I came to warn you." I lifted my hand, urging him to keep his distance in hopes it would help me think. "You need to leave your village."

"Leave my village?" Asa shook his head and then moved forward despite my raised hand. "What do you mean? What are you saying, Indra?"

"I can tell you nothing else." Shame flared through me, and for the first time in a long while, I was met with guilt over what I intended to do. I had to look away from him when I said, "Do not ask me to say more, because I cannot. But I need you to listen, and I need you to do as I say." I lifted my gaze from the ground and found him watching me, his eyes still clouded with confusion. "You must leave here as soon as possible. Tomorrow. Pack your things and get out."

Understanding bloomed in his eyes, and this time he took a step away instead of moving closer to me. "What have you done, Indra? What are you planning?"

"I am planning to stand up for my people." All the atrocities I had witnessed came back, the abuse and death, and I pushed the guilt away. I straightened my shoulders, trying to make myself taller, and met his gaze head on. "I am setting my people free."

"No." He ran his hand over his head in frustration. "You're killing *my* people, Indra. Can't you see that? You've been hunting and killing my people for more than a year now."

"I am killing the people who have abused and oppressed us for centuries," I spit at him, suddenly angry. "I am trying to save my people, one dead Fortis at a time."

Asa blew out a long breath like he was trying to keep his temper in check, but it did not matter because I was already mad. My blood was already boiling. These were his people and he should stand up for them, but I was beyond the point where I could listen to excuses. I had seen too much, bore too many scars.

The thought of those scars made me drop my knife to the ground. It clanged against the floor and Asa's eyebrows pulled together, jumping up only a moment later when I undid the leather ties that helped secure my shirt.

"What are you doing?" He shuffled toward me, his hand out.

"I am showing you what your people have done."

I turned so my back was to him as the fur slipped from my body. It fell to the floor, and the cool air in the room sent a chill through me, but I did not move. I stayed where I was, my back to Asa so he could see the scars I wore. He had seen them before, had looked at them the last time we were together, but we had not talked about what they meant.

"Indra," he whispered, his voice pained. "Please."

"No." I looked over my shoulder and found his eyes focused on the floor. "Look at me, Asa."

He lifted his gaze and met mine.

"Look at my scars," I whispered.

He swallowed then focused on my back.

We had lain together in the caves, had spent time naked and in each other's arms, but we had not spoken about the scars. Not even after he had looked at them. He had run his fingers over them, a feather light touch that had sent shivers shooting through me, but he had said nothing about the scars or the day I received them.

"You were there," I said, still looking at him over my shoulder. "You saw what they did to me. What they took from me. The scars on my back are nothing compared to the ones I carry on my heart. The scars for my father, my mother, my husband. My whole tribe. How can you continue to question me when you *know* what I have endured? When you have witnessed it?"

Asa lifted his gaze to mine, but even the tears shimmering in his eyes were not enough to make me feel guilty. "We're not all bad. Aren't I proof of that? Haven't I helped you enough?"

I bent down and picked up my knife and the discarded shirt then turned to face him. "I have never seen another Fortis like you," I told him, holding the fur against my chest. "No one has. As far as I know, they do not exist."

"You're wrong, and if you do what I think you're going to do, innocent people will die. I've turned a blind eye to everything you've done so far, but Indra, I can't sit back and watch you do this."

"Are you telling me that you plan to turn me in? That you plan to bring the Sovereign down on me? To lead the charge into the forest and kill me?" I kept my voice level as I worked to secure the shirt around my body once again. Asa would not turn on me, but I was not ready to walk away yet. Not until he understood what I was doing. Not until I was sure he had heard me. "I will not let them take me back into that city. I will not let them kill me for show the way they did my husband."

Asa put his hands up and stepped back. "I could never turn you in, Indra. You have to know that."

His gaze swept over my face, and I saw the measure of his feelings for me swimming in his eyes. It caused a tickle in my stomach. Made me think about how he had held me after we were together, how warm his skin had been against mine.

I looked away before the memories distracted me again.

"You know what I have been through." I kept my gaze off his face, instead looking past him. "It is nothing compared to what my people have endured. Think of Ronan, a ten-year-old boy, getting his hand cut off for a piece of bread. His family was starving and his little sisters too sick to sleep most nights, so he tried to help them, and they took his hand for it. He is not alone. You know that. For centuries my people have gone into the city and served the Sovereign, have done everything they said because we had no choice. Do you know Lysander cornered me in that pantry the very first week I worked in the house?"

Asa winced. "Indra, don't."

"I must, because it is true. It is what happened, and it did not just happen to me. It happened to almost every girl in that house, and I was there. I stood on the other side of the door and listened to their cries for help, and I did nothing. But I will not do that anymore. I will not stand by and watch my people get wiped out and imprisoned."

"The Sovereign did that, Indra. Not the Fortis. We are as much at the mercy of Sovereign City as you are."

"Are you?" I forced my gaze to meet his, and my heart pounded harder. "I know you are a good and honorable man, Asa, and you may be telling the truth. There may be others like you. But do not turn a blind eye to what your people do. They take pleasure in it."

Asa looked down then, and even if he did not say the words, I could tell he knew I was right.

"I am sorry if you feel like you are caught between two worlds," I continued when he said nothing, "but the time has come for you to pick a side. My fight with the Fortis has just begun, and very soon I will take it to the Sovereign."

"You don't have the numbers to beat us, Indra."

"You would be surprised what I have."

Asa's head jerked up. "What are you saying?"

"I am telling you to get out of the village while you can. That is why I came here. You risked your life to come into the forest and find me, and I have not forgotten it." My gaze traveled to his lips, and I paused as thoughts about our night together came back. When I spoke again, my voice came out softer. "I do not want you to get hurt. If there are innocent people here, get them out. Run. Leave this village and the monsters who live in it and do not look back."

Asa's gaze moved to the floor like he was thinking it through, but only a beat passed before he was once again focused on me. "Where would you have me go?"

"If you are asking to come to the caves, I cannot allow it. You know my people would never accept it. That they would never trust you."

"I know." He turned his gaze back to the floor. "I understand."

"You will have to find your own way in the wilds. Your people have boasted of their strength for centuries. Now is the time to prove you are as strong as you say you are." I took a step back, and his head jerked up. "I need to go so I can make it home by morning."

He reached out. "Wait."

Even though I knew what would happen if I allowed him to catch me, I did not stop him from grabbing my hips and pulling me closer. Then his mouth covered mine. Unlike the other times, there was no hesitation in his kiss, and I threw myself into it as well, knowing I might not see him again after this. He might not run, he might be here when we attacked, and even if he did run, he very well could die in the wilds.

Our lips moved together hungrily while he held me in a crushing grip. I did not want this moment to end, did not want him to ever let me go, but we both knew it could not last.

When he broke it off, he did not release me, and he did not pull back before whispering, "I love you, Indra."

Before I could stop them, the words I had barely acknowledged to myself came tumbling out. "I love you, Asa."

I pulled out of his grasp and fled the hut, refusing to look back as I once again left him behind.

IT WAS EARLY MORNING, JUST BEFORE DAWN, WHEN I returned to the caves. I had expected everyone to be asleep, had expected to be able to slip back into my alcove unnoticed, but I found Emori waiting for me. She was by the fire, pacing, and she spun to face me when I stepped inside.

"What have you done, Indra?" Her dark eyes were wide and accusing as they raked over me.

"What I had to," I said as I stripped my weapons off.

Her eyes flashed like they were full of lightning. "He will warn his people. You must know this."

"I know nothing except that I cannot let innocent people die for the sins of others. That is what happened to Bodhi, and I will not sit by and let it happen again."

I tried to walk past her, exhausted and hoping to steal a couple hours of sleep before training, but Emori grabbed my arm, refusing to let me pass.

She pulled me close, her face inches from mine as she hissed, "You cannot think this is right. He is a Fortis, and he cannot be trusted."

"Enough." My voice boomed off the cave walls and I jerked my arm from her grasp, holding her gaze as I said, "I am Head of this tribe, and I will decide what is best for our people."

"What is best?" Emori's eyes flashed again, and this time I saw darkness in them that made the hair on the back of my neck stand up. "Your actions may have killed us all."

"I do not think so." I straightened my back. She was taller than I was, but I was stronger, and we both knew it. "But if it is so, I will carry it with me into the afterlife where it will pull me down to the deepest depths of the underworld. I know what is at stake here. I burned the bodies of our people, too. You were not alone in that, and I have not forgotten what that felt like. I never will. But I also know what it feels like to watch the man I love be punished for something someone else has done. I will not do that to Asa. He has gone out of his way to help me, to help Mira, and he deserves a chance to flee."

I turned my back on her but stopped when Emori called, "You are letting your feelings for him affect your judgment."

Her words froze me in place. I could not help it because she could have been right. There *was* a chance I had allowed my feelings to steer my decisions. But I did not think so. Asa was a good man, better than most, and being born Fortis did not change that.

"Perhaps I am," I said, not looking back at Emori. "Or maybe I am simply doing what is right."

"So you admit that you care for this man? This *Fortis*?"

The words I whispered to him before leaving his house haunted me in the face of Emori's accusations, but I refused to talk to her about it. She was too full of hate to understand what love was.

"I admit only that I cannot turn my back on him. He did not do that to me, and I will not do that to him. He is trustworthy, Emori."

"For the sake of what is left of our people, I hope you are right, Indra."

"So do I," I said before continuing to the tunnel.

Twenty-Two

THE NIGHT AIR COOLED MY SKIN DESPITE THE oppressive heat from the people at my back. I traveled at the front of the group with my two greatest allies, Roan and Ontari. Having them at my side made me more confident not only in how this battle would go, but also what the future held for us. The Outliers would not return to the old ways, not after this.

Cruz alone gave me pause. He marched at the back of the group with the warriors from the Trelite tribe because he still refused to cooperate with the women. Although we had not spoken since our last meeting in his village, I believed Roan was right. Our alliance with the Trelite would end as soon as we finished our battle with the Fortis and Sovereign. They would not work with women, and no matter how much our world was about to change, that was something that would remain.

But even with the tension brewing between the Trelite and the women in our war party, we were united as Outliers. Only a short time ago, the warriors from the four tribes had met at the fork in the river, gathered together for the first time. With the four tribes combined, we had twice as many people as the Fortis and Sovereign put together. Already I could imagine the life in front of us. The walls of the city torn down, the Sovereign pulled from their thrones and forced to grovel in front of us for once. Victory was within our reach, and I had no doubt it would be sweeter than anything I had ever tasted.

When the Fortis village came into view, it was silent and dark. We had waited until halfway through the night to attack, wanting to be sure all the Fortis were in their homes, and it had worked. Not a single person emerged from the houses as we crept through the village, and there were no sounds other than the howl of the wind as it swept across the wastelands and between the buildings.

Upon entering the village, the other Heads and I split up, each of us leading our group in a different direction. My tribe was small, so we headed for the living quarters on the far end of the village. Inside that building hundreds of Outliers were being held, locked away and possibly starving, and very likely being abused. After tonight, they would be free.

Xandra walked at my side as usual, with Anja and Mira behind her. Emori's anger toward me had only grown since our last confrontation, and since then I had worked hard to keep distance between us. I grew to distrust her more and more every day, and had even begun to watch my back as her hostility toward me intensified. It would not be long before she challenged me as Head, and when that happened, I knew what would need to be done. It was a reality I was not happy to be faced with, but for my people, I would do it.

The fighting started before my tribe had even reached the quarters. A cry echoed through the night, and when I glanced over my shoulder, the light from the moon was just bright enough to illuminate figures darting in and out of houses. Inside those buildings, people were losing their lives, and even though I had killed so many Fortis that I had long ago lost count, I could not help the pang in my stomach. What we were doing was not right, but we had reached a kill or be killed point. We had to make the first move. More than anything else, though, I could not help thinking about the things Asa had said to me. I could only hope he had heeded my warning and fled the city.

We reached the quarters to find the building unguarded, but it was no surprise. No one had ever challenged the Fortis before, and even with their hunters being killed, it would never have occurred to anyone to post guards outside the cells. No, neither the Fortis nor the Sovereign would have guessed the Outliers would join forces and rise up against them. It was unheard of.

But it was happening.

When I saw the conditions our people were being held in, I remembered what Asa had said about the building being *almost* done. It had walls and doors, but the windows were only bars, which did nothing to keep the weather out. There were at least ten people crowded into each room, and they were so cramped that even if they had not needed to sleep curled up together to keep warm, they would have been forced to due to lack of space.

A metal clank echoed through the air when the first lock was broken, and inside the cells, people began to stir. At first they were afraid, but their fear turned to hope when they realized we were Outliers. Lock after lock was broken, and door after door flung open. People rushed out, throwing questions at us that we did our best to answer in low voices in case anyone was around to hear us.

One of the first cells I came to held several Winta men, the first we had seen since our people were slaughtered. The sight of them filled me with both pain and relief, as well as another feeling. Dread.

A few rushed to the window, Atreyu and Linc among them. Both were about my age, and Atreyu had at one time been good friends with Bodhi. Seeing them alive was a relief, but the reprieve was short lived.

"You are alive!" Linc called out. "The Fortis said you were all dead."

I slammed the stone I had gripped in my hand against the lock before answering him, and it broke, clattering to the floor. Not only did I want to delay relaying news that would most certainly hurt Linc, but we also needed to hurry.

"They killed most of us." I yanked the door open and the men rushed out. "But not everyone. Twenty-three women and children are all that remains of what was the Winta people."

Linc's face fell when he looked behind me and saw the small group of women freeing the other slaves. "It is true, then?" he asked when his gaze was back on me. "Inara is dead?"

"It is," I said softly. He had been a prisoner for over a year now, and in that time had probably come to accept that he would never again see his wife, but finally having it confirmed no doubt stung. "I am sorry, Linc. But we are here to wipe out the Fortis, and when that is done, the Sovereign will be next."

"You are wiping out the Fortis?" Confusion momentarily overshadowed his despair. "Who is leading you?"

"It is a long story and one that will have to wait. For now, you must help us free the other Outliers."

I turned away from the men and moved to the next cell before Linc could say anything else. When I looked back, I found him and the other Winta men behind me.

Linc and Atreyu stayed at my side while I worked to liberate the prisoners, and before I had even reached the last cell, more than a dozen Winta had been freed. When I opened the final door, more Winta women rushed out, throwing out thanks and relieved exclamations as they passed me. I paid very little attention to who they were, but the last woman to step out gave me pause. It took a moment for me to put a name to the face, though. Gaia. She looked older than she had before, much more than ten years Xandra's senior, and she was thinner, too. Her face was gaunt, her hair wild and shining with gray in the light of the moon, but her eyes were wide when she looked around.

"Gaia," I said, pulling her gaze my way. "Xandra is here."

"She is here?" Gaia froze and blinked a couple times like she did not understand me. "Xandra is alive?"

"She is."

The other woman's expression crumpled and tears came to her eyes. She swayed, and even before it happened, I knew she was going to collapse. I reached out, grabbing her arm just before she fell.

"I have you," I whispered to the sobbing woman. "It will be okay now."

Gaia was frail, light, but still much too big for me to carry. Thankfully, Atreyu was at my side, and when he realized she lacked the energy to walk, he scooped her into his arms.

"Thank you," I said, smiling up at the man who had at one time been a boy I played with.

"Thank you, Indra." He pulled Gaia closer and looked past me into the cell she had just been liberated from. "We had almost given up hope of being saved."

"I am sorry it took so long."

Behind him stood the other members of the Winta tribe. Twenty in all, a handful of them men. I had never taken the time to consider what would happen to our newly formed tribe if some of our men had managed to survive. Now, though, it occurred to me that Emori might have someone to back her up if she did decide to challenge me, and the thought was not a welcome one. I had no desire to fight my own tribe. Especially not when we were in the middle of waging a war against the people who had oppressed us for centuries. I would do it if I had to, though. For my people, I would do anything, and after the last year, there was no way that the women of my tribe would go back to what they had once been. Weak and dependent on men.

Atreyu and the others followed me down the stairs where we found the Windhi women, as well as dozens of newly freed Outliers. The men and women who had been held prisoner stood out even in the darkness. Like Gaia, they looked thin and sickly, and shivering as a breeze swept in from the wastelands.

I spotted Xandra among the crowd, talking with Anja, and called out to her. My friend turned, and her eyes grew wide when she spotted Gaia.

She moved without speaking, rushing toward the woman in Atreyu's arms. "Gaia. Are you okay? Gaia, tell me you are okay."

"She is weak," Atreyu said, and the expression on his face said he did not know what to make of this exchange.

Gaia turned toward Xandra, reaching out with a shaky hand to wipe the tears from her face. "You came for me."

"I would not have left you for anything." Xandra reached for her, not even looking at Atreyu. "I will take her. Give her to me."

He handed the woman over without comment, and at his side, Linc watched it all take place with silent allegations burning in his eyes.

When he turned on me, the accusations in his gaze were no less violent. "What is happening here?"

With all the prisoners now free, I felt comfortable taking a moment to explain the situation, but only a moment. There was more to do, and these people needed to be led to safety.

"We have unified the Outlier tribes," I said, but looked not just at Linc, but at everyone gathered around, "and we have come to wipe out the Fortis."

The man in front of me lifted his eyebrows in confusion, pushing his passage markings up so they disappeared under the fringe of dark brown hair covering his forehead.

I turned my back to Linc before he could say anything. "Xandra will lead the prisoners back to the wilds. She will make sure you get out of here safely."

"I will." My friend's gaze was focused on the woman in her arms. "I will make sure nothing happens to them."

Xandra headed off with most of the other women from the Windhi tribe, leading the dozens of Outliers we had just freed toward the valley that led to the river. As my sister passed by me, she paused long enough to give my hand a squeeze before turning to help an older Huni woman.

I watched for only a second before focusing on the Fortis village. The war was in full swing, and through the darkness figures were visible, darting between houses and running from open doors. We had the advantage both in numbers and because the Fortis had been taken by surprise, and just as we had expected, there seemed to be very little resistance. It would not be long until it was over, or at least that was what I hoped. All I could do now was join the fight and pray I had not unified the tribes and brought them here only to be slaughtered.

The occasional strangled scream still echoed through the darkness as I ran. Here and there I spied a bulky figure that had to be a Fortis, but most of the people I came across were Outliers. Without my bow, I felt inadequate. Useless. Still, I knew bringing it would have been impractical. In the darkness of the village, not only would it be difficult to get a good shot off, but in the confusion it would also be too easy to mistake an ally for an enemy.

I was only one street away from the center of the village when a man dove from the shadows and slammed into me. I went down, letting out a yelp of pain, and he landed at my side. He lunged a second time, but I rolled away before he managed to get his hands on me. My own hand moved to my hip, and my knife was out before he was able to jump at me again. I slashed at him, and blood sprayed across his face when the blade made contact with his cheek. He let out a sound that could only have been described as a growl and dove for me again, but I was ready. When my knife sank into his chest, I let out a battle cry that echoed through my head and left a ringing behind in my ears.

The man collapsed half on top of me, and I had to shove his body off so I could get free. I rolled him over to retrieve my knife, still panting from the struggle, and in the light of the moon, his face came into view. It was Thorin. This was the man who had threatened me in the streets as I was trying to carry Ronan home, and the one who had beaten Asa until he was unconscious, making it impossible for him to be at his post. Because of this man, no one had been around to protect me inside Saffron's house, leaving me vulnerable. Giving Lysander a chance to attack me.

I pushed myself up off the ground and stood over Thorin's now lifeless body. The rage that radiated through me when I looked at him had not lessened with his death. It was like the sun had come out and was beating down on my head. If I could, I would bring him back to life so I could kill him again. Not just once, but again and again. I would watch him bleed and not care if it pulled me down to the underworld.

It was impossible, though, so I chose instead to spit on his corpse. The act did nothing to alleviate my rage.

"Indra." I turned as Mira jogged up. "It is over."

"And we have won?"

"We have won," she said.

The news did not bring me the relief I had expected, and I slid my knife back into its sheath, knowing what I had to do next. "I must check on something."

Mira followed as I headed across the village. She did not ask what I was doing, but she also did not look surprised when I stopped outside Asa's house. The door was open, which was to be expected. The Outliers would have searched every building in the village to be certain they had missed no one. I just hoped they had found this one empty.

The hinges squeaked when I pushed the door open the rest of the way. The room was dark, unlike the other night, but I did not need light to be able to tell that it had been cleared out well before we arrived in the village. The blanket was missing from the bed, and there was no lantern in sight. Asa had fled.

"He made it." The knots in my stomach loosened and unraveled. He had listened to me. He was safe.

"He will come find you," Mira said from behind me.

I turned to face my friend. "Should I want him to?"

"You love him, Indra." Mira said it with confidence even though I had never uttered the words to anyone but Asa.

"There is no shame in that. No matter what Emori wants you to think."

"I do not care what Emori thinks." I made no attempt to deny my feelings. "The problem is only that I do not know what I think. I know I am glad he is not dead, but he is still a Fortis, and I do not know if we can make our two worlds fit together."

"You are wrong, Indra." My friend put her hand on my arm. "He is not a Fortis. If he were, he would be here. And thanks to you, the Fortis are no more."

"Perhaps you are right." I looked past her, over the village that now brimmed with death. "For now, we must focus on the next move."

Mira and I found the other Heads gathered in the very square where we had been harassed so often over the years. The dusty earth beneath us was painted red, as were Ontari's face and arms. Roan, too, was splattered with the blood of his victims, and in the light of the moon it almost appeared as if his piercings were bleeding.

Cruz, alone, seemed unmarred by the battle. I had been on the other side of the village, so I was not sure what part he had played in the fight. Perhaps he had left the majority of the killing to his men. Or, perhaps, his tribe had not contributed as much as we had hoped.

"We have done it." Roan smiled when I stopped in front of him, and at his side, Zuri did as well. "Just as you predicted, we have taken out the Fortis."

"I knew the Outliers could do it." My gaze once again moved over the silent village. "We are much stronger than we have believed."

"That we are," Ontari said. "And after this, the Sovereign will be easy."

I had to agree. Without the Fortis to defend them, the Sovereign would be as helpless as children. Assuming we could get inside the city. That would be the difficult part.

Cruz, who stood a little separate from the group, said nothing, and even though the disgust when he looked at Ontari and me was obvious, I could not figure out what he was thinking. If he agreed, if he planned to help us when we fought the Sovereign, or if he was already considering breaking our treaty now that the prisoners had been freed.

We broke off into groups once again so we could raid the homes for anything that might be useful. There were enough of us that it did not take long, and after we had freed the houses of everything we wanted, we set fire to the village.

Most of the Outliers left once the fire got going, but I stayed with a few others and watched as it spread. Seeing the flames light up the night sky filled me with satisfaction, but it gave me a small sense of closure as well. This village and these people had been a stain on the earth for too long. But no more. We had made sure of that.

The flames jumped higher, lighting up the sky until the wall just beyond the Fortis village was clearly visible. It was impossible to know if the Sovereign were already aware of what had happened, but it did not matter one way or the other. They would find out soon enough. Dawn was not far off, and when it came, the people inside the city would expect the Fortis and Outlier workers to show up. But they would not. I just wished I could be there to see how Saffron and the other women reacted to the realization that their world was about to come crumbling down around them.

"Will the Sovereign do anything to retaliate?" Mira asked as we made our way through the valley and back toward the wilds.

"I do not think they will be able to," I said. "Without the Fortis, they have no chance against us. Even they have to know that."

The sun had begun to rise over the wilds by the time we reached the point where the river forked off. Right now, the Sovereign were waking up to a reality they had never faced before. One where they had no servants and no muscle. One where they were vulnerable even behind their walls.

The other Heads and I stopped, as did a few stragglers from each of the tribes. I spied Xandra among them, still holding Gaia. At her side stood Atreyu and Linc, as well as a couple of the other Winta men we had rescued, and their uneasy expressions reminded me that my fight for the day had not yet ended.

"It has been an honor to fight with you," Ontari said.

She grasped my arm with her hand, wrapping her fingers around my forearm as I did the same with hers. It was the first time we had touched, but seemed like the perfect way to end the battle. It also felt like it was sealing us as allies, not just now, but for decades to come.

"We will meet again soon to discuss our next move." I released Ontari's arm, and grasped Roan's in the exact same way. "The Sovereign must pay for what they have done."

"Thanks to you," he said, "they will."

Cruz kept his distance, but he nodded when I turned toward him. "Our treaty will continue, Indra of the Windhi people," he said, addressing me for the first time since the day he slapped me. "We will tear down the walls with you."

Electing to stay silent, I merely nodded in response. I had not forgotten the sting of his hand against my cheek, nor would I ever, but it was the disgust in his eyes that made me the most uneasy. Once this was all over, I would not continue our alliance even if he chose to. I had no desire to be allies with someone like Cruz.

The tribes parted ways, promising to meet after a day of rest, and I headed off into the woods with my own people. I had little hope that rest was in my future, though. Not with the way Linc was watching me, and not with the anger that still burned inside Emori.

My tribe was loaded down with supplies when we returned to the caves. The possessions we had lost when our village was burned to the ground had at last been replaced, and with much nicer items. The Fortis had lived like animals, but because they had received the Sovereign's castoffs for centuries, they had items we had never been able to get ahold of before. Things like pottery, such as bowls and plates, cups, pots and pans, and even silverware. Luxuries I only knew existed because of my time working inside the city.

The women who had stayed behind to watch the children, Isa among them, had already prepared a stew and were busy dishing it out, while around the room, the remaining members of the Winta sat huddled together, covered in furs. They seemed shaken and unsure about our new home, the men especially, and I had barely had time to set down the supplies I had carried back when Linc was on his feet.

"Who is Head?" his voice rang through the cave, bouncing off the walls.

I held back a sigh as I waved to the floor. "Sit, please. Eat. We have much to discuss, and we might as well do it on a full stomach."

Linc frowned, but he did as he was told. With everyone we had saved gathered in the room, I discovered we now had seven men. It would have been a welcome addition since we would need them if we had any hope of growing in numbers, except I had a feeling most of them would not be receptive to the changes.

"The Winta tribe is no more," I said once everyone was sitting. "The Fortis burned our village to the ground, leaving only women and children. This made it impossible for us to continue as Winta. How could we? The Winta told us we were weak, that we needed a man to look after us. But there were no men." I paused and looked around, meeting the shocked, confused, and even angry gazes of the newcomers. "We have formed a new tribe. A tribe of hunters and strong women. We have called ourselves Windhi, both to honor the Winta, and to honor Bodhi, who taught me to be strong. I am Head of the Windhi."

"This is an outrage." Linc jumped to his feet, knocking a bowl over in the process and spilling the stew across the floor of the cave. "You are a woman. You cannot be Head."

Xandra moved to stand at my side, leaving Gaia for the first time since their reunion. "She can in the Windhi tribe, just as Ontari is Head of the Huni tribe."

"And you all agreed to this?" Atreyu looked around, his eyes wide but not angry like Linc's. "You have decided the Winta should be no more?"

Around the room, the other members of the Windhi nodded.

"We have lived without men for more than a year now," Mira said gently. "If we had not done this, if we had not decided to be strong, we would have all died."

For a moment, the group in front of me was quiet. I looked the men over slowly, taking my time to meet each of their gazes. While Linc's anger was the strongest, he was not alone. Still, I had to believe all was not lost. That they could see reason just as the women had after our tribe was wiped out.

Linc's face scrunched up. "You are still a woman, and now that we have returned, so can the old ways." He looked around, maybe waiting for someone to agree with him, but no one spoke up. Not even Emori.

"Women cannot lead!" Linc threw his hands up in exasperation. "They are not strong enough."

"We were strong enough to save you," Anja spit at him. "Where would you be right now if we had rolled over and given up?"

"Not only that. We have also unified the Outliers." Tris waved toward me. "Indra did that. She brought us together, and because of her, you are here and the Fortis have been destroyed."

"This is how you want things to be now?" Atreyu looked around at the women who had been following me for more than a year over. "You want Indra to lead?"

All the members of the Windhi tribe — except Emori — nodded. Linc's gaze was on her, and I saw it when he registered the discontent in her eyes. He would use that to his advantage, just as she would use him if she needed to.

"This is the new way, the way of our new tribe. The old way told us women were not strong, but we now know that was not true. We are strong, and we have owned our strength." I paused and looked the men over again, holding Linc's gaze longer than anyone else's. My eyes were still locked on him when I said, "Now we just need to know if you can accept the changes. If you can accept me as Head of our tribe."

My words bounced off the walls of the cave, but when they faded away, I was met with silence. Most of the men seemed more exhausted than angry now, and I started to hope they would see reason once they had gotten some rest.

Linc was the main exception to this. He glared at me like I had been the one to lock him up, not free him.

"What if we cannot?" he asked. "What if we refuse to go along with this?"

At his feet, Atreyu shifted uncomfortably.

I had to fight against the exhaustion in my body so I could straighten my back, but I did not blink when I said, "Cruz, Head of the Trelite, has offered to allow any of the remaining Winta people to join their tribe. That is your right."

"But these are our people." Atreyu looked around the room, at the other people gathered in the cave, and shook his head. "I have lost almost everything. I cannot stomach the idea of losing anything else."

"Then you are welcome here." I gave him a grateful smile, and then looked the other men over again. "There is no reason to make a decision now. You are tired, you are hungry, and we all need rest."

I hoped Atreyu's presence among the men would be a blessing, and I was sure that, Like Bodhi, he would be able to understand that teaching women to be strong benefited everyone. Only time would tell if the other men would be able to adjust, but I had to hope they would. Atreyu was right. We had lost too much already. Throwing more away would be reckless.

Twenty-Three

ONE DAY OF REST WAS ALL I COULD ALLOW MY tribe, but I could not allow myself even that much time. The day following our attack on the Fortis village, I met the other Heads in the clearing to plan our next move. The fact that the Sovereign had no training and could do nothing for themselves made them weaker, but taking them out would still be complicated. They were hidden behind an impenetrable wall, and even with all the other advantages we had, that wall remained a problem.

"We cannot climb it or get the gate open from outside," I told the other Heads. "Which leaves only the secret tunnel at the back of the city."

We were circled around a small model of the city I had made on the ground, using rocks and sticks, and I pointed to the area behind the wall where the tunnel sat.

"You fled the city through this tunnel?" Ontari asked me, her eyes on the small city.

"I did." I tilted my head toward Xandra, who once again stood at my side. "Xandra helped me get out. The mistress of the house connected to it is sympathetic to Outliers."

"I did not know any of the Sovereign were sympathetic to Outliers." Zuri lifted her gaze, and the frown she wore contrasted with her usual happy appearance.

It was no surprise that Roan had brought his wife to the meeting, but as predicted, Cruz was not thrilled by the addition. Especially since her presence meant we now had twice as many women as men. Not that the Trelite Head had done or said anything to add to the discussion. He might as well have been one of the rocks on the ground in front of me.

"Aralyn is not the only Sovereign sympathetic to us." Indicating where Aralyn's house was, Xandra tapped the fake city with the stick she was holding. "There is a group inside who wishes for reform, but it is small."

I had worried that she would not want to leave Gaia so soon after their reunion, but thankfully Xandra had insisted on coming with me today. After seeing how gaunt the woman she loved now was, it seemed as if her determination to wipe the Sovereign out had doubled.

"She will help us?" Roan tore his gaze from the city in front of us and looked between Xandra and me. "Will this Sovereign woman help us, knowing it may cost her everything?"

"'I believe she will." Xandra pressed her lips together, her gaze once again going to the small rock that represented Aralyn's house. "We will have to promise to spare her. Not just her, but her family and anyone else who is sympathetic to our cause."

"That is not a problem." I spoke up before anyone else had a chance to reply. "Anyone who helps us is worthy of redemption."

I was thinking of Asa, wondering where he was and how long it would take for him to come find me. Not long. I was sure of it, just as I was certain his thoughts were as much on me as mine were on him.

Xandra's gaze met mine, and as if she knew what I was thinking, she covered my hand with hers. One quick squeeze was all she gave me before once again focusing on the city of rocks in front of us, but it was enough to give me comfort.

"Can we all go into the city through this tunnel?" Roan was asking.

"It is much too small to send an entire army through." Xandra pressed her lips together and stared at the ground thoughtfully. "I think it would be wise for me to go in first so we can get a better idea of what is happening. We killed many Fortis, but there is no way of knowing if we got them all. Some may have fled into the wastelands. If there are survivors and they have been welcomed into the city, they might be ready for our attack."

"You cannot go alone." Cruz spoke up for the first time since the meeting started, his outrage over the proposition apparently overcoming his desire to avoid dealing with women. "It is too dangerous."

"I came out of the tunnel on my own many times." Xandra kept her voice level even as her brown eyes flashed with a fierce hatred for the man in front of her. "However, I did not plan to go by myself. I intend to take someone with me."

We had discussed all of this before leaving the caves, and it had been Xandra's idea to send a small party inside, as well as to volunteer for the job. But no decision had been made about *who* would go with her. Someone from our tribe made sense because they would already know and trust one another, but we had a feeling the other Heads might want to send one of their own people. Cruz, especially.

The Trelite Head lifted his chin so he could look down at Xandra. "One of my men will go."

Her expression did not change, but her gaze did flick my way. We had anticipated this, and even though we were not happy with the idea, we knew agreeing to the plan would be wise. Our treaty with the Trelite was shaky, due to their extreme dislike of women in authority, and if we refused to let them help us now, it could damage things permanently. While the alliance could not last, I hoped we could at least keep our numbers up going into the next battle.

Both Ontari and Zuri frowned at the idea, and Roan did not look much happier. He seemed on the verge of saying something, but was cut off when Xandra spoke up.

"That is acceptable."

Cruz crossed his arms and what could be called a smile pulled up his mouth, although it looked more like a scowl. He was the only one who seemed happy about the decision, but if he noticed, he did not care.

"I have just the man." The Trelite Head had gone back to avoiding Xandra's gaze. "Bowie will be a good ally to have."

Xandra nodded even though neither of us believed any of the Trelite men would be a good ally. Still, keeping the peace was the most important thing at the moment. We needed to maintain our numbers, especially since we were unsure about what we were going to face once we got inside the city.

"We will leave tomorrow, then," Xandra said. "At sunrise. We can meet at the fork in the river, just outside the valley."

"We will be there," the Trelite Head replied, but once again did not look directly at her.

While the others in the clearing shifted as if uncomfortable about the arrangement, I was not concerned. I was confident in Xandra's ability to look out for herself, and even if the Trelite did not view women as equals, I did not believe the man Cruz intended to send would put her in danger because of it. If anything, he would work harder to protect her because he did not believe she could look out for herself.

The planning lasted only a little longer, and then we broke up. Cruz left without a word, while the rest of us said our goodbyes.

"You and Gaia have just been reunited," I said as Xandra and I made our way back to the caves. "Are you sure you want to do this?"

She did not look at me, and the way her jaw clenched told me she was fighting against her emotions. "She was held in that prison for a year, Indra. The Sovereign had them locked away like animals." Xandra's jaw tightened even more, barely opening when she said, "I will go, and I will find a way to get us into the city so they can pay for this."

"I believe you will," I said.

We walked for a few minutes in silence, and it must have been enough time for her to relax a little, because when she spoke again, her jaw was no longer clenched.

"And what of you? What of the Fortis man? I know you warned him about the attack." When I looked her way, Xandra shrugged. "Emori likes to hear her own voice."

"She was very angry at me."

"She is wrong," Xandra said firmly. "Asa is not a threat to us."

"I knew that before the attack, but this proves it. He ran. Asa could have warned his people, but instead he fled. If that does not prove to Emori that he is on our side, nothing ever will."

"No," Xandra replied, "I do not think anything will be able to prove that to her. She is blinded by her hate."

"Maybe I can understand that." When Xandra shot me a questioning look, I shrugged and said, "We both know the things she went through inside the city."

I thought of the baby that had nursed at Emori's breast and how the child had come to be. The girl was walking now, and happy, but even after all this time, I could not look at her without seeing Lysander. Maybe that would change once I knew for certain he was dead, but I doubted it. No matter how much I had healed, I would always wear those scars.

It was probably the same for Emori, which was why her hatred of the Fortis made it impossible for her to see Asa clearly. Lysander had been the one to violate her and give her a child, but Fortis guards had no doubt also abused her. I had no way of knowing exactly what she had endured. I did not think I wanted to know.

THE NEXT MORNING, AS PLANNED, MIRA, XANDRA, and I met Cruz and Bowie where the river forked. The man accompanying the Trelite Head was only a few years older than Xandra, but like his leader, nearly every bit of his exposed skin was covered in passage markings. Indicating that he had lived a very eventful life. Hopefully, his experience helped on this journey.

When we stopped in front of the two men, Bowie did not greet us with the disdain we had come to expect from Trelite men, but instead simply bowed his head and introduced himself. The lack of hostility helped ease some of my worries about sending him into the city with Xandra, but not all of them. That would have been impossible.

"Be careful," I told my friend as she prepared to leave.

"We will not be gone long." Xandra looked behind her toward the river, which stretched out through the valley. "Aralyn will be able to tell us what is going on, but more importantly, I will be able to warn her to be ready."

"That is important," I said, thinking once again of Asa.

Xandra's hand covered mine, and I looked back to find her eyes on me. "Watch over Gaia."

"You have my word," I said.

She squeezed my hand. "And yourself, my friend. Watch over yourself."

"I have no plans to do anything else," I replied.

It was not long before Xandra and Bowie headed out, and Mira and I stayed where we were, as did Cruz, until they had disappeared from sight. Once they had, the Trelite Head turned away, barely nodding a goodbye before taking his leave. Mira and I, however, stayed where we were.

"Are you worried about what will happen next?" she asked once Cruz had disappeared into the trees.

"Not about Aralyn. We were in that house, and we know she can be trusted. I am concerned that some of the Fortis did manage to sneak away during the battle, though. Our attack on their village was easy, but that was because they did not know we were coming. If the Sovereign are prepared for an attack, and if they have even a small group of Fortis to help them, it could be much more difficult this time around."

"The Sovereign are not fighters. What can a small group of Fortis do? How can they stand up to us when we are so many?"

She was right, but I could not shake the feeling that something was happening in the city, and that we were in for a surprise.

"I only know the Sovereign have things we do not even understand. Power and technology from the old world. What if they have something we have never seen before? Something worse than the electroprods? What if they use it against us?"

Mira shivered and wrapped her arms around herself. "We must pray that is not the case."

I DID NOT EXPECT XANDRA TO RETURN THAT DAY, but halfway through the following day, I began to watch for her. When I was out in the woods hunting for game, when I was eating my dinner in the main chamber, after the sun had set and the caves had settled down. She did not come back. By the third day, I began to suspect something had gone wrong, and I could tell by how shaken Gaia looked that she harbored the same worries.

"We need to visit the Trelite," I told Mira. "To talk to them about Xandra and Bowie."

"Should we go to the Mountari first? You know Cruz will not like it if we come alone."

"I know." I let out a deep breath, thinking it over, and then shook my head. "Our people are the ones missing, not the Mountaris', and in this instance, I have a feeling Roan will not be able to help."

"You think Cruz will pull out?" When Mira's gaze met mine, the worry swimming in her eyes mirrored my own.

"I do."

She exhaled. "As do I."

Only the two of us went, and just like every other time we had visited the Trelite, our arrival was announced by the sounding of a horn, followed shortly by Zaire meeting us, a group of men gathered behind him.

"Indra of the Windhi." His words were laced with even more hostility than we had ever been greeted with before. "What brings you to our village?"

"Our people still have not returned," I replied, ignoring the threatening looks from the men at his back.

"The Head has been concerned as well." Zaire turned, nodding for me to follow as he made his way back into the village.

"We must meet with the other Heads," I said, hurrying after him with Mira at my side.

Zaire glanced back, and the look in his eyes told me what I already knew. That would not be happening. Not now, and not ever.

"That will be up to Cruz," was all he said.

Mira and I waited in front of the wooden throne, sitting on the ground as usual, only this time when Cruz appeared, he did not take a seat. "I can no longer take my people into this battle."

I stood, not caring if Cruz was offended by the action. "You are backing out of our treaty?"

"I am making a decision for my people based on what I know." He straightened his shoulders and glared down at me, giving me a look that was meant to be punishing, but only succeeded in making me angry. "I sent a man into the city as you requested, and now he is gone. Without more information, I cannot send anyone else inside."

"If we are going to find out what is happening in the city, then we must send another group in," I argued.

"Then you can send one of your people," Cruz barked. "You do not need us to defeat the Sovereign. We are not fighters, and the Trelite have risked enough."

I looked past him, back to where the men stood, and then up at the trees. High above us, the women of the Trelite tribe peeked from windows, looking down like scared children. It made my stomach twist. Made me want to kill not just Cruz, but all the men in this tribe.

Only I had not started this alliance with plans to alter the customs of the Trelite, and as much as the men disgusted me,

I could not change my mind. It was not my place to tell these people they were wrong. No matter what I thought.

I took a step back and once again focused on the Head. "This is the end, then?"

"It is," he said.

"Then consider our treaties over. All of them."

Cruz frowned, and a moment went by before he said, "You have decided not to join our tribe?"

"Joining your tribe is nothing I would have ever considered. We only needed your vegetables. Now that we have formed a relationship with the Mountari and the Huni, we will do our trading elsewhere."

The expression in the Head's eyes hardened and he waved his hand in my direction, as if shooing me away. "It is time for you to leave, Indra of the Windhi people."

I did not even bother nodding before I turned my back on Cruz.

Mira and I were silent as we left the village. The Head's decision to back out of our treaty had nothing to do with Bowie going missing. Cruz did not like taking orders from a woman, and even if I had decided to take Roan with me today, nothing could have changed that. The Trelite prisoners had been freed, and Cruz knew we would attack the Sovereign with or without him. Pulling out now meant he risked nothing, but he would still gain his freedom from the Sovereign, just like the rest of us.

"He is a coward," Mira said as we walked.

"Yes. It should not come as a surprise. He refuses to associate with the women from other villages because he knows it will challenge his views." I scowled but worked to push my anger at Cruz aside. As much as I hoped that one day he and I would come across each other in the forest, I could not focus on him right now. "We need to come up with a plan. We will have to send another group in."

"Can we risk it?" Mira's eyes darted my way. "We have already had two people disappear."

"What if they never even made it to the city?" I argued. "What if they were killed by a lygan or some other creature? Even if they made it, we need to know what is happening inside the walls before we make our next move. There is no way around it."

Mira ran her fingers through her blond hair and exhaled. "You are right."

"I do not think we should send someone straight into the city, but we do need to send a small group that way to check things out. We need to see if there are any clues about what happened to Xandra and Bowie, or if there is movement in the Fortis village. We need information."

I stopped walking and looked up at the trees. Spring was in full bloom, and the branches above us were proof of that. The buds that had sprouted only a couple weeks ago were now well on their way to engulfing the limbs, turning the bare branches into a sea of green.

"We need to talk to the other Heads," I said, my gaze still on the buds as I thought about how much had changed so quickly.

"I agree," Mira said.

I tore my gaze from the tree and looked at my friend. "We are closer to the Huni."

"Then we will go there."

Twenty-Four

EVEN UNEXPECTED, OUR ARRIVAL AT THE HUNI village was met with warmth. Arkin was one of the first to spot us, and when he led us through the village, very few people even looked our way. Those who did smiled or nodded. It was a far cry from the reaction we received on our first visit, and yet another example of how much had changed not just for me, but for all the Outliers.

We found Ontari in her hut. It was the first time we had been allowed entry into her personal space, and the fact that she did not even stand when we stepped inside said a lot about how comfortable she had become with us.

"Sit," she said, waving to the floor at her side.

Mira and I did as we were told, taking a place across from her, a steaming pot of stew sitting between us. Arkin took his place at Ontari's side and began to dish out the food, making a bowl not just for himself and Ontari, but one for Mira and me as well.

"What is it you have come to discuss with me?" Ontari said as Arkin passed out the bowls.

"The scouts we sent into the city have not returned." I took a bowl when it was held out to me, but my focus was on the Head. "We went to visit the Trelite today, hoping to discuss the next course of action. It made sense, to me, to go to them since Bowie was their man."

"They have pulled from the alliance," Ontari said before I could give her any further details.

"They have," I replied.

She exhaled and set her bowl down. "I am not surprised. Cruz was never comfortable with it. It challenged his views too much."

Mira paused with a bowl poised in front of her mouth. "It showed him that his views are wrong."

Ontari's lips twitched, but I could not tell if it was from amusement or pride. "Yes, it did."

"What will your next move be?" Arkin's gaze was focused on me, his own bowl clasped in his hands and seemingly forgotten.

The thin man was twice my age, and even after all the changes, after becoming the leader of my new tribe, killing Fortis hunters, and unifying the Outlier tribes, having him turn to me for strategy decisions still did not feel right. But I knew the responsibility rested on my shoulders more than anyone else's. I started this when I chose to defy Lysander, and when I released that first arrow and killed the Fortis hunter in the woods. It was up to me to see it through, even if I was not confident in my abilities.

"I think we need to send another group out," I said, my gaze moving between Arkin and Ontari. "We have no idea if they even made it to the city, or if all the Fortis are dead. We need to see what is happening."

"I agree," Ontari replied. "Will you go yourself?"

"I will." Putting myself at risk when my tribe was on such shaky ground might not have been the best idea, but I wanted to see what was happening—if anything—with my own eyes. "As will Mira."

Ontari turned her gaze on Arkin. "We will send men with them." She looked back at me. "Not because you are not capable, Indra of the Windhi, but because a larger group will be better. Especially if the first two ran into trouble."

I gave her an appreciative smile. "Thank you."

Arkin loaned us the two best hunters in the tribe, and together the four of us headed off. We did not go straight to the valley, though, but instead headed for the Mountari. Not just because I wanted to let Roan know what had happened with the Trelite, but because I wanted to keep him informed of our plans.

Like Ontari, he agreed that we needed to send another party out and gave me two men. Also like the Head of the Huni tribe, Roan did not express any surprise that Cruz had broken our treaty.

"He is a coward," Roan said, mimicking Mira's words.

"He is afraid of what he will lose."

"As he should be." Roan gave me the same appreciative look he always did, unconcerned that Zuri stood at his side.

"You have shown his people what strength is, and he does not like it."

"I am not alone in that," I said, nodding to Roan's wife.

To her credit, Zuri only smiled placidly at the exchange, once again seemingly unconcerned by her mate's obvious admiration for me. It was a difficult thing to wrap my head around, knowing I would not have liked it if Bodhi had shown another woman the same kind of attention, but I understood why it did not bother Zuri. Their customs said I would have to challenge her if I wanted Roan, and since I was not from their tribe, it was not an issue.

With the four hunters in tow, two from the Huni and two from the Mountari, Mira and I headed out. The Valley that would lead us to Sovereign Lake was lined by the wilds on one side, and the lygan Cliffs on the other, with the river running through it. Since the scaled creatures living in those cliffs came down often to hunt, I was careful to keep an eye out not just for them as we walked, but also for any signs that Xandra and Bowie had been attacked. There were none, though. No blood, no torn clothing, no bodies. We made it to the lake at the end of the valley without finding a single clue as to what had happened to our friends.

Not far from the edge of the lake sat the outskirts of the Fortis village. Now nothing more than charred remains and ashes, it was crawling with grizzards that had come in from the wastelands to pick the bones of the dead Fortis clean, and the sight of the large, black birds caused a shudder to go through me as I thought about how close I had come to being speared by one of these very creatures the day the city had been under attack.

Seeing the birds made me think of Asa again, made me wonder where he was and how he was doing. As I thought about him, a sense of guilt washed over me that I had not experienced in a long time. The sight in front of me felt irreverent. My former tribe, the Winta, had held human life in high regard, yet we had left the bodies to rot in the hot sun. Even worse, these had been Asa's people, and despite my burning hatred for the Fortis, I could not help feeling remorse that their remains were currently being picked apart by birds. We should have gathered them as we had done with our own village. We should have burned them. It would have been the right thing to do.

I did not say this to the others, though, not even when we paused beside the lake to eat. The sight of the birds picking their way through the fallen city made it difficult for me to choke anything down, but I could not look away. Not when I was searching both for signs of our missing friends, as well as for any indication that some of the Fortis might have survived the attack. Thankfully, the birds seemed to be the only things moving, and from where we were sitting, there was no sign that anything other than animals had been back to the village since we burned it a few days ago.

"What next?" Mira asked, drawing my attention from the sickening sight in front of me.

I exhaled as I thought it through, knowing what had to be done but not savoring it. "The tunnel."

The men from the Huni and Mountari tribes looked at me, but they did not speak, and I could not tell what was going through their minds, if they agreed with me, or if they thought going so close to the city was reckless.

"We said we would not go into the city today," Mira reminded me, but like the others, she did not act as if she was going to resist me.

"And we will not." I stood so I could gather my things. "I just want to see if there are any tracks around it or other signs that Xandra made it this far."

Both the Huni and Mountari men nodded, and Mira visibly relaxed.

"That makes sense," she said.

After we had gathered our things, we moved around the wall of the city, not bothering to keep our distance the way Mira and I had before. With the Fortis gone, there was no one to spot us, and I wanted to take the fastest route possible.

The sun was already setting, and the mirrors I had spied the last time we were here were visible in the distance. They reflected the pink glow of dusk, making it seem as if the tower in the middle was glowing.

"What is it?" one of the Mountari men asked as we walked.

"We do not know," Mira replied, her gaze fixed on the building despite the blinding glow.

I was too focused on my task to respond, especially on the footprints in the sand that seemed to tell me Xandra and Bowie had in fact made it here. We reached the boulders that shielded the tunnel from view, and I climbed over. The door was just as I remembered it, and around it there were footprints in the sand.

"They were here," I said.

"How do you know?" a Huni man asked.

"If these tracks were older, the wind would have blown sand over them by now."

"I think you are right," Mira said. "Now what?"

"We cannot go in." I looked regretfully toward the wall. "It is too dangerous. We will have to go back and discuss the next step with Ontari and Roan. We need a plan."

It was the right decision, but as I stood by the rocks, staring at the walled city I hated so much, I could not help worrying that my hesitation would doom my friend. Whatever was happening inside the city, I knew for sure Xandra was suffering, and leaving her to be tortured did not sit well with me.

I turned my back on the city anyway and said, "Let us go."

As much as I wanted to go through the tunnel and save her at this very moment, I could not afford to make an impulsive decision. I was a leader now, and I had a treaty. Whatever the Outliers chose to do, we would need to do it together.

Twenty-Five

WATCH AND WAIT. THAT WAS OUR PLAN. IT WAS the right decision even if it made me feel powerless. We could not afford to run off without more information, and unless we went into the city, there was no way to get it. The Sovereign were sealed in tight, but we were convinced someone would eventually come out. They made and grew nearly everything inside the city, but even the Sovereign would need the meat the wilds provided.

We sent people out in shifts, each of our three villages taking turns. Three days passed, and we still had little information. It was wearing on me, and I was not alone. Gaia, like me, was having a difficult time focusing on anything else. When I got up in the middle of the night, my spinning mind making it impossible to sleep, it was not uncommon to find the older woman sitting alone in the main cave. Like she was waiting for the moment when Xandra would step through the opening.

That was where I found her on the third night after my visit to the wall, sitting by the fire and staring at the opening. She had looked ragged when we rescued her from the Fortis village, and she seemed to have aged another ten years since Xandra left. Or possibly it was just the light from the flames flickering across her face playing tricks on my eyes.

Gaia looked up when I entered, her eyes wild as if she had gotten caught doing something wrong. "You startled me," she said, and then her gaze went back to the opening of the cave. "When you freed me, I swore I would never be away from her again."

"We will get her back," I said. "I promise."

The other woman nodded, but did not look my way. "I know the two of you have become close, and I have tried to find comfort in knowing you would not leave a friend to die. But it is not easy. Not after everything I have seen the Sovereign do."

"I understand." I could only manage a whisper because she was not alone in her fears for Xandra's safety.

Gaia glanced my way again, this time her gaze lingering on my face. "I believe you do." She paused for a moment, hesitating before finally saying, "Xandra told me about your friend. The Fortis man. Is that why you can so easily accept who we are?"

"Perhaps," I said and then exhaled as I lowered myself to the ground on the other side of the fire. "Or perhaps it is because I have learned that the Winta did not always know what was best. Right or wrong, it is not for me to judge you. I will leave that up to God."

Gaia nodded, but said nothing before turning back to stare at the cave entrance.

I stayed at her side, knowing I would be unable to go back to sleep, and together we stared at the opening in silence. Her worry was focused on Xandra, but after our conversation, I found my own thoughts focused on Asa. Wondering where he was and if he was okay, as well as when I would see him again.

Fortunately, I did not have to live in suspense for long. Early the next morning, shortly after Gaia had given up her vigil and retired to Xandra's alcove, someone burst through the cave entrance and stumbled inside. My heart jumped and I was on my feet in seconds, my first thoughts of Xandra as I spun to face the intruder.

Tris was standing in front of me, red in the face and out of breath, and I took a step toward her, my hand already on the knife at my waist. "What is it?"

"We have someone," she gasped out. "A Fortis man."

"A prisoner?" The news caused my heart to leap. This was what we had been waiting for.

"No." Tris shook her head and swallowed before saying, "The man you know. The one who came here once before."

Asa.

Thinking of him made my heart soar again, but in a different way this time. I had known he would find me eventually, and had it not been for Xandra going missing, the wait probably would have been agonizing. But I had been too focused on my missing friend and the upcoming battle to think about him much before. Now, though, all I wanted was to see with my own eyes that he was okay.

"Take me to him," I demanded, already heading for the cave entrance.

Tris popped out of the cave in front of me, and I followed on her heels as she led me through the wilds, winding between blooming bushes and trees now bursting with green. We reached the same clearing I had found Asa in before, and even though I was thankful he was not bleeding this time, the sight of him kneeling in front of Emori was just as bad. His hands were bound behind his back and he was blindfolded, and Emori stood over him with a knife, holding it against his throat. The fierce expression on her face and the fire in her eyes told me she wanted nothing more than to cut him open and watch him bleed. Thankfully, Tris had been present to stop it from happening. She may have been the only thing that saved Asa.

"What is this?" I demanded when I stopped in front of Emori.

"This man was found in the woods," she spit out.

"You know who this is." I waved at him angrily. Exasperated that I had to tell her yet again that Asa was not a threat. "Why are you pretending you do not know him?"

"I know he is a member of the village we wiped out only a few days ago," Emori sneered.

Behind the blindfold, Asa jerked at the venom in her words, and I almost reached out for him. The blade was pressed against his throat, threatening to slice him open if he made one false move.

"Get that knife away from his throat and untie him," I ordered. "Take the blindfold off. *Now*."

Even Tris hesitated at the last command. "You cannot take him to the caves without the blindfold, Indra."

"If he wanted to destroy us, he would have done it already. He could have warned his people we were coming, but he did not." I looked from Tris to Emori. "If that is not a sign that we can trust him, what is? Now untie him."

Emori's gaze stayed focused on mine. She pulled the knife back, but she made no move to untie Asa. Tris, however, did as I requested and untied the ropes binding his wrists together, but the expression on her face said she was not happy about it.

When Asa's arms were free, he yanked the blindfold off. Immediately, his gaze searched me out, and when his brown eyes met mine, it felt like we were standing in the middle of the wastelands with the hot sun beating down on us.

"Indra." Asa climbed to his feet and moved toward me, stopping an arm's length away.

I wanted him to take me in his arms almost more than I wanted to wipe the Sovereign out, but I was relieved he showed restraint. No matter my feelings for this man, I had no desire to anger Emori any more than I already had.

Asa looked as healthy as always, as big and as broad, although dirtier than ever before. His clothes were smeared with black residue that could have only come from the Lygan Cliffs, and his fingernails were caked with dirt. He looked weary, too, as if he had not slept much over the last few days.

But he was whole, and he was here.

Emotion clogged my throat, but I managed to say, "I am glad you are okay."

"I ran just like you told me to," he whispered. "With a small group of my people. We've been hiding in the cliffs."

The thought of him living among those creatures filled me worry. The Fortis had very little experience hunting lygan. "You should be in the wilds. The cliffs are too dangerous, Asa. Here the trees will provide you with food and shelter, and keep you safe from the lygan."

"That's why I'm here."

At his back, Emori snarled, but it was almost drowned out by the pounding of my heart. I knew what he was going to ask, and what I *wanted* to say to him. The only problem was, I had no idea what I should do.

Asa and I had a lot to talk about, but it would have to wait until we were alone—something I had been longing for since the last time I saw him. Whatever happened next, whatever decisions were made or declarations uttered, I had no desire to let it play out in front of Emori, so I waved toward the trees.

"Come with me," I said as I began walking. "We will talk."

Tris frowned as we passed her, and even though I understood her uncertainty, Asa had proven himself to me time and time again. She followed at a distance, but I looked back to discover Emori had stayed behind. We had spoken very little since the attack on the Fortis village, but I was aware that she and Linc had been spending time together. It was not a surprise, just as it would not be a surprise when they finally decided to challenge me.

Asa and I said nothing on our way back to the cave, and when we reached it, I ducked inside without hesitation. He followed behind wordlessly, as did Tris.

The main chamber was not empty when we stepped inside. More than a dozen people were gathered around the fire, eating the stew that had been cooking for the last several hours, but only a couple looked up, Linc and a few other men among them. Shock rippled through the room at the sight of Asa, and their expressions ranged from outrage to terror. Linc went for his knife, and Atreyu looked around as if he, too, were searching for a weapon.

Before either of them could do anything, I raised my hand and said, "He is a friend."

"Friend?" The fire that flashed in Linc's eyes was no less intense than the real one burning in the center of the room. "You cannot be serious, Indra. He is a Fortis."

"And he saved me. More than once. I trust him more than I trust you right now, Linc. Remember that."

Atreyu stood frozen, staring at me like I was a stranger. Despite how understanding he had been about all the changes to our tribe, there were accusations in his eyes. He was thinking of Bodhi, and possibly remembering the rumors that had followed my husband's death.

"He is an honorable person," I said, more calmly this time.

Atreyu's gaze moved to Asa, but his expression did not change. "I do not understand what is happening with you, Indra."

"It is something we will have to discuss later." I turned away from him, heading toward the tunnel that would take us to the largest chamber. "Come, Asa."

There, people were busy working, and to my relief no one seemed to care that Asa was with me. Gaia was among the group, as forlorn as before, as well as Mira. My friend's blue eyes lit up when she saw Asa with me, but she said nothing. She was giving us space, I knew, and time to be together.

Asa followed me in silence just as he had the last time he was here, his heat wrapping around me more and more with each step. His nearness, his size, and his comfort engulfed me, dragging memories from the past. The times he had saved me from disaster, as well as the times he had comforted me when he had been unable to stop disaster from destroying my world. The night we spent together here in this very cave, and even the last time we spoke, in a hut that was no longer standing, and in a village that existed no more.

"Indra," he began once we had reached my chamber. "I—"

I said nothing as I turned to face him, cutting his words off with a kiss.

Whatever he had planned to say was forgotten as he kissed me back, his hands already working to remove my clothes just as my own were working on his. I pushed myself up on the tips of my toes, trying to get closer to him, my fingers working on this pants while our lips moved together.

When we had both undressed, he lowered me to the ground, his body already on top of mine. I kissed him with a fever I had not known I could possess, remembering the fears that had tugged at my insides as we marched on his village. How scared I had been that he might not have run.

When he kissed his way down my neck, I took the opportunity to say, "I was scared you would not listen to me."

"I was scared you'd get hurt during the battle."

His mouth once again covered mine as he settled his body between my legs, and it was just as it had been before. His muscled warmth making me feel whole, his body fitting against mine in a way that made no sense. His heat comforting me and pushing my worries away.

We stayed that way, undressed and in each other's arms. His body and the furs wrapped around us warmed the alcove, and I found myself wishing he could stay here with me. That he could be at my side every night when I lay down to sleep.

"My village is gone," Asa said after a long silence.

"I am sorry for what you have lost, but I cannot be sorry for what I have done."

"I know." He kissed the top of my head as if to reassure me he was being sincere. "It isn't over. You know that, right?"

"We know. We sent two people into the city and they have not returned. We have no way of knowing what is going on, but I fear we have underestimated the Sovereign."

"Some of the Fortis survived," Asa said.

I pushed myself up so I could look him in the eye. "You know this for sure?"

"We saw them," he said. "The next day. When you attacked, they fled into the wastelands and the cliffs, and when they were sure you were gone, they went to the city."

"The Sovereign allowed them to enter?" I asked even though I knew they had not hesitated. The Sovereign needed the muscle and the numbers, despite their electroprods and technology.

"They did. They're inside the walls right now."

"It is what I feared." I sighed and settled back down, but I was not as relaxed as I had been. "It will make our attack much more difficult, but we cannot back down now. If we do, they will see us as weak and send the remaining Fortis out to destroy us. If that happens, we could be the ones taken by surprise."

"You'll figure out a way to get inside." Asa twisted onto his side so he was looking down at me. "That isn't why I came here today, though."

His dark eyes held mine, so soft and gentle they seemed to defy his status as a Fortis man. I knew what he was going to ask, and I knew how I would be forced to respond, but I stayed quiet and let him say it anyway.

"My people are suffering, Indra. We aren't used to living outside the village, and we have nothing. No shelter. No food other than what we kill. We need help."

I lifted my hand to touch his face, running my fingers down his scratchy chin. The stubble there was longer than usual, but no less abrasive.

"I am sorry for your suffering," I whispered, my hand still on his cheek, "but there is nothing I can do. I have to make my people a priority. You know this."

"You've unified the Outliers," he said, his eyes searching mine. "What about my people? We left the Fortis because we believed in your fight more than our own. Shouldn't we have a place in your alliance?"

I let my hand drop from his face. He had a point, but not everyone would agree. It would be a fight, and adding another battle to my life right now might not be a wise thing to do. Still, I was part of the reason he was suffering, and to do nothing was wrong.

"It is not up to me alone, and I am not sure if the other Heads will agree," I told him. "They have not seen the same side of the Fortis I have, and even I have only seen you."

"Take me to them," Asa said. "Let me plead my case and see if we can work out a deal."

"Is this why you came today?" It felt like the claws of a lygan had scratched across my insides when pain surged through me. His actions proved he had wanted to see me, but I still needed him to say the words.

"Yes," he whispered, "and to see you. I wanted you to know I survived, and I wanted to make sure you were okay."

It was not his words that made my throat tighten with emotion, but the expression in his eyes as he looked me over. The love that had shimmered in them before had deepened until it threatened to overwhelm us both.

"I knew you survived because I went to your house after the fight to make sure. I had to know."

He leaned down and kissed me again, and I wrapped my arms around him. For just a few moments we were lost in each other. The dangers outside this cave did not exist, and there was no death or war. There was just the two of us.

But it could not last. Not when Asa's people were suffering, and it was not long before he pulled away.

"I need this, Indra," he said, pleading with me this time. "My people need this. You once told me you were a ghost, and you're not alone in that."

It was true, I realized. Because of me, Asa's life and the lives of the other Fortis who had fled with him were now upside down. They were as much ghosts in this world as I had been after losing my tribe. If he came here, if the other Heads allowed him to join our treaty, things between us would be less complicated. He could be here with me every night.

It felt like the question Asa had asked me the last time he was here was hanging hung over our heads, and my insides stirred from the possibilities. Would I consider marrying someone outside my tribe? Could I marry Asa, or would it destroy everything?

I was not sure of the answer, just as I had no idea what the future held, but I had to try. And not just for myself. For Asa and his people as well.

"Do not get your hopes up," I said. "I will take you to meet the other Heads tomorrow, but they will not be easy to convince."

"All I ask for is a chance," he said.

Then he settled down next to me again, his long body flush with mine, and wrapped me in his embrace.

Twenty-Six

WITH CRUZ NO LONGER IN OUR ALLIANCE, THE decision to allow Asa and his people to join us would be up to Roan and Ontari. The three of us had fallen into a trusting relationship, one I never could have foreseen, but more than anything, this would test what we had built. It would not be easy to convince the other tribes that even one of the Fortis were trustworthy, let alone a whole group of them.

Even worse, I had withheld my relationship with Asa, and I worried they would see it as betrayal instead of what it was. A desire to keep my feelings private until I understood them myself. I did not care what anyone thought about Asa and me, my bringing him to the cave proved that, but I also did not want others weighing in on it until I had decided for myself what I wanted. Ontari and Roan had no idea I had gone to the Fortis village three days before our attack, and even though everything had turned out okay, it could very well seem like a betrayal to them.

It was hard to say who would be more difficult to convince. Both Roan and Ontari trusted me, but Asa was still a Fortis. To many people, like Emori, it did not matter that he and his group had fled his village, or that they had not warned the others. It only mattered where he had been born.

When I left the caves, I took only Mira and Asa. We went to the Mountari village first since it was closer, and despite my joy at knowing Asa was alive, as well as having him at my side, the weight on my shoulders seemed to increase with every step we took.

I had not expected the same warm welcome we were used to receiving, but I was still unprepared for the hostility that met us when we arrived at the Mountari village. Even during our first visit the people had done little more than look at us with curiosity, but now, as we approached the outskirts of the village, they moved out of our way like they expected an attack, and a few of the men even went for spears or knives.

After everything we had been through, Asa's first instinct was to put himself between me and danger. In this instance, however, it would only make him seem like a threat, not a guest.

"Let Mira and me take the lead," I whispered as I stepped around him and continued into the village.

Every single Mountari man and woman stopped to stare, their gazes mostly on Asa. If his size had not marked him as a Fortis, the passage markings on his arms did. No Outliers, not even the Trelite, had such thick, dark lines on their skin.

Roan and Zuri met us halfway through the village, each of them carrying a spear. "What is the meaning of this?" the Head demanded when he had stopped in front of us. "You have brought a Fortis into our village, Indra? Is this an act of war?"

"No. You must hear me out, Roan." I raised my hands to show I was not armed, and Mira did the same. I looked back to find Asa copying us. "He is a friend."

"Friend?" Zuri's usual smile was gone when she spit the word at me. "He is a Fortis!"

She glanced behind her, and in the distance I spied a teenage girl I had never seen before. Her daughter. The girl's gray eyes gave away who she was, as well as what she had gone through in the Fortis village. It brought back memories of my own defilement, and I suddenly found I could not keep my head up.

"I know it does not seem likely," Mira said when I did not reply, "but it is true."

I kept my head lowered, but lifted my gaze from the ground. Roan looked at me, and then at Mira, saying nothing. Even when he looked past us, studying the large man at my back, the Mountari Head did not utter a word.

A long time seemed to pass before he finally looked at me again and said, "Explain yourself."

The fire in Zuri's gaze did not lessen as I began my story. I recounted my time working in the city and how Asa had helped me, as well as the many times he had saved both Mira and me from other Fortis guards, and how he had made sure I got safely back to my village after I was whipped.

"Even when I did not return to my job in the city, he made sure to watch over Mira," I finished.

Roan had listened without interruption, but his gaze had not softened when he turned it on Mira. "You can confirm this?"

"I can," my friend replied.

The Head frowned, and he once again looked past us to where Asa stood, taking in his surroundings, studying the people in front of him, as well as the lygan bones decorating the village. He had worked in the city just as I had, and had seen members of the Mountari tribe before, but not like this. Not in their home, surrounded by the remnants of the lygan they had killed. Not with their chests exposed, showing off the piercings that proved what great hunters they were. It had to be intimidating, had to make them look savage and threatening. I knew, because I had entertained the same thoughts before getting to know these people.

"Step forward, Fortis." Roan's voice boomed through the village.

Mira and I moved aside, giving Asa room to walk by. He said nothing as the Head looked him over. Behind Roan, Zuri's expression had softened, and it both surprised and unnerved me to find that her gaze was focused not on Asa, but on me.

"I am Roan, Head of the Mountari," the Head began, "Indra tells me that you fled your village with other people and can be trusted."

"That's right." Asa shot a quick glance my way, but I could not read his expression. "There are nearly fifty of us, mostly women and children. We've been in the cliffs since our village was destroyed, but we can't stay there. We need help learning how to live in the wilds. We've never done it before. In exchange, we will help you fight the Sovereign."

"Why would you do this?" Roan's hand tightened on his spear. "Why would you betray your people so quickly and with so little thought?"

Asa's gaze moved to me again, this time lingering a little longer. "Because I'm not like those other men, and I'm not the only one. Because I don't think anyone should be treated the way the Sovereign treat the Outliers."

"And because you are in love with her," Zuri said.

All eyes were on Asa now, waiting for his response. Roan's, Mira's, everyone else in the village. Zuri, however, was still staring at me.

It only took a beat for Asa to murmur, "Yes, I am."

The heat that flared across my cheeks grew more intense when Roan turned his gaze on me. "And what about you, Indra, Head of the Windhi. Do you love this man? This Fortis?"

I looked down, focusing on the sprigs of grass in front of me so I did not have to look Roan in the eye. I had said the words to Asa only once, and had admitted my feelings to no one else since then, not even Mira. Saying them now, in front of the entire Mountari tribe, made it too real. I owed Roan the truth, though. I was asking a lot of him, and if I wanted him to trust Asa, I would have to put my trust in him as well.

After a beat, I tore my gaze from the ground and looked at Asa. He was watching me, waiting for me to answer, and his gaze, so steady and sure, gave me strength.

"I do love him," I said, still staring at Asa, and I had never been more certain of my feelings.

Roan sighed, breaking the spell Asa had on me, and I looked back at the Head to find his expression troubled. "This is a difficult thing you ask of me, Indra. More difficult than anything you have asked so far."

"I know," I said. "I would not ask if I did not believe Asa could be trusted. I have put everything I have in his hands, and he has never let me down. I know he is worthy of our trust."

"I believe you believe that," Roan replied, "but I cannot put my people in this kind of danger. Not without some proof we can rely on this man. If he fights the Sovereign with us, I will be willing to consider the matter more. But for now, I must tell you no. I cannot align my tribe with a Fortis. Not after everything they have done to our people." Roan stepped back, signaling that the discussion was over, and even though I could tell he was confident in his decision, there was real regret in his eyes. "I am sorry, Indra."

"I believe you are," I replied.

At my side Asa stood taller. "I will fight with you, and I will prove I can be trusted."

"I hope that is true." Roan's gaze moved from Asa and me. "For both your sakes."

Silence followed us out of the village, and my scalp prickled from the knowledge that the gazes of every member of the Mountari tribe were watching us. At my side, Mira was silent, but it would not last forever. She would have something to say about this.

She said nothing the whole way back, though, and when we reached the cave, she went inside alone. Asa and I had things to discuss, but I had no desire to revisit the argument with Emori or Linc. Not when my mind was already so troubled.

"I am sorry," I told Asa once we were alone. "I warned you it would not be easy."

"I'll prove to them that I can be trusted," he said. "I have to."

"I believe you can."

Asa reached out to me then, his fingers brushing the passage markings on my chin and setting my skin on fire. "You told me you loved me that night in my house, but I wasn't sure if you meant it."

My gaze moved to the ground, focusing once again on the sprigs of green poking through the long dead leaves dotting the forest floor. "I would not have said it if it was untrue."

Asa's hand dropped from my face. "Why does loving me make you turn away?"

"It feels wrong." I ventured a look up, but being so close to Asa while we talked about this tore my insides up, and it was only a beat before I was once again staring at the ground.

"Because of your husband?" he murmured, the question barely louder than a whisper on the wind.

"And because you are a Fortis and I am an Outlier. Because my tribe, even those who did not complain when you came to the cave today, will not accept it. We have never married outside our tribe, and you are—"

"The enemy," he said with a sigh.

"Yes," I whispered.

Asa exhaled, and only a moment later said, "What's your next move?"

I let out a deep breath as well, blowing the discomfort away and finally managing to lift my head. "I may have to sneak into the city. We need more information, and I have to find out what happened to Xandra."

Worry clouded Asa's vision. "How will you get in?"

"There is a back entrance, a tunnel behind the city."

"Behind the city?" His eyebrows furrowed. "Where the mirrors are?"

My back straightened as my heart beat faster. Asa knew about the mirrors? It made sense. He was a Fortis, and their village had been close to the walls, close to the lake. But did he know what they were?

"You know about the mirrors?" I asked. "What are they? What do they do?"

"I do," he said, nodding. "The mirrors collect sunlight, and the tower moves it to the city. It's how the Sovereign have electricity." Asa hesitated, and something in his expression made the hair on the back of my neck prickle. I had a strange sense that I was about to learn something new, something important. "There are people there, living in the tower. They maintain the panels in exchange for help from the Sovereign."

"What people?" My mind spun not only with the new information, but with thoughts of what it could mean. This could be the answer we had been looking for. "Who are they?"

Something in my excitement must have made Asa uncomfortable, because he took a step back and shook his head. "It doesn't matter."

He was wrong, though. Already a plan was forming in my head. This was the answer we had been looking for, the missing piece that would help us defeat the Sovereign.

"It does matter." Irritation coated my words, and I did not try to hold it in. "Going into the city is too risky right now, but if we take out their power, it will give us an advantage. We have to hit the tower next. We need to destroy the mirrors."

Asa's brown eyes widened, and for the first time since we met, he looked scared. "No, Indra. You can't. The people living there, they aren't like us. They're defenseless."

We had already had this conversation, and I may have given in then, but I would not this time. Not again. Not when Xandra was missing. Not when this would give us the advantage we had been looking for.

"I have heard that before, Asa, and I listened to you then, but I cannot this time. *This* is the only way. If we cut off the power to Sovereign City, they will be at our mercy. It will help us win the war."

I turned toward the cave, anxious to tell Mira what I had learned, but Asa blocked my way. "You can't do this, Indra. If you destroy the mirrors, the Sovereign will send the rest of the Fortis to the tower. They'll kill everyone there. Those people are only useful to the Sovereign because they need someone to watch the mirrors. Their blood will be on your hands."

Anger flared through me and without thinking, I shoved him. When my palms landed against his chest, it was like slamming them into the wall of the cave, but I managed to catch him by surprise. Asa stumbled back a few steps, freeing my way to the entrance, but I did not move. I was too angry.

"Do not tell me what I can and cannot do," I spit at him. "Those people may die if I do this, but it will mean my people live. That they will live freely for the first time in centuries! The sacrifice is worth it to me."

It was Asa's turn to be angry. "I can't support this. I won't."

He was so much taller than I was, but it did not stop me from moving closer, from lifting myself up on my toes so we were almost face to face. "You *just* swore you would find a way to convince the Huni and Mountari your people are trustworthy. *This* is it, Asa. *This* will convince them. If you fight with us, they will see you as an ally."

The anger faded from his eyes, but he did not back away. And I could tell just by looking at him that he never would.

"I can't," he said. "You once told me it was time to choose a side, and that's what I'm doing."

"You would stand against me?" The shock of it forced me to take a step back. I wanted to be angry. I wanted to scream at him, maybe push him again, but I was too stunned. After everything we had been through, I had not thought he would stand against me on anything.

"I have to stand with whoever's in the right, Indra. It's why I supported you before, why I fled my village and left my own people to die, but I won't do it this time. You're wrong. You'll know it when you get there and see the people. You'll understand then."

He took a step back, and the movement pushed my shock away, making room for anger once again. "What does this mean? Will you try to stop me, Asa?"

His face scrunched up, reminding me of someone who had just been bitten by one of the many bugs living in the wilds. "I'll do what I have to."

My hand went to my knife, and his gaze followed the movement, but he did not pull his own weapon. I needed to stop him from warning the people in the tower, only I could not. Emori had been right. My feelings for Asa were clouding my judgment, but I could do nothing about it now. I had gone too far, given him too much of myself.

"If you do this, the other tribes will never trust you. You and your people will be outsiders for the rest of your lives. Think about that, Asa. Then think about what you can gain if you work with us. If you march on the towers with us, the Huni and Mountari will let you in on our treaty, and you and your people can come here to live. In the caves." I wanted to tell him we could be together if that happened, but the words were impossible to get out in the light of what was about to happen. Just looking at him told me that he would not back down.

"I can't do what you ask of me, Indra. I'd do almost anything for you, almost anything to save my people, but this is impossible."

Pain pulsed through my heart as if it had been slashed in half by his words. My hand dropped to my side, and I looked away. "Go before someone else shows up. I cannot kill you, Asa, but others would not hesitate."

Out of the corner of my eye, I saw him nod once. He was still looking at me when he took a step back, and a fresh wave of pain pulsed through my heart. Still, I could not change his mind. The choice had been his to make, and now we were both going to have to live with it.

Twenty-Seven

MIRA WAS WAITING WHEN I STEPPED INTO THE cave. "Did Asa leave?"

"He did." I passed her, nodding for her to follow. We needed to speak, but in private. "Come with me. We have things to discuss."

It was unclear whether Mira thought I was referring to my confession of love for Asa or something else, but she followed with no other comment. Which I was grateful for. I would tell her everything, but first I needed to work it out in my head and accept what had happened. Asa had walked away from me. Again.

We reached my alcove, but my brain still had not acknowledged what was about to happen, and my heart was even more in denial. Even so, despite my feelings for Asa, my people had to come first, which meant destroying the mirrors. Without power, the Sovereign would be helpless, giving us the advantage once again. Even with the remaining Fortis on their side.

There were no lanterns in the city and few candles. The buildings were too close together for fires, and even the electroprods would eventually stop working since they had to be plugged in every night. We would take out the tower, wait a day, and then send a small party in through the tunnel after the sun had set. That would enable us to open the gates, letting our army into the city so we could take the Sovereign down once and for all.

"Tell me what is going through your head," Mira said when I did not speak. "Is it about Asa?"

"It is. You heard me say I love him, and it is true. I did not intend for it to happen, but it has. Only now, I know for sure we are not meant to be together."

"Indra—" Mira began.

"No. You must listen, then you will understand." She closed her mouth and nodded for me to go on. "Remember the mirrors we saw in the wastelands? Beyond the city?"

"I remember," she said.

"The mirrors are what give Sovereign City power. They collect the sunlight, and the tower converts it to electricity."

"Magic," Mira whispered, her eyes wide with wonder.

"No. It is technology from the old world," I said. "But if we destroy the mirrors, they will have nothing. It will give us the advantage once again."

"Then we do it." Her blond hair swished when she nodded. "We must, Indra."

"I know. Except Asa did not agree. He said if we do this, the Sovereign will kill everyone living in the tower, and he could not let that happen. I am afraid he will take his tribe there and try to stop us."

Mira's brows furrowed over her blue eyes, pulling her passage markings together. "If he does this, the other Heads will never trust him."

"I know." When I looked down, my gaze landed on the bed where only last night Asa and I had lain together. "I told him, but he refused to take my side in this."

Saying the words to someone else, even Mira who knew firsthand that Asa was a good man, weighed my heart down even more. Everyone would see him as the enemy now, and no matter my feelings for him, I would be forced to do the same.

"We need to go there." Mira's expression was fierce, like that of an animal about to attack. Or that of a warrior. "Soon. Tonight. Before he has time to plan a defense."

"I am afraid we will be too late regardless. I should have stopped him from leaving, but I could not." I let out a deep sigh. "Emori was right. I have let my feelings for him cloud my judgment, and now it has put us in danger."

"There are more of us, Indra," Mira said firmly. "We can beat Asa and his people."

"I know," I whispered as pain squeezed my heart. She was right, but I also knew what this could mean. There was no protecting Asa from this, no convincing the other Outliers not to kill him. Not after this betrayal.

Mira's fiery expression softened. "But you are afraid of what will happen to him."

"He will be a traitor in the eyes of the other tribes. They will not let him live."

"He had a choice to make, Indra, and he has. Now you must make a choice. Will you lead us or will you stay behind? Either way, we must march on the mirrors tonight."

This time when pain throbbed through me, it was from guilt. Not from what I was about to do, but because I had never considered turning my back on my people. I loved Asa. Maybe even as much as I had loved Bodhi, which was not an easy thing to admit even to myself. But everything I had done since my husband's death had been for my people, and no matter my feelings, I could not stop.

"The Outliers are my priority, no matter how difficult the consequences will be. I will go." I turned to leave the alcove. "The sooner we meet with the other Heads, the better."

"Will you tell them what Asa is doing?" Mira asked, stopping me in my tracks. "If you do not, they will be at a disadvantage."

I closed my eyes, fighting against the anguish over the decision that now faced me. "If I do, they will think him a traitor even if he is not there."

Mira said nothing.

I exhaled, but it did not help. My heart had turned to a boulder in my chest. "I will tell them to expect resistance. That is the best I can do. Asa said the people living there are defenseless, and he has fewer than fifty people who can fight with him. We will be okay." I opened my eyes and turned to face Mira, anticipating judgment or disappointment. When I met her gaze, only sadness greeted me.

"We will figure out a way to fix this," she said.

"There is no way to fix it. Not if he cannot stand with us." I turned and headed out of my alcove.

I HAD SEEN THE MIRRORS TWICE BEFORE, BUT BOTH times had been from far away, and the sunlight had made them blinding. In the darkness with the moon shining down on them, they were utterly brilliant. I had worked in the city for years, but had never known where the Sovereign got their power, and other than the few Outliers who had come out through the back tunnel, no one had known about these mirrors. It was impossible to know for sure since Xandra was not with us, but I assumed she and people like her had never told anyone about the tower out of the need to protect the location of the tunnel.

The group was smaller tonight, but we still had over a hundred men and women traveling across the wastelands toward the mirrors. Asa had said he had fifty people with him, but that his group consisted of mostly women and children. Who lived in the tower was a mystery, one that would very soon be solved, but I was confident that no matter what their numbers were, we could take them. We all carried weapons, but our main goal when we reached the mirrors was to smash them. Hopefully, we would be able to achieve that without bloodshed.

My eyes swept the area as I moved, looking for any sign that Asa and his people were nearby. There was nothing. No movement, no shadows, and no sounds greeted my ears other than the howl of the wind. It was possible he had decided against trying to stop us. That he had allowed his feelings for me to get in the way of duty just as I had.

Then we reached the mirrors, and the shadows moved. Figures emerged from the blackness, hulking even in the dark night, and I raised my bow. I hesitated, though. All I could think about was Asa and if he was one of the dark forms in front of me. All I could imagine as I ran beside the men and women from the wilds was how devastated I would be if my arrow were to pierce the man I cared so much about. It made it impossible to strike.

More figures moved through the darkness, their large frames colliding with the smaller ones of the Outliers, and the clang of metal on metal filled the air. The grunt of people hitting the ground and the scuffling of feet followed, but I still had not released my arrow. Instead I moved cautiously through the dark night, between the mirrors as the people around me went down. Outlier after Outlier.

A figure appeared in front of me, large and familiar even in the surrounding blackness. I flipped my bow around and swung it at his head, striking the figure in the shoulder. He let out a grunt, and the familiar sound made me freeze. Then he had my bow and he was jerking me forward, making me his prisoner.

The bow disappeared, and his arms went around me. He twisted me until my back was to his chest, pressed tightly against his giant body. I gasped when the cold point of a knife pricked at my neck. All around us people struggled and fought, but in the light of the moon, it was clear Asa's friends were winning. There were more of them than I had realized, more than I had ever imagined. But there was no blood. My people were on the ground, held down by larger men and women so they could not move, but it did not seem like anyone was injured. The Outliers were still struggling under the hulking frames, reminding me just how capable the Fortis were, but they were not hurt.

"Stop," Asa bellowed, his face close enough to mine that his voice echoed through my head.

The Outliers still left standing came to a stop in staggers as those on the ground eased in their struggles, but they did not stop completely. I could not focus on the faces of my people, making it impossible to figure out who was up and who was down, not with the knife at my neck, held there by a man who claimed to love me.

"Fortis!" Emori's scream drew my attention her way.

She was up and angry, her sword in her hand as she rushed forward. I wanted to reach out and stop her, to shout for her to stay back, but I could not move with the blade pressed to my neck.

Thankfully, Mira grabbed Emori's arm when she rushed by. The other woman reeled around, her expression hard and her sword still up.

Mira did not blink. "Stand down."

Emori jerked her arm from Mira's grasp and spun to face me. In the moonlight her eyes shone like the fire that burned in the underworld. "I told you he could not be trusted."

Roan was on the ground, held down by a Fortis man twice his size, his face twisted in my direction. He was looking at Asa, though, at the knife held to my neck, and the expression in his eyes reminded me of the way Greer had looked at me in Saffron's house. They were full of fire and hate.

"Stand down," Roan called to Emori, his voice strained from the knee in his back. Then he focused on Asa. "Only a few hours ago you claimed to be on our side, Fortis. Tell me the meaning of this."

"I can't let this happen." Asa took a step back, pulling me with him. "And soon you will see why." He stepped back again, and this time the blade was pressed harder against my neck, forcing a cry out of me. "Don't move."

Asa turned, taking me with him. He tightened his grip before he started walking, and my feet left the ground as he carried me toward the tower. The knife was still up, but the point was no longer touching my skin. He moved faster, and the desert air seemed especially cool against my hot skin.

Anger pulsed through me, but also shame. Not only had Asa proven he was not trustworthy, but he had also humiliated me in front of my people.

He entered the tower through the only door, dragging me into thick darkness. The air was musty and damp, somehow defying the dryness of the earth. Two steps in, and my feet were once again on the ground. The knife was no longer anywhere near my neck, and I wiggled from his grasp before shoving away from him.

I stumbled forward when he released me but caught myself, then spun to face him. "How dare you?" I spit in his direction.

"You knew I wouldn't hurt you."

He was right, although I refused to acknowledge it. Outside, with the knife held to my throat, I had not been afraid he would kill me, only that someone—especially Emori—would kill *him*.

Something scuffled to my right, and I turned just as Roan was shoved inside. He stumbled forward a few steps before turning to the man who had dragged him in, only there was nothing he could do. The man in front of him was huge, taking up the entire doorway, and he was also armed while Roan had nothing.

The Mountari Head spun to face Asa. "What is the meaning of this?"

"You wanted me to show you why." Asa waved toward the tower at his back. "Follow me and you'll find out."

He turned away from Roan, not looking at me as he moved deeper into the black depths of the building. It was silent other than his footsteps, and no more than a few shapes were discernable through the oppressive darkness. Doorways, a chair of some kind. That was it.

I watched Asa for a beat before glancing back the way we had come. Roan had not moved, and Asa's man still stood in the doorway. Something about his red hair tickled a memory, but I could not grasp it with so much else happening. His frame seemed to take up the entire opening, but there was nothing threatening about him.

"Follow him," the man said, nodding in the direction Asa had just gone.

I did not follow Asa because I had been ordered to, but because I knew if he had gone to this extreme, something big must have been happening inside this building. He had killed none of us, and if any of the Outliers had been injured in the skirmish, it was no doubt by accident. Asa had come here to stop us, but also to show us why.

Still, I refused to let him off the hook so easily. "You took a real risk doing this."

Footsteps thudded at my back, telling me Roan was coming as well, but the Head said nothing.

Asa glanced over his shoulder, his eyebrows raised. "You're going to talk to me about risks?"

"You have a valid point," I reluctantly conceded.

He turned into a doorway, and I followed, only to find a staircase that wound up into the darkness of the tower.

"Do the people living here not have electricity?" I asked.

"Only what they need to keep the tower and mirrors going. The Sovereign don't give them lights."

"Why do they not demand it?" Roan's voice dripped with rage. "It seems like these people hold a lot of power in their hands. Why are they not using it?"

Asa looked past me, toward the other man, but in the darkness of the stairwell, I could not make out his expression. "They're just trying to survive."

He said nothing else before continuing up, and even though it was too dark to see Roan, his footfalls echoed through the stairwell as he followed Asa and me.

We went only as far as the first landing before Asa stopped. "You should prepare yourself."

"What do you mean?" My hand moved to my hip as if going for a weapon even though I had none. "Are they dangerous?"

"No." Asa was invisible in the darkness, but I could not miss the sadness in his voice. "It's just that it can be shocking to see."

He pushed the door open, and a dim light penetrated the stairwell. Before I could utter a word, Asa stepped inside.

My heart was pounding at Asa's words and I did not move. The room was dimly lit, making it difficult to see much from where I was. Shocking, he had said. What did that mean?

"It is a trap," Roan hissed.

Asa's soft voice, whispering reassurances that everything was going to be okay, floated from the room.

"No." I took a deep breath, hoping to calm my pounding heart. "You do not know Asa, but I do. He would not put my life in danger."

"You still think that after he held a knife to your neck?"

"Yes," I said calmly, "I do."

Then I stepped inside.

Twenty-Eight

I WAS GREETED BY THE STINK OF TOO MANY BODIES living together. Sweat, dirt, human filth, the smells brought to mind the Fortis village and how my nose used to wrinkle in disgust when Mira and I walked through it.

A handful of lanterns were spread throughout, casting shadows across the people and playing tricks on my eyes. At least I thought I was seeing things. I had to be, because it looked as if the girl in front of me had an extra arm, and just past her sat a man who appeared to have a horn growing out of his forehead, and beyond that I spied a growth protruding from a young boy's neck.

I blinked, but my eyes did not clear. Instead, they focused on other things that made no sense. Two girls who seemed to be attached at the hip, a boy with no legs, a woman without a neck. It was like this with everyone, all of them having some kind of deformity similar to the few I had seen in the Huni village.

"What is this?" Roan said from behind me.

"This is where the untouchables go," Asa replied.

I pulled my gaze from the people in front of me and focused on him. "I do not understand what that means."

"It happens a lot," he said. "Babies both in the city and in our village are born with something wrong. Extra limbs, or hands or feet that have shriveled up like fruit dried in the sun. When it happens in the city, they are turned out, left by their families to die. When it happens—happened—in our village, they came here to live. It's been going on for centuries, and this building is full of them."

"This happens often?" I asked, looking around again.

This level was full and the tower was high, ten stories, perhaps. If every floor housed this many people, there must have been hundreds of them living here. Hundreds of people who had been born with something wrong, and because of it they had been cast aside. Their living conditions were even worse than ours, and their existence could not have been anything short of miserable.

"Every fifth baby," Asa whispered. "At least that's what the healer told my mother when she gave birth to an untouchable."

I spun to face him. "Your mother?"

Asa's eyes focused on someone behind me. "This is my sister, Elora."

The girl with the extra arm was only a couple feet away when I turned. She was in her late teens and probably a good ten years younger than her brother, but they resembled one another a lot. She was broad and tall like all the Fortis, and her skin was the same shade of brown as Asa's, her eyes just as big and beautiful. When she smiled, she reminded me so much of her brother that it brought tears to my eyes. Everything about her was perfect except the extra arm protruding from her right side. It was much smaller than the others, but still looked functional.

"Asa has told me about you," Elora said.

"This is why I stopped you from killing these people." My attention was drawn back to Asa. "They are innocent, Indra. The Sovereign have rejected them and made them feel like they should stay hidden here because of how they were born. Killing them would accomplish nothing."

Shame filled me. I should have listened to him. Should have given him more of a chance to explain. I should have known that if Asa told me not to come here, he had a good reason.

"I am so sorry." The urge to go to him, to wrap my arms around him and kiss him and tell him how wrong I had been, pulsed through me, but shame forced me to keep my distance. "I should have listened."

"This is why I'm not like the other Fortis. I saw my sister when she was born, saw that she was just a baby with a small defect, and I wanted her to stay. But the village was superstitious. They believed allowing the untouchables to stay would only cause more to be born, my parents included, so they sent Elora here."

I looked back at the girl, the sister Asa had risked everything to protect, and the expression in her brown eyes squeezed at my heart. "How old was she?"

"A day old. I brought her here myself so I'd know she made it okay, and even though my parents didn't want me to, I visited her as much as I could. I'm not alone in this. The other people who fled the village with me, most of them have family here, too. Children, brothers, and sisters. I told you we weren't all the same."

"I know. I should have listened."

My gaze moved over the pathetic people living here. Most were like Elora. Most could have had led completely normal lives had they not been sent away. But they had, and because of it they lived in horrible conditions. They were hidden away from the world and totally dependent on the Sovereign. Asa had been right. Bringing the fury of the city down on these people would have been wrong. They deserved to be liberated just as much as we did.

"We will not attack you," Roan called out, drawing my attention to him.

So focused on Asa and his sister, I had completely forgotten the Mountari Head was here. Sorrow shimmered in Roan's eyes, but there was fury, too. Only, it was not directed at Asa anymore, but at the Sovereign.

"We will not destroy the mirrors and send the Sovereign down on you," Roan continued. "We will find another way, and once the Sovereign are no longer in charge, you will be free to leave this tower."

My gaze moved to Elora, and I gave her a small smile. "You will be able to return to your family."

Asa's hand touched my back, and the contact was more welcome than I ever would have guessed. After our earlier confrontation, I had worried there might never be any intimacy between us again. Knowing we could still find common ground was a relief even though some of the other Outliers might not be able to forgive Asa for the part he had played today. More than that, it made me more certain of things. For years, Asa and I had been traveling down two separate paths that were destined to cross. Sooner rather than later, if I had anything to say about it.

But that would have to wait. With our promise delivered, it was imperative that we returned to our people. They needed to be told this had not been an act of hostility, but an act of love.

"We must go," Roan said, as if reading my mind.

He was already walking to the door when I turned to Asa. "We need to explain to the others what is happening here before someone gets hurt."

As he so often did, Asa nodded in response. He gave his sister a goodbye hug, and then together we joined Roan at the stairs so we could head down together.

"It isn't just the Fortis who have children like these," Asa said when we were halfway to the first floor. "It's the Sovereign, too. Don't the Outliers have this problem?"

"No," Roan replied. "We have never had this happen in our village."

I opened my mouth to agree, but paused. What about the children in the Huni village? Could these two things be connected?

"We do not have babies born like this, but the Huni do." I stopped as realization dawned on me. "They live closer to the wastelands than the rest of us. Maybe that is why this happens. Maybe it is because you live in the wastelands.

Nothing will grow there, and the earth has turned to dust. Maybe it is poison. Our water comes from the wilds, closer to the source, which I now know is in the caves where we live. From there it runs through the valley and to the lake, half of which is in the wastelands. Maybe the water there is as poisoned as the land is."

"It is possible," Roan said.

"The reason doesn't matter to me," Asa replied. "I just want to keep my sister safe."

"We will make sure it happens," I said, answering for both Roan and myself.

People stirred when we stepped outside. The Outliers were no longer held down by the Fortis, but instead sitting on the ground, waiting for our return. Asa's people stood over them with swords and spears, but their stance was defensive. Now that I was able to look them over better, I noticed the ones closest to the tower were untouchables. They kept mostly to the shadows, but a few small defects were visible among them. Still, though, they were large and impressive like all the Fortis, and no doubt could have contributed in so many ways had they not been forced to live in hiding.

A few of Roan's people moved as if to go for their weapons, but he lifted his hands as a signal for them to stop. "It is okay," he called. "There is no need for weapons. We will not be attacking the tower or the mirrors."

"What?" Outrage rang in Emori's voice as she got to her feet, shoving her way by the Fortis man in front of her despite her lack of weapons. "You cannot do this. This is how we will win."

I stood tall and met her gaze. "The people here are not a threat, and they need our protection. We must find another way."

All around me, the Fortis and untouchables relaxed. They lowered their weapons and moved as the Outliers began climbing to their feet. Emori was still fuming, but it was something I was almost used to.

At her side, Mira only looked curious. "Who is it?"

"They are called untouchables." I searched for Ontari in the crowd. "Like the children I saw in your village, these people have been born with deformities. Only they have been cast aside because of it."

Roan spoke up next, telling them about the people living in the building who had nowhere else to go and no chance of surviving if we destroyed the mirrors. Asa stopped at my side, and I glanced back at the tower to find the other Fortis still present while the untouchables had retreated into the building.

"Asa did not come here intending to kill us—" I looked to Ontari, knowing she, too, would have to concede in order for us to walk away now. "—but only to stop us from making a mistake we would not have been able to recover from. He did what he thought was best. Would you be able to condemn helpless people to death?"

"No," the Huni Head said. "When children like this are born in our village, we teach them to be strong. Many grow up to become great hunters despite their disadvantages."

Asa visibly relaxed at my side. "Thank you."

"This is not over, Fortis." Roan turned on Asa. "You have still risen up against us only hours after pledging to stand with us."

"His sister is here. You saw it with your own eyes." I stepped between Roan and Asa. "I would not listen to him. This is my fault. I pushed him to make this decision."

Ontari lifted her hand. "We will discuss this tomorrow at the pond. For now, we must retreat before we are spotted by anyone in the city. We have no way of knowing if they are watching for us."

I lowered my head. "You are right."

Roan and Ontari turned away. They called for their people to follow, and the Outliers standing around the mirrors began to retreat, some of my own people with them. Mira stayed behind, though, and Anja as well. My sister stared up at Asa as if trying to figure out who he was, and it occurred to me that I had not yet confessed my feelings to her. It was partly because I was still uncomfortable with the sentiment, but also had a lot to do with Bodhi. He had been like a brother to Anja, and I worried she would not accept Asa.

The red haired man came to stand at Asa's side, and once again, the feeling that I had seen him before came over me. It was not until he slipped his sword into a sheath on his back that I remembered.

"I saw you once." I thought back to the first day Bodhi had taken me out into the woods. "I was hunting with my husband, and you killed the forest cat I was about to shoot. We hid so you would not see us."

The man's eyebrows lifted, and he gave me a smile that was partly hidden under his beard. "Then I'm lucky you hid instead of killing me."

Heat flared across my cheeks. If I had come across him only a few months later, I would not have hidden, but would have instead shot him and not thought twice about it. I would have assumed he was just like the others—a Fortis man who wanted nothing more than to oppress and hurt my people.

"This is Nyko," Asa said. "He's a friend."

Shame made it impossible to meet the large man's gaze. "I am sorry."

"There's nothing to be sorry about," Nyko grunted. "I'm not a fool. The Fortis were bastards, and I know what they've done to your people. If you had shot me that day, my blood would've been on their hands, not yours."

I peered at him through lowered lashes, finding it impossible to lift my head despite his words. "How can you be so forgiving?"

"Because," his grin widened, showing off his white teeth, "I'm not a bastard."

"Indra," Mira called to me. "We need to leave."

"Yes." I glanced back to find the remaining Outliers waiting for me, but I did not move to join them. Instead, I looked back at Asa. "Where will your people go?"

"We'll sleep here tonight and head into the forest tomorrow. We can't stay here permanently or we'll be discovered." He looked toward the tower as if uncertain, then said, "One night shouldn't be too risky."

"You will come to the caves."

Asa's brown eyes flicked back to me. "The other Heads won't allow me into your treaty after this."

"I will make them."

He opened his mouth to protest, but I cut him off when I pressed my lips to his, and only a beat passed before his hands were on my hips. We had never kissed in front of anyone else before, but after today, I no longer cared. Like my people and like the untouchables, I had decided I needed to stand up for Asa and the other Fortis who had chosen to stand with us.

Twenty-Nine

THE NEXT DAY, WHEN THE SUN WAS DIRECTLY overhead, Mira and I met the other Heads in the clearing. Ontari brought Arkin as usual, while Roan had Zuri accompany him. Asa brought Nyko.

While he needed the backup, I could not help wishing Asa had chosen someone less imposing. Nyko was young, thirty at the most, and he fit the physical description of a Fortis guard perfectly, even more so than Asa. His height made even Arkin seem short, and he was broad, with arms like tree trunks. Despite his size, the softness in his blue eyes told me he was as trustworthy as Asa, but I was an exception when it came to Outliers. Most would only see a Fortis man when they looked at Nyko.

"I ask again that you allow Asa's people to join us," I began once we were all assembled. "They have proven they are not like the rest of their people, and they need our help.

Not only that, but they will also be an asset when we go into the city."

"He has betrayed us." The way Ontari shook her head made it seem like she was more sad than angry. "He asked to join our treaty, but then took his tribe out into the wastelands to stop us."

"He did not attack," I pointed out. "He only wanted to show me why we could not destroy the mirrors. Who he was protecting."

"Ontari is right." Roan's voice came out much harder than I had expected, considering how he had acted in the tower. "Asa did not attack us, but he would have if necessary."

"Last night you said you agreed with him. Have you changed your minds?" I looked back and forth between the two other Heads. "Would you have attacked the people in that tower?"

"That is not the point," Roan said.

"It is to Asa."

"Enough, Indra." Ontari lifted her hand. "We know you care for this Fortis, but he has proven he is not on our side. Not completely. We cannot bring his people into our alliance knowing he might take sides against us again."

Behind me, Asa and Nyko stood quietly, waiting to learn their fate. Going into this meeting, we had suspected the other Heads would not be as forgiving as I was, but I refused to let it go without a fight. It was not in my nature to do nothing. Not anymore.

"He would never side with the Sovereign," I said firmly.

It was Roan's turn to stop me, only he did it with his sharp gaze. Even though I was grateful the admiration had disappeared from his eyes, there was nothing welcome about this look. "It has been decided, Indra. We cannot trust the Fortis, and we are wasting time arguing about it. We need a new plan. We need to figure out how we will get into the city."

"I'll go," Asa said, speaking for the first time.

The other Heads looked his way, but they did not speak.

"Asa—" I could barely hear my own voice over the thumping of my heart. "It is too dangerous. Xandra and Bowie have not returned, and we have no idea what is happening in there."

He focused his gaze on Roan, avoiding looking at me. "I understand you don't trust me and accept that you won't allow my tribe into your alliance, but it makes sense for me to go. There are no more Outliers in the city, and sending someone from one of your tribes will only risk them getting caught. Inside those walls there are only Sovereign and Fortis. I can get in and move around without raising too much suspicion."

"He is right," Ontari said.

"Yes," Roan agreed with a sigh. "Only I still do not know if we can trust this man."

Asa stepped forward until he was standing at my side. "You may not trust me, but you have to know I'd never do something to put Indra at risk."

Ontari leveled her sharp gaze on him. "Only last night you held a knife to her throat."

"That's true," Asa replied, his voice as even as before, "but it was the only way to get you to listen. I wouldn't have hurt her. She knew it, and I think you did, too."

Roan frowned and looked me over. Despite the terror rushing through me at the thought of Asa heading into the city, I held my head high as I met the Mountari Head's gaze. I had no idea how I wanted this discussion to go. If Asa went into the city, it could end in disaster, but his logic was sound, and it could be the only way to get the other Heads to trust him.

A beat of silence passed before Roan nodded, but before he said anything, he turned to face Ontari. "Do you accept these terms?"

"If he is untrustworthy, he will give us away to the Sovereign," she said.

"The Sovereign already know we are out here. They already know we want them dead," Roan replied. "We have no plan yet, which means there is nothing to risk by him going inside. It is only his life on the line."

I swallowed, trying to hold my emotion in until later.

"That is true." Ontari looked at Asa, and then me. She pressed her lips together before nodding once. "I accept this plan."

"As do I," Roan said.

At my side, Asa exhaled. His relief was palpable, but I could not be as grateful, not when I thought about how Xandra had already disappeared. Not when I thought about Asa going into the city where, if he were discovered, he would most certainly be seen as a traitor.

"Nyko will go with me," he said.

"And you know where this tunnel is?" Ontari asked him.

Asa's gaze moved to me, and my heart beat faster. "No."

"We will lead him there," Mira said before I was able to find words.

"Very good." Ontari nodded, as did Roan, and then she said, "We will head there tonight. Our whole army. After the Fortis men go inside, we will camp in the valley so we are ready." Her eyes focused on Asa. "You will open the gates."

"What if I can't?" he asked.

"If you cannot, you will come back through the tunnel and tell us what's happening inside the city."

Asa's only response was to nod.

"Until then," Roan said, "we will prepare our armies."

"It is a good plan." Mira's words were firm, but the worry in her blue eyes when she looked my way matched the emotion swirling through me.

"We will leave before sunset." How I managed to get a single word out, I did not know, but somehow I did. The others needed to know I was with them, that despite my feelings for Asa and my fear that something might happen to him, I would not back down from this fight. "The rest of you can follow behind."

"We will leave shortly after the sun has set," Roan said.

"After the sun has set," Ontari agreed.

The other Heads took their leave, and the four of us did as well. The walk back to the caves was silent. Mira and Nyko walked ahead of us while Asa kept stride with me. The dread and hope swirling through me made for a nauseous combination, and I found it impossible to talk. My thoughts, too, were jumbled, and it was not until Mira stopped outside the cave that I remembered Nyko was with us, and that I had promised Asa's people shelter.

"What now?" Mira asked.

At her side, the man with the brilliant red hair shuffled his feet like he was unsure of how to handle himself in this situation. The cave entrance was covered, and having never been here before, he must have been wondering what we were doing. Perhaps he even wondered if he had walked into a trap and was about to be killed by a group of Outliers.

I turned to Asa, lifting my head so I could look him in the eye. "I promised your people sanctuary."

"I don't want you to do anything that might get you in trouble with your people."

I took his hand, my eyes still on his. "You are my people."

Asa looked down at our entwined fingers, and I followed his gaze, once again marveling at the contrast in both our size and the color of our skin. The summer sun had made me tanner than usual, but I was still pale compared to the man in front of me.

After a moment, Asa said, "You would take me as one of your people?"

"If it is what you desire," I whispered.

When he lifted his eyes, his brows were raised, but he said nothing. He was waiting for me to take the next step, the one I had told him I could not take. Things had shifted since then, and now everything was different. Again.

"I will marry you, Asa." My voice came out amazingly calm and sure, and there was not an ounce of doubt inside me. "Not only will it unite our tribes, but it will also make the other Heads see how much I trust you."

"And what about your people?"

I looked toward Mira, who stood silently next to the cave opening, and she nodded once. Her approval meant more to me than I could say, but I would have made this decision regardless. At Mira's side, Nyko wore an expression of amusement, but there was relief and even understanding in his eyes as well.

I turned my gaze back to Asa, and his grip tightened on my hand. "By now my people should know I would never do anything to risk my tribe. Not after everything we have been through."

Asa smiled, and it was such a rare sight that it caused a flutter in my chest. "Then we get married?"

"We get married," I said, returning his smile.

I KNELT AT ASA'S SIDE, MY BACK TO THE FIRE. OUR two tribes stood in front of us, the remaining Fortis men, women, and children, and the remnants of what had once been the Winta tribe. Not only would this unite us, but it would also heal a part of me that I had been certain was damaged beyond repair.

For the most part, my people were not upset by the union—it had even seemed as if a few of them had expected it—but they were still reluctant to get too close to the Fortis. Most were women and children, and I had to hope the memories of how vulnerable we had felt when our own tribe was first wiped out would help them accept these new members. It would not always be easy, but nothing we had done since our village was attacked had been. And yet we had come so far. Thrived, even. We could do this as well.

My future husband's hand was wrapped around mine when Anja stopped in front of us, setting the bowl of ink on the ground before kneeling. We had spoken at great length about what was to come next, if we would continue our tradition of passage markings, or if we should start anew. The markings I wore on my face were a source of pride for me, and the idea of leaving the tradition behind did not sit well. But Asa was not Winta or Windhi, he was not even an Outlier, and while his people had decorated their bodies with markings much like our own, they had been for show and not to commemorate moments in their lives. It was for this reason that we had decided to alter our traditions, but only slightly.

Anja lifted the tebori as I pushed the fur covering my chest aside, revealing my collarbone. My sister tapped the tool against my skin, over and over again, and each prick against my flesh reminded me of a moment Asa and I had shared. How he had saved me, stood up for me, and watched over me. How he had come to see me in the forest, and how I had given myself to him. Not just my body either, but my heart. He had helped me heal, and I hoped to do the same for him. Together we would be stronger, just as our tribe would be.

When Anja finished with my new marking, she rubbed the dye into my skin before turning to my husband. He was naked from the waist up, showing off his chest and arms, both of which were crisscrossed with lines. Anja did not put

Asa's marking in the same place she had put mine, but instead placed it on his bicep, between a few other lines.

I watched as my sister began tapping the tool against his skin, practically holding my breath until she had finished. Then she rubbed the dye into it just as she had with me, using a piece of fur to wipe it clean so I was able to get my first glimpse of the marking we shared. It was an arrow. No bigger than my little finger, thin and delicate, it had a sharp point at one end and wispy feathers at the other.

"You are now one," she said as she stood.

Asa and I stood as well, our hands still joined as we faced our new tribe together.

"This is a new beginning for us," I said, my voice bouncing off the walls of the cave and coming back to greet me. "We have had many new beginnings since the Winta were wiped out, but this is the one that will define us. Will we be as narrow-minded as our enemies?" I looked around the room, taking the time to focus on my people. "Or will we prove we are better by embracing those who are different than us?"

Around the room, people nodded or shifted, or even looked down. No matter how they reacted, I could tell they were thinking my words through. I only prayed the people standing in front of me would be able to understand what the words meant.

As I turned away, Emori's eye caught mine. No one had attempted to dispute my marriage, and only a few people had shown displeasure in it, but it had come as no surprise that she and Linc were the biggest dissenters. I had expected it, but the anger in her gaze acted as a reminder to keep an eye on her. She would not evolve to fit our tribe, but she would never consider leaving us to join the Trelite. Emori would not make it in a tribe that did not validate her, but she would not be able to make it here either.

I did not want to waste time worrying about it now, though, so I pulled my new husband past her and toward my alcove. Soon Asa would be leaving, heading into the city where he would risk his life, and I wanted to be alone with him before we had to say goodbye.

Alone in our alcove, we undressed one another in silence. The man before me seemed imposing in size, but the look in his eyes told me who he really was. He was gentle and kind, and loving and brave, and it was all those things that had captured my attention back when Bodhi was still alive, and then my heart later when I when I been certain I would never love again.

When he wrapped his arms around me, I kissed him with more force than I ever had before. In no time at all we found ourselves on the ground, which was much softer than it had been due to the things we had scavenged from the Fortis village. Asa rolled me onto my back, his body on top of mine, and I sank into the soft cushion.

"I've wanted you to be mine for so long," he said.

"I have been yours for a while now."

"Not like this." Asa's eyes moved over me, down my chest, between my breasts and to my stomach, and his hand followed. "Before, I had no real right to touch you." He paused and pressed his lips to my collarbone, right over the arrow. "To kiss you. But I do now."

"You had every right," I told him, "because I wanted you to touch me. I wanted you. I have wanted you for so long, much longer than I allowed myself to accept. And now you are leaving me."

"Not forever."

I had to whisper because my throat felt as if it were locked in the grip of a Fortis soldier. "For long enough."

Asa leaned down, and his mouth covered mine. I wrapped my arms around him, and then my legs. We kissed, enveloped in one another's embrace as our bodies moved together.

A tear slid down my cheek when I thought about saying goodbye. "Do not leave me," I whispered against his neck, thinking of another time I had said those words and how it had turned out. "Please."

"I'll never leave you," he lied. Just as Bodhi had.

Thirty

WE LEFT BEFORE SUNSET AS PLANNED, MIRA, ASA, Nyko, and I. The four of us did not speak, and to our right the Lygan Cliffs were just as silent. Almost like the beasts knew we had much bigger things to worry about.

Our army would not be far behind, the three Outlier tribes and Asa's people, now part of the Windhi tribe. It was something I had not yet told the other Heads, and something I might pay dearly for, but I could not regret what I had done. I had made the decision to be true to myself when I decided to form a new tribe, and this was no different. I loved Asa, but more importantly, I knew him, and I knew he was trustworthy.

We did not pause until we had reached the end of the valley. Here the cliffs had died away, and in their wake the ruins of the Fortis village sat, their remains dark against the brown dirt of the wastelands. I had expected the grief radiating off Asa and Nyko, but not the shame that squeezed my heart. I had done what was necessary, but the necessity of it did not alleviate my sorrow at the lives I had taken. Not completely. Now all I could do was hope the guilt did not follow me into the afterlife and drag me down to the underworld where I would burn for eternity next to the very people I had killed.

The break in our journey was a quick one, just long enough to make sure nothing was moving. Wind whipped across the ruins and blew ash into the air, grizzards cawed in protest at the disturbance, and I spied a few marsoapians in the distance, but otherwise, the landscape was still.

"It's clear," Asa said.

He grabbed my hand as he started walking, moving faster than before like he was in a hurry to get to our destination. But as we reached the wall of the city and the ruins of his home faded from sight, he slowed, and I realized he had only been trying to run from his ghosts. Like me, he carried the blame of what had happened on his shoulders. He could have warned them, could have saved hundreds of lives, but he had chosen not to.

Behind us, Mira and Nyko were quiet. In the distance, the setting sun reflected off the mirrors, and beyond that the wastelands stretched out until they faded into nothingness, and I found myself wondering if anything existed beyond our world. If Bodhi and I had left the way he had wanted to, would we have found another place, or would we have died in the wastelands? Were we all that was left in this world?

"What do you think is out there?" I asked Asa, nodding toward the horizon where the sun sat, hovering just above the wastelands.

"In the desert?" I nodded, and he shook his head. "I don't know. Nothing."

"Do you think it is possible that somewhere beyond this place there are other people?"

"Yes," he said thoughtfully. "But far away. In Saffron's library there are maps of what the old world looked like. It was massive, and there were great bodies of water separating other stretches of land. There have to be other people who, like us, descend from survivors of the cataclysm, but they're far away. Too far for us to reach."

I supposed he was right. If someone else existed, we surely would have seen them by now.

We stopped when we reached the rocks that sheltered the tunnel, and Asa's gaze moved from the wall surrounding the city to the tower where his sister lived, and then to me.

"If I don't come back, you'll watch out for her?"

Once again, it felt as if someone was choking me, and I was forced to swallow before I could talk. "You will come back."

"I'll do everything in my power to get back to you."

He reached out and grabbed me by the hips, pulling me against him. When he leaned down, I closed my eyes, concentrating on his warmth and size as his mouth closed over mine. My heart pounded harder, and I found myself grabbing hold of his jacket, clutching it like I was afraid if I did not hold on tight enough, he would be swept away by the breeze blowing across the wastelands. I lifted myself up on my toes, moving closer to him. Not wanting to let him go. Ever.

But it was over too soon, and then he was pulling back. Mira had already removed the tunnel's cover, and Nyko was descending. His red hair disappeared into the darkness, and Asa extracted himself from my grasp. I did not want to let him go, and I had to force my hands to relax.

Mira was at my side before Asa had climbed over the rocks, her arm around me as together we watched him move to the opening. He looked up, his eyes holding mine, and I remembered that first day I noticed him in Saffron's house. How I had stumbled, and he had almost reached out to catch me. How I had assumed he was a brute like all the other men and women in his village. It seemed impossible that we were those same people. So much time had passed and so many things had changed that I almost could not remember what it had felt like to be that meek girl.

"I love you," he said.

I swallowed. "I love you."

Asa nodded, and my heart swelled at the familiar gesture, and then he began to climb down. I did not move, not even after he had disappeared into the darkness of the tunnel. It felt like I was about to be a widow again, and the pain of it made my legs wobble.

"He will be okay," Mira said.

"There are no guarantees."

She turned to face me. "He would destroy the whole city by himself before he allowed the Sovereign to keep him from getting back to you."

"Let us hope it does not come to that."

WE HAD NOT BEEN IN THE VALLEY LONG BEFORE WE spotted the army in the distance, and my back stiffened at the sight of Roan and Ontari. With my focus on Asa, I had nearly forgotten what I was about to face. The other Heads had declared Asa was not to be trusted, yet I had aligned myself with him anyway. The confrontation was not going to be a pleasant one, but it was a stand I had to take. Just as Asa's stand at the tower had been one he had had to take.

When the group stopped in front of me, the warriors from our tribes began to settle down. It would be at least a few hours before we heard anything from Asa, and we all needed our rest if we were going to be ready to face what came next.

"Your Fortis man has entered the city?" Ontari asked.

I nodded, but then shook my head. "He has, but he is not Fortis any more."

Roan stiffened. "What have you done?"

"What I had to, just as I have since the day my husband died." I swallowed even as I straightened my shoulders. "Asa and I are married." I pulled my fur aside to reveal the passage marking my sister had given me only a few hours earlier. "His people are now members of the Windhi tribe."

Ontari turned her gaze on Mira. "And you agree with this? The Winta have never married outside their tribe. No Outlier has."

"And look where that has gotten us." Mira's gaze moved back and forth between the two Heads. Ontari had her mouth open as if to speak, but she shut it when Mira lifted her hand. "If we had trusted one another more, perhaps things would have been different. Perhaps we would have won our freedom decades ago. Perhaps the Winta would still be here. We know Asa, even better than we know you, and we are certain of his loyalty. Leaving his people to suffer and starve when we could do something would be wrong, just as allowing the Sovereign to continue to oppress us would be. Asa and his people are Windhi now, and if you accept us, then you must accept them as well."

Although I had known my friend supported my choice, and that she trusted Asa, I had not expected such strong words from her. It obviously took the other Heads by surprise as well, because neither one spoke at first. I held my breath, waiting to find out what they would say, uncertain if they would be able to see our side or if they would pull their armies out.

After a moment, Roan let out a deep breath, seemingly blowing all his frustration out with it. "If you are willing to put the safety of your people on the line, you must be very sure of this man. You have risked a lot for them, have done everything to ensure they survive. You would not risk that for nothing."

"My people are everything to me," I said, "but so is Asa. Which was why I had to join our tribes. He is my people now."

Roan nodded again, and it was followed a beat later by Ontari mimicking the gesture. My body relaxed as tension melted off me the way snow melted off the trees in spring.

"You have proven yourself trustworthy, Indra of the Windhi," the Huni Head said, "but you cannot keep things from us if you wish this alliance to continue after we have killed the Sovereign. We must be open with one another so things do not return to the old ways."

I had never thought about them returning to the old ways, not when I was on such good terms with Ontari and Roan. But I also had not taken much time to reflect on what came next. On what our lives would be like after we completed this mission and freed our people. I had been too focused on the now, on the next step, the next kill.

"What will we do after this?" I looked past the Heads to where our army sat.

It was dark now, but fires had been lit, illuminating the valley and the people gathered there. Mountari, Huni, and Windhi intermingled, gathered together around fires as if there had never been a gorge between our tribes. They looked very different from one another, the picrced faces of the Huni contrasting with the passage markings of my own people and the pierced bodies of the Mountari, but we were all the same. People who wanted to be free. Here and there I spotted one of Asa's people, the former Fortis men and women. Their large frames stood out among the much smaller Outliers, but they were a part of us now. Asa and I had made sure of that with our union.

"What do you see becoming of our tribes when this is over?" I looked back at Ontari and Roan. "We are on good terms. Do you see us intermarrying?"

Ontari's back stiffened. "The Huni do not marry."

"What if they wanted to?" I nodded to the group gathered behind her. "What if one of your men decided he liked one of my women?"

She blinked and her shoulders relaxed. "I would not stop them. We embrace all ways of living."

I turned my gaze on Roan, and his lips were already pursed as if thinking the question through. "Our women fight for their mate."

The corner of my mouth quirked up. "Do you not think some of my women could defeat some of yours?"

Roan returned my smile. "I believe they could, Indra of the Windhi. And if they wanted to challenge someone in my tribe for the right to a mate, I would not stop it." He paused and looked me over, and I was reminded of how he had expressed his admiration for me in the past. Thankfully, he said nothing of it now, but instead nodded again. "Yes, I believe we could create something much stronger than we had before by allowing our tribes to mix in this way."

"As do I," Ontari said.

"I agree," I replied as I once again looked past them toward the army gathered in the valley. "No matter what, I want to ensure that our people stay strong. That even when the Sovereign are gone, we will never again be held prisoner."

"HOW LONG DO YOU THINK IT WILL TAKE?" MIRA asked.

The horizon glowed orange in the distance, but the sun had not yet risen, and behind us in the valley our army was waking up. Asa and Nyko had been in the city for hours now and should have had more than enough time to get to the gate, and yet they still had not opened it. I was beginning to worry that something had gone wrong. That like Xandra, we would never see them again.

"Any time now," I said despite the worry clawing at my insides.

My eyes had barely strayed from the gate since Mira and I had settled in for the night, and it felt as if I had hardly blinked. They were beginning to burn, but still I could not look away. It was like I thought looking away would doom Asa to death.

"Hopefully—" Mira's words were cut off by a hum.

I stood, looking around as I searched for the source. It reminded me of the sound the electroprods made, or how I had sometimes been able to hear the buzz of the lights in Saffron's dining room when the house had been very quiet.

The hum started low, but it grew louder as the seconds ticked by. It echoed across the wastelands until it seemed like the ground would begin to shake, and I covered my ears.

At my side, Mira did the same. "What is it?"

Just as I shook my head, a brilliant light began to glow, pulling my gaze from the gate at last. I turned to face the tower, pressing my hands harder against my ears. The light was blinding, brighter than the slowly rising sun. I squinted, trying to get a better look at it, but it was too brilliant. Too intense.

"Something is happening!" I called, raising my voice to be heard over the hum.

A boom vibrated through the air, and I ducked like I thought I was going to be struck down by a bolt of lighting. A burst of light shot from the tower, quivering through my body as it spread across the wasteland toward the wall. I could feel the electricity from it, moving over my body, and it reminded me of the time I had shocked myself trying to plug in a vacuum inside Saffron's house.

The current moved through me, and all around the valley a cry of surprise rose up. People dropped to the ground and covered their heads, but I stayed standing. Facing the city with my hands over my ears. Too stunned to do anything but stare.

The buzz of electricity had felt strong enough to knock the walls down, but they had not fallen. They stood tall and strong, and what could only be described as a bubble now stretched over the entire city. It was translucent, shimmering blue in the dim light of the early morning, and I instinctively knew we would never be able to penetrate it. Not with our bodies and not with our weapons. Even worse, there was another much smaller bubble surrounding the tower, making it now impossible to destroy the mirrors.

"What is that?" Mira said.

She stood at my side, as stunned as I was. My hands were still over my ears, but I lowered them when I realized the hum had died down. It was still there, but like the lights in Saffron's house, it was low and I had to strain to hear it.

"I do not know," I whispered, staring at the bubble in disbelief and shock.

All around me, the other members of our army began to climb to their feet. There were hundreds of us, all of us staring up at the bubble. No one spoke for a long time, and when the silence was finally broken, it was with a shout of fury.

Emori slammed into me a second later. I hit the ground, too stunned to move as she pulled out her knife and pressed it to my throat.

"I told you he was not trustworthy. You sent him into the city, and now he has warned them that we are coming!"

I could not speak. Asa had not done this, of that I was certain, but I was in no position to argue with Emori. Not when I had no proof, and not while she had a knife to my throat.

"Emori!" Anja screamed. "Get off her!"

The woman on top of me did not look away. "You have the blood of our village on your hands, and you have allowed the Fortis to twist your mind. You are not fit to be Head."

Someone grabbed Emori from behind, but she fought against them, and the blade of the knife stung against my skin a second before she was pulled away, followed by the warmth of my blood spilling from the wound.

My hands went to my neck, but I did not move. I was frozen, lying on my back and staring up at the sky as the sun moved higher, spreading its rays across the blackness. All around me there were voices and shouting, but I could not focus on them. I felt the afterlife coming for me, and I knew with certainty that all the sins I had committed over the last two years would pull me down to the underworld. There was so much blood on my hands, just as Emori had said. Bodhi, our village, hundreds of Fortis hunters, and the rest of their people on top of that. I was responsible for all their deaths, and as I lay bleeding in the sand, I suddenly found myself wondering how it had all happened. How had I ended up in this position? This was not the place I had set out for two years ago when I married Bodhi. I had looked into our future and seen a lifetime of happiness, but instead all I had gotten was blood and death. And it was my fault. No one else could be held responsible for where I was now, not even Emori, who had been the one to slash my throat. No, it had all been up to me.

"Indra." Mira's face appeared in front of me. "Hold on. Please."

When I swallowed, it hurt more than I had expected. "I am sorry, Mira. I did not plan for all this to happen."

"Stop," she said, sobbing. "You did nothing wrong. You taught us to be strong. You taught us how to stand up for ourselves. Emori is wrong."

More blood gushed from the wound when I shook my head. "I was wrong. I wanted vengeance, and I risked all of you."

Another face appeared at my side, Roan this time, and at his right a man I recognized as the Mountari healer.

"Hold still, Indra," Roan said. "Kale will fix you."

He moved aside, allowing the healer space, and my hands were forced away from my neck. A fresh gush of blood followed, and with it the sound of Mira's sobs grew. I wanted to look at her, but I could not. All I could focus on was the bubble in the distance, the one that had enclosed the city. Not only had it cut off our chance of taking out the Sovereign, but it had also trapped the man I loved inside. He would die within those walls, just as Bodhi had. Maybe everyone who loved me was destined to die. Maybe I had already died myself and been dragged down into the underworld, and the punishment for my many sins was that I would spend eternity watching the people I loved die one by one.

Acknowledgements

Once again, I have to thank my sister-in-law, Rebekah, for telling me to watch *The 100* – am seriously obsessed with this show now. More thank yous go out to Netflix for making *The 100* available to me, and the creators and cast who have made it so awesome. Yes, I borrowed a lot of names from the show, but credit also goes to *Outsiders* for giving me the name Asa, and *Point Break* for allowing me to think of the name Bodhi.

A very special thank you goes out to my author bestie, Diana Gardin, for allowing me to borrow the term *passage markings*, which she used in her own novel, *The Lilac Sky*, and my SIL, Rebekah, who helped me come up with the name for my city guards, the Fortis.

This book was so much fun to write, but also a huge undertaking since the world is so complex, and I want to thank everyone who has taken the time to give me such great feedback. The enthusiasm of people like Cheer Stephenson-Papworth and Mysti Holsinger-Stitt, who rallied the participants in the BOD Reads group to make Outliers the April book, means more to me than I can possibly say. All I can say is: thanks for being so awesome!

Jan Strohecker, thanks for being that first critical eye after I finished writing the novel, and reading it again before I hit that ever important publish button. Thanks to my first readers and typo hunters: Courtnee McGrew, Rebekah Caillouet, Cheer Stephenson-Papworth, and Erin Rose.

Thanks also to Lori Whitwam, who answered some of my editing questions with book one when the person I hired dropped the ball, and for being super pumped to take over editing duties for the second one! And last but not least, a big thank you goes out to Amber Garcia, my PR Goddess, for setting everything up last minute.

As always, I am forced to acknowledge my husband and kids and how amazing they are. Whenever I'm really into a project, they get neglected, and I appreciate not only what good sports they are, but also how supportive they are. My husband especially has no problem picking up the slack, doing laundry and running the kids to events, so I can get just a little more done, and I couldn't ask for a better support system!

About the Author

Kate L. Mary is an award-winning author of New Adult and Young Adult fiction, ranging from Post-apocalyptic tales of the undead, to Speculative Fiction and Contemporary Romance. Her Young Adult book, *When We Were Human*, was a 2015 Moonbeam Children's Book Awards Silver Medal winner for Young Adult Fantasy/Sci-Fi Fiction, and a 2016 Readers' Favorite Gold Medal winner for Young Adult Science Fiction. Don't miss out on the *Broken World* series, an Amazon bestseller and fan favorite.

For more information about Kate, check out her website: www.KateLMary.com

Made in the USA
San Bernardino, CA
08 September 2018